WHATEVER MAKES YOU HAPPY

In William Sutcliffe's new novel, naive gap-yearers have given way to three men in their early thirties who are not (in the eyes of their mothers) properly settled.

Matt works for lads' mag *BALLS!* and is a serial dater of girls half his age. Paul lives in a mysterious commune, and is bafflingly secretive and evasive around his mother. Daniel spends his Saturday nights alone in his flat reading novels, pining for the love of his life, his ex-girlfriend, Erin.

Their mothers, three close friends, decide to launch a co-ordinated attack: they will arrive without warning, and stay with their sons for one week. During the visit, they will find out why their sons have gone so wrong, and will do what they can to set things right. As Matt's mother puts it, 'You're never too old to be in need of a little mothering.'

WHATEVER MAKES YOU HAPPY

William Sutcliffe

WINDSOR
PARAGON

First published 2008
by Bloomsbury Publishing
This Large Print edition published 2008
by BBC Audiobooks Ltd
by arrangement with
Bloomsbury Publishing Plc

Hardcover ISBN: 978 1 405 68740 9
Softcover   ISBN: 978 1 405 68741 6

British Library Cataloguing in Publication Data available

Printed and bound in Great Britain by
CPI Antony Rowe, Chippenham, Wiltshire

For Maggie and Saul

*A child came out of me. I cannot understand this,
or try to explain it. Except to say that my past life
has become foreign to me. Except to say that I am
prey, for the rest of my life, to every small thing.*

Anne Enright

My mother—she isn't quite herself today.

Norman Bates

CAROL AND MATT

SEVEN FROZEN LASAGNES

'What's happened?'

'Just thought I'd pop in.'

Matt stared at his mother, aghast. He couldn't think of a single thing that might have prompted her to turn up, here, at his flat, on a weekday evening, uninvited, without even giving him a warning. There was no precedent for this behaviour, and he immediately assumed that something terrible must have happened, something too awful to discuss over the phone—an event to be spoken of in hushed voices, with a chair at the ready and hot, sweet tea to hand. At the very least, someone must have died.

'What's wrong?' he said.

'Nothing's wrong.'

'Is everyone OK?'

'Everyone's fine,' she said.

They stared at one another across the threshold, both at a loss as to what to do next, like hikers suddenly realising they are lost.

'Aren't you going to invite me in?' said Carol eventually.

'Yes, yes,' said Matt. 'Come in. I'll make some tea. Sorry, I'm just a bit surprised to see you. Are you sure you're OK?'

'Yes. I'm fine.'

Hearing his mother say those words, with that particular high, clipped intonation, took him back twenty years, to his adolescence, when the word 'fine' had been a key weapon in his mother's emotional arsenal. This one word had a huge variety of meanings, depending on various faint nuances of tone, as if the word was not English but Chinese. 'I'm fine' could mean 'I'm tense', or 'I'm upset', or 'I'm angry', or 'Why does no one ever listen to me?', or even 'Look, I'm clearing away the breakfast things that you said you'd clear away but never did.' The statement, in fact, had a near infinite range of meanings, all of which had only one thing in common. They all meant, in essence, 'I'm not fine.'

Matt's interpretation skills were a little rusty but his best guess at her meaning on this occasion was, 'I'm tense.' This was something of a catch-all for a number of subtler meanings and didn't say much in relation to his mother's mood, since tension played a role in her life of comparable importance to oxygen. Matt could barely imagine her not being tense. She even relaxed tensely, reading the newspaper at the kitchen table, sitting erect on a hard chair. If you persuaded her to attempt relaxed relaxation, by forcing her on to the sofa in front of the TV, within a quarter of an hour she'd be fast asleep. If you looked closely enough, at her eyeballs flicking rapidly around under their lids, you could see her dreaming her tense dreams. The only TV programme she ever watched from start to finish without dozing off was the news, which she liked to see twice a night, perched on the edge of an armchair, her face a twitching mask of empathy, horror and dismay at the ever more lurid and unpredictable ways in which the world was becoming scarier.

Anxiety held Carol together. To deprive her of it

would be like removing the mortar from a house.

At this moment, the fact that she appeared merely tense, rather than on the point of psychological meltdown, probably indicated that her visit had not been prompted by anything truly dire. There would be a reason that in her head was clearly something of urgent importance— undoubtedly something bizarre, possibly something incomprehensible—but Matt was beginning to feel reassured that it was nothing too close to the death/divorce end of the family-crisis spectrum.

'Take a seat,' said Matt, knowing she wouldn't.

She didn't. She followed him closely to the kitchen area, in the furthest corner of his open-plan apartment.

'I'm not interrupting, am I?' said Carol.

'No, no. Nothing too important, anyway.'

At the precise moment the doorbell had rung, he'd been playing on his PlayStation, but he'd been about to send a couple of emails, and there was a football score he'd been on the point of looking up on the internet. There was also a girl he'd been half-intending to ring. All in all, he had a plan for the evening—there were things to get done—and thanks to his mother there might not be time for any of them. She really did have a knack of always managing to be inconvenient.

Matt filled the kettle and tossed a couple of teabags into the cleanest two mugs he could find. He saw his mother register, with a rueful glance, the lack of a teapot. The way Carol saw the world there was an easy way and a right way of doing things. To take the route of convenience, in her eyes, was expressive of fundamental moral degeneracy. She was not just a teapot woman: teapot, milk jug and biscuits laid out neatly on a plate constituted, for her, the barest minimum of hospitality.

Naturally, she had never succeeded in passing on these ideals to her son. In fact, Matt had grown up with an aversion to milk jugs so strong that they awoke in him a desire to commit physical violence.

Matt knew precisely what Carol was thinking as he handed her a mug of morally degenerate tea, and he didn't care. In fact, he enjoyed her disapproval. At thirty-four, he knew he ought to be too old to enjoy this kind of rebellion by domestic niggle, but he was still fond of his inner teenager and couldn't bring himself to definitively kill him off. Perhaps he'd do her another cup later in a teapot, just to make her happy. Assuming he could find one.

'Let's go to the living room,' said Matt.

'Is that what you call it?' said Carol.

'Call what?'

'The living room.'

'I don't know what you mean.'

'I'm pleased, that's all. I mean, it's good. That you still call it a living room, when the whole place is . . . well . . .' Carol swept her arm around Matt's warehouse apartment, in the manner of an estate agent feigning enthusiasm for a tasteless, hard-to-shift property. Matt adored his flat, and loved it all the more for the fact that his mother hated it. He found it funny how the whole idea of living in a warehouse was simply baffling to her, twenty years after everyone else in the world had got used to the idea.

Whenever she visited—a rare occurrence—Matt

4

found it amusing to sense Carol's slight pity for him: it was as if she felt he had been conned by a deluded property cult, robbed of all his money and left in a state of penury, squatting in an abandoned industrial space like a fugitive from justice. If he'd made her tea on a camping stove perched on a couple of bricks in the middle of the floor, she probably wouldn't have raised an eyebrow. She might even have been pleased to have her suspicions confirmed.

'I've never really thought about it,' said Matt.

'Because I was just wondering if this is a kitchen.'

'Of course it's a kitchen.'

'Good. I'm glad. I thought maybe you had another word for it.'

'No.'

'You are brave. Living like this.'

'Brave? It's a desirable flat, Mum. It was expensive.'

'Well. As long as you're happy here.'

'I am,' Matt replied, a little more tetchily than he intended.

It was natural that she'd feel uneasy here. She looked as out of place in his apartment—in her dowdy clothes, with her body the shape of a beer keg—as his forty-two-inch plasma TV would look in her chintzy living room. If she felt how she looked, it was hardly surprising she wasn't at ease.

Matt closed the blinds on the floor-to-ceiling glass doors that led out on to his balcony. He didn't usually bother, since he liked being able to see and hear the traffic below, and the fact that he was overlooked never worried him. It wasn't as if he'd ever meet the people who lived in the block opposite, so what was there to hide? The view from his flat was the whole point of the place, especially after dark, when London twinkled and buzzed. You felt like you were part of the city, even when you were at home. But that was hardly to his mother's taste, who'd decorated her mock-Tudor suburban semi—which backed on to the Pinner high street's Poundstretcher—to give the impression to visitors that they were in Edwardian Hampshire, right down to the Edwardian TV cabinet, the logical inconsistency of which she always refused to discuss.

With the blinds drawn, he joined her in the centre of the room. Carol was perched on the front edge of his sofa, resisting the slouch-inducing pull of its soft, expensive, stain-resistant (yet stained) cushions. Matt threw himself into an armchair, showing her how it was supposed to be done.

'So what's up?' he said.

Carol looked at her hands. She was having trouble catching Matt's eye. Already, her confidence was faltering. She'd been hoping it would be possible to sit with him for a while, chatting about neutral topics, before broaching the real reason for, and intended duration of, her visit. Stupidly, she hadn't realised in advance how Matt's shock at her sudden arrival would put him in a position where he wouldn't be able to relax until he knew why she had come.

But she couldn't tell him. Not yet. Her mouth was too dry, and her heart was beating too fast, and she knew it would come out garbled and confused. She wouldn't be able to explain herself until she felt a little less on edge.

'I should have brought a bottle of wine,' she

6

said. 'I mean, it's a bit of a special occasion, this, isn't it? Just me and you. When did we last have a good old private chat?'

'Wine!' said Matt, jumping at the bait. He sprang up from his chair and began to clatter through the cupboards in his kitchen. 'I've probably got a bottle stashed away somewhere. Actually, why don't I pop out and get a nice one? There's an offy just downstairs. I'll be back in a mo'.'

He already had his coat on by the time Carol could answer, 'No, no. No need. I'm very happy with this.'

'It's no trouble. Really. If I'd known you were coming I'd have had one ready. It'll only take a minute.'

The door slammed. He was gone.

Matt needed a drink.

*   *   *

Nothing was going to stop him getting that wine, least of all his mother's feigned preference for tea.

The man behind the counter eyed his purchase, the most expensive red in the shop, suspiciously.

'*Wine?*' he said.

Matt was one of the shop's most regular customers, and in five years he had only ever bought beer.

'The mum's popped round.'

'Oh, right,' said the shop assistant, a hint of commiseration in his voice.

'Thought I'd treat her to something nice.'

'Well—enjoy.'

Matt wasn't sure whether this referred to his

mother's visit or the wine, but either way the intention seemed vaguely sarcastic, so he slipped away with only a grunt for a goodbye.

On his way back in the lift, he started to pick off the price sticker, then changed his mind and left it on. This short time outside the flat had given him a chance to gather his thoughts. His mother clearly had something to tell him, but she didn't want to do it straight away. Her wine hint had really not been very subtle, but he was glad of the suggestion. After all, if she needed a glass of wine to say it, he probably needed two to hear it. Whatever it was, it couldn't be good news.

The best he could hope for was that it would be something that seemed bad only to his mother. He tried to lift his sense of foreboding by reminding himself that there were many, many things his mother considered appalling that were in fact utterly normal, such as drugs, swearing, all music recorded since 1965 and chewing-gum. Whatever might be on her mind was clearly horrific to her, but that meant nothing. As yet, there was no reason for Matt to panic.

A light nausea, however, had settled into the pit of his stomach, and no reasoning with himself could shift it. This visit was deeply irregular. His mother would not appear at his flat without warning unless something fundamental in the order of things had altered. By this stage of life, with his parents now both in their sixties, any change could only be involuntary and for the worse. If the last ten years had proved anything, it was that his parents didn't do change, not by choice. Like skiing and Japanese food and furniture that isn't brown, it simply wasn't to their taste.

'I got a nice Italian red,' he said, as he strode back in.

Carol was still perched on the sofa. She was looking at the *Grand Theft Auto* box, which Matt had left on the coffee table.

'Is this a film?' she said, while Matt searched for a bottle opener and some wine glasses.

'It's a game.'

'A video game?'

'Yeah.'

'That's nice. Have you had children visiting? Friends of yours?'

'It's mine,' he snapped. 'I play. It's not for kids. It's an adult thing. The video games industry is worth more than the movie industry, Mum. In fact, I was playing it when you rang the bell.' He didn't know why, but a tone of petulant defiance had crept into his voice.

'Oh. I thought they were for children.'

'Well, they're not. In fact, that one's forbidden for children.'

'Really? Why?'

'Oh . . . it's not important.'

'No, tell me. I'm interested.'

'It's just . . . a bit violent, that's all.'

'Oh. And it's about stealing cars?'

'That's part of it.'

'What, you have to catch the thieves?'

'No. You nick the cars.'

'That's the game? Stealing cars?'

'Sort of. And other stuff.'

'Like what?'

How was it that his mother reduced him to a child so easily? Shame was not a part of his daily

9

life. He was thirty-four, successful, well-off, good with women; he was a swaggerer, not a skulker or a blusher or a stander-in-the-corner. His life was on track. He had made something of himself. He was living the life that most guys could only dream of. Yet within ten minutes of his mother turning up he felt like an evasive teenager, ashamed and embarrassed by his secret pleasures.

No, shame was not for men like him. He had to fight it. He wouldn't let his mother do this to him. He had nothing to hide. If she didn't like what she saw of his life, that was her problem, not his.

'Drug deals,' he said. 'You become a drug runner, and you go around the city doing bad things. It's fun.'

His mother stared at him with an expression that was part dismay, part bemusement. It was the same face she pulled during war reports on the news.

'And that's what you do with your evenings?'

'Usually I'm out. If I'm in, it's something I might do for a bit or might not. Like the way you listen to the radio. It's the same thing.'

'Is it?' she said.

Of course it wasn't the same thing. He knew that, and he instantly regretted the claim, which he now saw made him look even more corrupted and shallow, as if he really couldn't see the difference between engaging in a fantasy killing spree and listening to *Desert Island Discs*.

He toyed with the idea of confessing that he understood what she was getting at and he realised playing *Grand Theft Auto* was a dirty habit, but he didn't like where that would lead. After all, what he was doing was normal. Everyone did it. He did it less than most. And so what? It was just a game! He'd never deal drugs in real life. Not proper drugs. He had passed on the odd bit of this and that to friends, now and then, occasionally for a small profit, but that didn't make him a drug dealer. Compared to most people, he was extremely law-abiding. He would never so much as hit anyone, let alone rampage around a city with a gun, beating rival pimps to death with dustbin lids. It was just a bit of harmless fun. Only an idiot couldn't tell the difference between fantasy and reality.

His inner voice was already hitting a teenage squeal. He had to stay calm and remember that, despite the way his mother spoke to him, he was an adult.

'Cheers,' he said, offering up his glass for a chink.

'Cheers.'

'So,' he said, slumping back into the welcoming embrace of his armchair, the brand of which—La-Z-Boy—his mother could never be permitted to know. Ideally, she'd also never find out that the arms contained a hinged compartment for as many remote controls as a man could ever dream of. The nausea was still there. He couldn't wait any longer. He had to know the worst. 'What brings you here?' he said, with a tentative smile. 'Not that it isn't great to see you. I mean, it's lucky I was in. I'm usually not. But we're both in luck. That's what I mean. Just . . . to what do I owe this pleasure?' He was taking it too far, now. He was beginning to sound implausible, or perhaps even sarcastic.

'Well,' she said, allowing her body the slightest of yields to the temptations of modern upholstery,

11

'I've been having a long hard think, and you're my only child, and . . .'

'Is someone ill? Are you OK?'

'I'm fine. Everyone's fine. I'm just trying to say that I feel as if our relationship has fizzled away to nothing. I don't think I know you any more. And I'd like to rectify that.'

This was the scariest thing Matt had ever heard. The hairs on his neck prickled and his tongue went numb. Maori war dances were less frightening.

'So I thought maybe I'd move in for a few days,' continued Carol. 'You've got a spare room. I won't be any trouble. In fact, I'll help out. This place could do with a tidy. Just a week or so. Until we know who one another is again. I thought if I said it on the phone you wouldn't understand, and you'd think of some excuse, so I decided to just turn up.'

Carol downed the rest of her wine in a single gulp. 'I'm dog-tired,' she continued. 'Mind if I turn in?'

And with that, she stood and made for the spare room, pausing on the way to pick up a capacious bag she had concealed under a draped raincoat. 'I'm sure we won't be bored,' she said perkily, shutting the door behind her.

Matt was too shocked to respond, or even to move. He realised that his mouth was open, but no sound had emerged. Of all the apocalyptic scenarios that had been running through his mind since her arrival, this was one he had never even begun to imagine.

What on earth could have prompted this?

A week?

She came out of the spare room a minute or so

12

later, wearing a nightie, clutching a faded purple sponge-bag Matt vaguely recognised, and gave him a quick, thin smile as she walked rapidly past. As she was closing the bathroom door, Matt heard himself stuttering, 'But what about Dad?'

'Seven frozen lasagnes.'

The door clicked shut and locked.

When she re-emerged, the sight of his mother's legs rendered Matt speechless, and she disappeared into the bedroom before a word of protest passed his lips.

AWKWARD BREAKFASTS

Matt was already walking out of his bedroom, naked, yawning and tumescent, before he remembered he was not alone. He retreated and slammed the door, praying he hadn't been glimpsed, and jumped on the spot a couple of times to encourage gravity's help in redistributing his blood supply. When it could be done without excessive indecency, he wrapped a towel around himself and headed for the bathroom, stooping, with his eyes lowered, in the hope that he would not be forced into conversation while only one towel away from nudity.

'Morning!' came the chirp from the kitchen. 'Sleep well?'

'Mmm. Thanks. Just having a shower.'

'Is there somewhere round here I can get a croissant?'

'Er . . . yeah. There's a supermarket on the corner down that way.'

'Marvellous. I'll be back in two ticks.'

As Matt showered, enjoying the feel of his gym-hardened muscles slicking up under the shower gel, he began rehearsing maternal ejection speeches. The great-idea-but-just-an-impossible-week-for-it angle seemed most tactful. He could even propose rescheduling the visit for another time, knowing that other excuses would arise when he needed them.

By the time he had shaved—a prolonged ritual involving the application of more unguents than his father had purchased in an entire lifetime—he was feeling confident of the exit strategy. As he gelled his hair, it occurred to him that his mother's visit hadn't been too painful after all. Perhaps he should invite her back for dinner some day.

He took his time selecting an outfit for the day, and arrived at the breakfast table thinking more about the day's work that lay ahead of him than the task of dislodging his mother. He found that she had returned from the shop with a preposterous amount of food. An array of croissants, pains au chocolat, fresh bread, jams, yoghurts and fruit covered every square inch of the table, looking more like a buffet for ten than a meal for two. If he got started on a breakfast like this, he'd be late for work. A cup of coffee and a bowl of cornflakes eaten standing up in front of the TV was his usual morning routine.

He decided to let himself be late. One meal together wasn't so much for his mother to ask of him, even if it was at an awkward time of day. And in the course of the meal, having demonstrated that he was hospitable, patient and kind, he'd ease the conversation towards the lovely-idea-but-not-

14

this-week routine he'd perfected in the shower.

'I've made a pot of Earl Grey,' said Carol.

'Where did you find that?'

'I bought it.'

'What, the teapot?'

'No, the Earl Grey.'

'Oh.'

'The pot was under your oven, behind the pans.'

'Oh. Right.'

Matt was by no means unaccustomed to having awkward breakfasts with women he hardly knew, but for the woman to be his mother was an unusual twist.

'Sleep well?' she said, again.

'Yes, thanks.'

Matt reached for a croissant and picked up a fresh pot of Bonne Maman raspberry jam. He wasn't sure if she'd bought this brand as a joke, but he didn't like to ask. There was something in the homely shape of the pot and the gingham-patterned lid that took him back to his childhood. He had forgotten about this jam, about how much he used to love it, and was surprised that it had never occurred to him to buy it for himself.

He hadn't eaten jam for years. As it melted on his tongue, along with the fresh, buttery croissant, he felt a surge of unidentifiable emotion spread through his body.

The taste of this croissant, with this jam, transported him. It was not that he had often eaten croissants as a child, or even that this jam held a unique, nostalgic flavour, but something in that precise sensation on his tongue popped him out of the moment. From where he was sitting, at the dining table with his mother, for a split second he felt like a child, looking up at where the adult Matt would be on a normal day, standing over the coffee table, joylessly shovelling in a heap of over-sweet cereal, gazing at a shouty, uninteresting TV programme, alone.

Matt was not a lonely man. He was as far from lonely as it was possible to be. He had a desirable job, a beautiful flat, and a SIM card containing the numbers of many of the top people in the magazine industry, as well as a good-sized sample of the sexiest women in the country, many of whom he had bedded. If, aged sixteen, he'd been asked to write down a fantasy of everything he could have wanted from life, this would have been it. The idea that there could be any space for loneliness in his busy and frantically sociable life was preposterous.

But occasionally Matt looked around his flat— at the kitchen he never used, and the furniture he'd had chosen for him and his racks of this year's clothes and his gadgets and his wall of DVDs—and he wondered if these things had anything to do with him. There were odd periods, once every few months, when he simply didn't want to go out, or see anyone, or do anything.

This first mouthful of breakfast with his mother had, for some reason, reminded him of this sensation, not because he felt the mood descending again, but because of some tangential connection he could only half grasp—perhaps because eating breakfast with his mother reminded him of his childhood, of a time before these anxieties meant anything; perhaps because he saw in his mother's eyes a bleak prognosis of his life.

'That nice?' she said.

'Mmm. Very.'

Then Carol began to talk, telling Matt the latest news of his father, and of things that had been happening in Pinner, before reeling off local gossip about the families he had grown up among, focusing on marriages, jobs and hospitalisations, with the greatest level of detail reserved for babies born to childhood friends, people he would have entirely forgotten about were it not for these periodic updates from his mother. Carol somehow remembered every name, and even the odd birth-weight.

Matt half-listened, neither bored nor interested, waiting for an opening to arrive for his shower speech, but, as gaps began to appear in her chatter, he found that the phrases he had planned now escaped him. The balloon of righteous outrage at her invasion of his life was mysteriously deflating. Sitting at his heavily laden dining table, eating breakfast opposite this ageing, infinitely familiar woman, he realised there was something intimate in all this, something companionable, something not entirely unpleasant.

Was there really any desperate rush to kick her out? He'd be at work all day, after all. What would it cost him to let her stay one more night? There was no way she really wanted to visit for a week. She must have just said that to scare him, or maybe as a joke. By this time tomorrow, she'd want to go home. She'd do it of her own accord, without him having to make any difficult speeches. However gently you put it, whatever excuses you'd prepared, there was something tricky about kicking your mother out of your home.

Some things, in a family, are never forgotten. If he turned her away now, it might be held against

17

him for years to come. Taking the long view, he realised that perhaps it would be less hassle to let her have her way for just a short while longer.

When he left for work, he simply said, 'See you later,' heading for the front door without really understanding what had stopped him from even attempting to get rid of her.

'I brought my spare keys with me,' she said. 'So I can let myself in and out.'

Matt was annoyed to find how unannoyed he was to hear this.

'OK,' he said, closing the door behind him.

As the lift carried him down to street level, he felt how he imagined a shoplifter must feel, sneaking out into the daylight with a guilty secret. The thought of what his colleagues would say if they knew what he had done made him flush with shame.

HELEN AND PAUL

A LITTLE MORE OOMPH

As she lay in bed, listening to her husband crash around the kitchen, Helen knew she had to get up. She did not, on the whole, believe in pre-11 a.m. human interaction, but today she had no way out of facing Clive before he went to work. If she had been braver, it wouldn't have come down to a breakfast confrontation, but she had lazily left it until the last possible moment.

Helen dragged herself upright and put on her dressing-gown: the old, cosy padded one that had been mothballed for the interregnum between her two marriages but had come out again not long after her second honeymoon.

'Morning, darling,' said Clive, as she shuffled into the kitchen. 'Cup of tea?'

'Mmm.'

'You're up early.'

'Mmm.'

'Any special reason?'

'Not really.'

'You going somewhere?'

'Actually, that's what I wanted to talk to you about.'

'Oh?'

'I'm going to see Paul today.'

'What—for breakfast?'

'No. Around lunchtime.'

'OK,' said Clive, his intonation making it clear that Helen wasn't making any sense, but that he wouldn't attempt to force an explanation out of her. One of the things Helen had found most attractive about Clive was this incurious streak in his character. In the course of their marriage, she had carefully nurtured it. The last thing you want in a second husband is someone inquisitive. On occasion, though, a little more oomph would have made him easier to talk to.

'I'm staying for a while,' she said.

'Oh. OK.'

'A few days, I mean.'

'A few days?'

'A week. Probably.'

'A week? You're going for lunch and staying a week.'

'Lunch isn't important. I'm just going at some

point today, I don't really know when, and I'm staying a week.'

'What's brought this on?'

'I'm his mother.'

'I know that. I just . . . well . . . OK. Is it his birthday?'

'No. I'm just going because I want to.'

'Well . . . have fun. Give me a ring and tell me how you're getting on.'

Everything Helen had done in the course of their years together had taught Clive to behave like this. She had trained him to let her be. He had learnt (the hard way) that attempts to thwart her were futile. Yet part of her still yearned to be challenged and confronted, as she had been by her first husband.

Clive had accepted her explanation without even coaxing out of her that she was going uninvited, and could quite possibly arrive back home that same evening, spurned and humiliated. If he'd stopped to think about it for more than a second, he'd have realised that Paul would never invite her to stay for a whole week. He never even invited her for dinner. And having figured out that Paul was unaware his mother was about to descend on him, he would surely have tried to talk sense into her, tried to stop her attempting something so brazenly stupid.

You needed this in a husband. It was their job to help curb your crazier instincts and desires. Her friends had talked her into it, now she needed her husband to talk her out of it. But this was not Clive's department. She had never allowed him that role. It was too much to ask of him that the one time she actually wanted someone to stand up

20

to her, he should somehow sense it and step in.

With a kiss on the forehead and a jangle of car keys, Clive set off out of the house. Now she was committed. She'd hoped to spend most of the day mulling over whether or not to go through with her plan, but now she had told Clive, and he had so blithely accepted it, there was nothing more to think about. She couldn't not go, or put it off for any longer.

THE TWO BEST THINGS THAT EVER HAPPENED TO HER

Helen had no idea why she'd described her visit as lunch. There was no point arriving at Paul's house until he got back from work. Lunch had somehow sounded more plausible. She was used to having lunch with people, so it was the first word that came out of her mouth.

Now she had said it, the day stretched emptily ahead of her. She felt restless, too excited and nervous to think about anything other than her visit to Paul, but with nothing useful she could do about it until evening, when he'd get home from work.

In the end, she decided to set off and explore Paul's area of town before the visit. It would give her something vaguely relevant to do, and help screw up her courage. She hadn't yet been to Paul's new house, even though he'd been living there more than six months, and had never visited Hoxton before. It would be interesting, and the time she spent there would ease her into Paul's

21

world, before having to face him in person.

Hoxton, it turned out, was more stimulating than she expected. She had never seen anywhere quite so schizophrenic, so confused about whether to be rich or poor. The shop-fronts seemed to alternate between tiny supermarkets where nothing is fresh and everything is foreign, and the kind of restaurants where unnervingly good-looking waiters bring you teetering sculptures of shiny food on plates that aren't round. Some roads looked like there had been a riot the week before, others reeked of money. The people on the streets all seemed to be dressed in either high fashion or asylum-seeker tracksuits, with each group apparently invisible to the other.

It was as if some magical space-saving superimposition had taken place, and a rich area had somehow landed inside a poor area without either set of people noticing that half of everything around them was for someone else.

As her feet and her brain grew tired, Helen decided to sit out the remainder of the afternoon in a café. She had the choice between two on opposite sides of the street, one serving PG Tips in a styrofoam cup for 30p, the other offering more-froth-than-coffee cappuccino for two quid. She opted for the latter, even though she felt equally out of place in both. *If in doubt, go somewhere clean*, was her general rule of thumb in these matters. When she was younger, she had worked in a hotel, which had left her with an abiding certainty that everywhere was at least twice as dirty as it looked. This didn't worry her unduly, she just knew that the glass in your hotel bathroom had probably been dried on the dirty towel of the

22

outgoing occupant, that your food was largely composed of the previous day's leftovers, and that your bed cover had never been washed and contained every bodily fluid you could name and a few you couldn't.

She had been working as a waitress when she met Larry. She'd served him lunch and, like most men in those days, he'd flirted with her, but to her surprise she found herself flirting back. Back then, she had been a head-turner, her every step a little easier and lighter than it was now, as if her life was cushioned and levitated by the thrilling potency of her youth and beauty. The exact thing that she felt slipping away from her faster than ever, these last few years, had at that point been at its peak.

Men wanted her, and she knew they wanted her, and they knew she knew, and it was almost impossible to talk to any man without being aware of her own magnetism. Her hair was straight and dark, with one neat curl at the end made fresh every morning with her beloved curling tongs, after which she'd carefully draw round her dark eyes with heavy black liner. Without the curl and her liner, she didn't feel quite herself. Her legs, which as a teenager she'd always thought too long and skinny, also exerted a strange power over men, and as skirts got shorter, she found herself drawing more and more gazes. For a good ten years of her life, Helen forgot what it felt like to be ignored.

Her childhood had given her no preparation for what happened to her in London in her early twenties. Her mother had always put her down; her father had been unpredictable and cruel; her elder sister was jealous and sniping. Not one teacher throughout her schooling had ever been so much as slightly impressed by a single piece of her work. Everything in her early years had sown deep into Helen's heart a sense of her profound averageness. She had never even felt the lack of any superior qualities, since to be clever or beautiful or interesting had never seemed to be an option. Her life had been lived exclusively in a dreary town filled with people who felt their role in the world was to make up the numbers. Helen hadn't known there was any alternative.

Then, aged twenty, against the advice of her parents, she took the Derby to London train, heading blindly for the capital, having no idea what she would find. A friend of hers had done the same and had found work within a week as a waitress. Helen had enough money to last a fortnight.

Within two days, she had a bedsit off the Edgware Road and a job in a Chelsea café. For the first month, she spent her spare time simply walking around the city, plugging herself into the buzz and zip of a place that knew it was important, filled with people jostling for position. At first she felt like a spectator, but as the tin under her bed began to fill with wages and tips, which she spent with gleeful abandon on the King's Road, she gradually stopped looking and feeling like a hick. The sight of her own reflection in shop windows sometimes caused her to double-take. Her first thought was often, 'She looks good—what's she wearing?', before she realised that the unfamiliar form she had glimpsed was her reinvented self.

The two best things that ever happened to her took place that month. First, she discovered that everything her parents had ever taught her was wrong. Even though she had known this would happen, the revelation was still, as it is for everyone, an utterly joyous surprise, like a first-ever lungful of fresh air.

Second, she discovered men; specifically, the effect she had on them. They wanted her. All of them, it seemed, wanted her. They wanted her body, or, failing that, just a conversation, or a smile, or the shortest little gift of eye contact. Whatever she gave, however meagre, they lapped up. Even old men and bus conductors and cheeky schoolkids; almost every male gave her a look that she only now fully understood. She began to realise that, anywhere she went, men were at her service. This, she imagined, must have been how Clark Kent felt when he discovered he could fly.

Not only did she have the joy of exercising her powers whenever she felt like it; she also, even when she was alone, had the secret thrill of knowing that she possessed them, and could use them whenever she wanted. She could be happy simply sitting alone in her flat, listening to the muffled thrum of the city, privately relishing the knowledge that, despite everything her parents had led her to believe, she was, after all, someone special.

There was a quality to Larry she instantly liked. His flirting had an overtness, a directness that was unusual, and that made her smile. There was nothing veiled or oblique in his approach to her. You could barely even call it flirting; it was closer to simple, naked lust.

Larry had persuaded her to write her phone number on the bill, and later that week he'd taken her to what he described as a gig. She'd been expecting loud music in a seedy dive, but it had turned out to be a Prom at the Albert Hall, culminating in the Britten Violin Concerto, which she had never heard before, but which ever after caused her heart to race with the thrill of new love, and these days always made her cry. That night they had made love frantically at first, then again with slow and intense relish, then once more, because they couldn't quite believe they still wanted to and were capable of it. That third time, halfway through, he had whispered in her ear that one day they would get married. She had told him to shut up, biting his neck with mock annoyance, but he was right, and even at the time she suspected he might be.

He was an American by birth, and though he had left years before, he still carried something of New York in his bearing. Wherever he was felt like the centre of things. He was in no way a handsome man, his nose, lips, chin and brow being all too big to fit neatly on to one face, but he was astonishingly attractive, perhaps just because his own confidence that this was the case somehow made it true.

No other human had ever exerted such a pull over her, and she enjoyed watching him have the same effect on others, both men and women, which he did with ease. When they went to parties together, Helen loved staying by his side, feeling the centre of the room shift towards them. No room, however heavily populated, could remain unaltered by the presence of Larry. In fact, the bigger the audience, the happier Helen felt with him.

He had introduced her to a west London and Soho party scene, his gregariousness soon proving to be as oversized as his facial features and his libido. Their first two years together had been so sociable that Helen's first worry about their relationship was that, although they were rarely apart, they only ever seemed to be alone together in the bedroom.

When Paul was born, they bowed out of this demanding social regimen, but after a month or so, Larry simply carried on without her. The birth had left Helen bruised, sore and uninterested in sex. Despite his protestations to the contrary, Helen never believed for a moment that Larry was the type of person who could leave a party alone. Nor was he a man who could send his libido on vacation. His good intentions were just about plausible, his chances of seeing them through virtually nil.

But the rules were different then. She had even, at the time, thought herself irrational for finding his behaviour upsetting. As the pretence of fidelity slipped away, he even occasionally brought women back to the spare room of their flat. She was once woken up by the sound of them, late at night, and had put on the bedside radio to block out the noise. And it had all seemed normal. Among their peers, it was normal.

Helen was in no position to object to Larry's breach of their marriage vows, since she had done the same herself. It was the thing to do at that time, and by taking up with Larry, Helen had bought into an ethos and a way of life from which you couldn't pick and choose the elements you fancied. You were either in, wholesale, or you were out.

That she had never enjoyed her infidelities—

27

they had been performed more out of social obligation than anything else—was immaterial. She had done it, ironically enough, largely to please Larry: to show him that she was with it. She hadn't initially realised that, by doing so, she was handing Larry a passport to the bedrooms of all her friends.

She never regretted marrying Larry. Her main regret was simply that she had allowed herself to be so weak. At the time, she and her friends had thought their lifestyle was a historic leap forwards in the liberation of women. She now realised it was closer to being the final fling of patriarchy: the last time men had it all their own way, and had been able to con women into believing it was for the common good.

Her insistence that they move to the suburbs had been founded on the argument that a child needs a garden. Larry had resisted, but for once, on this one issue, Helen had refused to compromise. It was her attempt to extricate them from the social set she knew would destroy their marriage. She eventually got the house she wanted, but only really succeeded in moving herself and her child into it. Larry effectively only lodged there. In his heart, his home was always Soho.

Helen was astonished, sometimes, that she and Larry had stayed together so long. It was in the eighties that all these marriages fell apart. Every last one of them.

They had divorced almost twenty years ago, now, and every day she thought about him at least once. This long reminiscence, if she was lucky, could be today's thought, but on an idle day he was likely to haunt her more than once, and her visit to

28

Paul made the prospects worse. Paul was half-Larry; in looks he was three-quarters Larry, closer to how Larry had looked when she fell in love with him than Larry now was himself.

The sight of Paul was an exquisite torture for Helen, like scratching a rash or picking a scab. It made her think thoughts she knew were bad for her, it plunged her back into all the emotions she had worked so hard to be rid of, but in some way she relished the pain. She wanted as much as she could get. She wanted to hold Paul close and nuzzle herself into the Larryness of his neck; she wanted, just for a moment, for Paul to not be Paul, but to be the Larry he so resembled, the Larry before everything had turned bad.

How happy she'd be if there had been a daughter, if there was now a lookalike of the young Helen to match this time-capsule Larry. It would make everything so much fairer. Why did Larry not have to go through these agonies? If only this woman could exist, ready to bounce into his life every time he thought he was beginning to forget Helen, an ally to help make Larry suffer the way Helen suffered. Why had everything always been so much easier for him?

If there was a medical procedure by which doctors could erase a person from your head, Helen would be at the front of the queue. Larry was a poison in her brain. He still afflicted her because she couldn't make herself stop loving him, however much she also hated him. Paul sometimes seemed like an antibody, sometimes like more of the poison, often both at once.

Three coffees later, Helen was abuzz with caffeine-and-Larry-induced anxiety. She couldn't sit there any longer, and she couldn't allow herself to be alone with her thoughts for so much as one more drink. It was still only five o'clock, but she had reached the limit of her capacity to wait.

She'd go and ring the bell. See what happened. If no one was in, she'd take it from there.

ECCENTRIC AND VAGUELY
UNWHOLESOME GROUPS

Paul's door was answered by a handsome man in his early twenties who somehow managed to look both neat and scruffy at the same time. Scruffiness was the look he had chosen, but it had been put together with immense care. He was wearing a tight, short T-shirt and a pair of jeans so low and loose-fitting that they appeared to be held up only by his genitals. A good five inches of midriff were on display, though it was more low-riff than midriff, since the revealed band of flesh started at the navel and descended to what was unmistakably a frond or two of pubic hair.

The clothes, even to a woman who was no expert on these matters, said very clearly, 'I am gay'. The way he stood said, 'I am gay'; the hair said, 'I am gay'; even the way he opened the door somehow succeeding in saying, 'I am gay'.

He was gay.

'Are you the new cleaner?' he said, with a sceptical lilt to his voice, as if she didn't quite look poor enough.

'No,' she said. 'I'm Paul's mum.'

His mouth silently opened and closed, like a

30

fish.

The reason Paul had never invited her to his Hoxton house was suddenly obvious. Helen had thought Paul might be gay since he was eight, and had been pretty sure of it by the time he was fourteen. She had a fairly good idea of when he first came out to his friends, and a strong sense of when he had his first boyfriend. But not once had he ever so much as hinted at it to Helen. He only ever had 'lovers' or 'partners', never 'girlfriends' or 'boyfriends', and was frequently shifty with his pronouns, hiding behind an obfuscatory 'they' in place of a 'he' or 'she'.

Why he was like this, why he had never been able to talk to her about his sexuality, she had no idea. She was a modern, open-minded woman. Paul couldn't possibly have thought she was homophobic: she had gone out of her way to make clear to him that she wasn't, and to let him know that she would accept him whoever he was and however he chose to behave, but none of her hints had ever been picked up on, and he had never opened up to her, even though it often seemed that he knew she knew. She sometimes thought that perhaps he kept it private not because he was ashamed of it, or because he was afraid she would be critical of him, but simply to keep her at a distance.

The neatly scruffy man at the door was still staring at her, rendered speechless by her explanation of who she was.

'Can I come in?' she said. If this man didn't know anything about her, he wouldn't have any reason to be shocked. And for him to know anything at all about her, he had to know a fair amount about Paul. She was already certain this was Paul's lover, even though the size of the house suggested that more than two people lived here. Half an hour with him over a coffee—it might have to be a decaf if she didn't want to end up a twitching zombie—and she'd be prepared for Paul's arrival.

'Is he expecting you?' said the man. 'Cause he's not here.'

'Oh, yes. We spoke on his mobile a couple of hours ago. He said he was coming home early from work and I should meet him here.' Helen found it extremely easy to lie to men. It was a talent she had perfected during her waitressing years.

'Oh. OK. Shall I call him and tell him you're here?'

He was resisting. Lying to gay men, she remembered, was not as easy as lying to straight men.

'He'll be back any minute. He sent me a text. I'm dying for a cup of tea.' Less threatening than coffee. More harmless-old-womanish. 'I'm sorry, I didn't catch your name.'

'Andre.'

'With an accent?' If she made enough small talk and generally acted as if he had already invited her in, his defences would weaken.

'No, no accent. Just Andre. Like Andrex without the x.'

Helen laughed. 'Well, I think it's a lovely name. I always regretted calling Paul Paul. It was his father's idea. He deserves something more exciting, don't you think?'

'You'd better come in and wait here,' said Andre. 'I'll get you that tea.'

Inside, a sleek but doleful lurcher clicked over the floorboards towards the door and greeted her with a welcoming sniff. Helen went down on her haunches and gave the dog a friendly barrage of pats. 'Hello, beautiful,' she said in her dog voice. 'Who are you?'

'He's called Oscar,' said Andre.

'He's gorgeous,' said Helen. Be nice to the dog, and you're in. 'Is he yours?'

'He's everyone's,' said Andre, ambiguously. 'He belongs to the house.'

Everything Andre said was a clue. There were clearly several people who lived here, and the implication was that they were more than just flatmates. More than strangers, at least. Did people still use the word commune? Was this a gay commune? Or was it a homophobic fantasy that such a thing existed, that gay people clubbed together in eccentric and vaguely unwholesome groups to couple in ways that mathematically simple-minded heterosexuals could never even dream of? Helen had recently heard a physicist on the radio talking about calculations he was doing on a nine-dimensional universe. Maybe gay people were like that about sex. Maybe they could get their heads round forms of cohabitation that binary-thinking people like her weren't capable of comprehending. Maybe Andre wasn't Paul's boyfriend. Perhaps he was something similar for which there was no word, the workings of which she was as likely to understand as the formation of black holes.

'Kitchen's downstairs,' he said, leading the way. He walked without lifting his feet, like a figure-skater. Helen checked her hair and lipstick in the

33

large art nouveau hall mirror before following him down.

Helen was relieved to see that Andre made two cups. There was no way of knowing what kind of social rules prevailed in this place. For all she knew, he might easily have made one tea, then disappeared to leave her waiting for Paul. Whatever went on here, some common courtesies at least prevailed. Unless, of course, he didn't believe her story and was keeping an eye on her to make sure she didn't nick anything.

Oscar came down and joined them, which put Helen a little more at ease, helping the situation resemble something comprehensible and familiar. This was a man and a woman in a kitchen, drinking tea, in the company of a dog. If all else failed, the presence of a dog was a conversational safety net. If a silence went on too long, there was always dog-talk to fall back on.

Once they were settled across the table from each other, Helen decided to go for the big one, before he got in first and started exploring how much she knew.

'So how long have you been Paul's boyfriend?' she said. Anything less would have put Andre in a difficult position. Putting it like this, she bypassed the coming-out question and gave the impression there were no secrets Andre had to tiptoe around.

Andre appeared almost to choke on his tea. Helen pretended not to notice. She allowed the silence to run on, giving him no way out.

'About four months,' he said. 'Give or take.'

'Oh. And it's going well?'

Andre smirked, and nodded, then got up and fiddled in a cupboard, as if playing for time. He came back to the table with a packet of Jaffa cakes, which he offered to Helen, who declined. He then broke one up and fed it to Oscar, bit by bit, allowing him to duck the conversation without being too rude.

Helen refused to offer him a conversational lifeline. It was Andre's turn to speak, and she wasn't going to hand him a let-off.

'You're not what I was expecting,' he said, eventually.

'Oh?'

'I had the impression Paul hadn't come out to you.'

'Maybe he never had to. I'm not an idiot.'

'If someone doesn't want to see something, often they don't. That doesn't make them an idiot.'

'Why would I not want to see it?'

'Search me, but lots of people don't.'

'And Paul acts like I'm one of them, does he?'

'No. It's just the impression he gives. He doesn't talk about it, really.'

'He's very secretive,' said Helen.

'He is,' said Andre, and the two of them smiled at one another, sharing, at last, a moment of warmth.

'But we shouldn't talk about him behind his back. It's not really fair, is it?' said Helen.

Much as she would have loved to plug Andre for information, Helen wanted to make sure it was she who said this first. She had to show Andre that she wasn't as monstrous as Paul might have made out.

'Well, what else are we going to talk about?' said Andre, only half joking.

'The weather?' said Helen. 'The dog?'

'OK. Nice weather.'

35

'Nice dog.'

Paul hadn't even arrived, and already Helen had made significant progress. Both the boyfriend and the dog seemed to like her, and she liked them. From the moment he'd described himself as Andrex without the 'x', she had known he was OK.

A tiny but muscular man with a shaven head thundered down the stairs and began clattering wordlessly through the cupboards, without a glance at Andre or Helen. It was odd to be so small, and yet so body-built. Such wasted effort. It wasn't as if anyone that size could ever be physically threatening or even particularly strong. Why would anyone with that body pick the gym as their hobby? It reminded Helen of the deaf people who painstakingly attain some kind of mastery of a musical instrument. However good they are, you just want to ask, 'Why?'

Ripping open what looked like some kind of power bar, the muscle midget turned and glared angrily at Helen.

'Well, thank God you're here,' he said. 'You're two hours late.'

'Am I?' she said.

'She's not the new clean—' said Andre.

'Have you sorted out the wages and everything?' he said. 'And have you told her that if she touches a single fucking thing in my studio she's sacked?'

'You can tell her yourself,' said Andre, 'but there's not much point, since she's not the new cleaner.'

'Christ, do I have to do everything myself?' he said, and clomped back up the stairs, as if attempting to impress on them how much he weighed.

36

'You get used to him,' said Andre, after a pause. 'He's an acquired taste.'

'I thought he was charming.'

'He's OK. He just has bad days.'

Then, suddenly, there in front of her was Paul, looking as heart-stoppingly Larrylike as ever: his broad chin exactly replicating his father's, his curved, dark eyebrows frowning Larry's frown.

'I didn't hear you come in,' said Andre, standing, walking across the room and kissing Paul on the lips.

Paul recoiled from the kiss and stared from Helen to Andre and back again, in the manner of someone teleported without warning to a place they've never seen before. What had just happened, it appeared, simply did not compute. Andre, equally befuddled, gazed at Paul and Helen. The way Paul was staring at her made it clear that he absolutely wasn't expecting her, as Helen had told him, and the way he had recoiled from the kiss gave the distinct impression that he was not, after all, out to his mother.

Only Helen kept her cool, smiling warmly at Paul. 'Hello, darling,' she said. 'Just thought I'd pop in.'

GILLIAN AND DANIEL

WHY IS NOT HAVING A LEMON TYPICAL?

'That's a nice greeting!'

There is a window of truth in all relationships that exists in the fraction of a second between opening a front door and composing a polite response to an unexpected visitor. The more alert you are, the greater your chances of drawing the curtains over this window before anyone gets a chance to look inside. Women are swifter than men. Sociable men are quicker than unsociable men. The happy can move faster than the unhappy. This put Daniel in the slowest category of all. For a full second, at the unexpected sight of his mother on the doorstep, his face betrayed sheer, unadorned dismay.

'What's a nice greeting?' he finally managed. 'I haven't even said anything.'

Gillian had already walked past him into the flat, and was unbuttoning her coat in the living room by the time he finished speaking. She held out her coat and scarf (which she wore ten months of the year) without even glancing in Daniel's direction. She was looking around the room in the manner of a policeman at a crime scene. Daniel took the garments and tossed them on to a chair.

'What are you doing here?' he said, returning to the living room.

'I came on impulse.'

'Impulse? It's four hundred miles.'

'I'm your mother. Distance has nothing to do with it.'

'But . . . why didn't you phone?'

'I told you, it was a sudden impulse.'

'You still could have told me you were coming.'

Gillian's gaze suddenly latched on to the novel splayed open on the coffee table. 'What's *that*?' she said.

'It's a novel. You want some tea?'

'I can see that, Daniel. I'm not stupid.'

'So why are you asking?'

'What's it doing there? Are you reading it? I mean, is that what you were doing just now? That's your evening?'

'Yeah. It's good.'

'This is worse than I thought. I need to sit down.'

'What's the big deal?'

'You're thirty-four!'

'Yes.'

'It's Saturday night!'

'So?'

'You're single!'

'I'm aware of that.'

'And you're sitting at home, on your own, reading a . . . a . . . *novel!* What's wrong with you? I mean, have you given up? Is that it? Thirty-four isn't young, but it's not old. It's too early to give up. Isn't it? Tell me you haven't given up.'

'Do you want tea or not?'

'Of course I want tea, and I want to know why you're sitting around like a pensioner when you should be out there finding yourself a nice girl and getting ready to give me some grandchildren.'

'Grandchildren. Here we go,' said Daniel, walking to the kitchen, closely followed by his mother.

'It's not a lot to ask.'

'So ask Rose.'

'Don't worry, I ask her every week. But I don't see why you should get off so lightly.'

'Whatever you say won't make any difference, Mum. Nagging doesn't make people breed.' He flicked on the kettle and began searching a high cupboard for some biscuits.

'What did I do to get such selfish children? Before I've even spoken, my own son tells me nothing I can say will make any difference.'

'You have spoken, Mum. You've spoken plenty. I've never met anyone who's managed to stop you speaking.'

'Every woman deserves to be a grandmother. It's half the point of being a mother in the first place.'

'Oh, so we're just machines to make your grandchildren?'

'Not machines, but you do have a job to do, yes.'

'Mum, your life is your life, my life is my life. It's up to me to—'

'That's the stupidest thing I ever heard.'

'What, my life isn't my life?'

'Of course it isn't!'

'Whose is it, then?'

'I don't know,' she said. 'But you're not just here for you. You're here to . . . pass on the flame.'

Daniel slammed the cupboard door, abandoning his biscuit search, and turned back to his mother. 'What flame?'

'If we were all just here for ourselves, life would be pointless.'

'Life is pointless.'

'Don't be ridiculous. Lemon, not milk.'

'I don't have any lemons.'

'Typical.'

'What does that mean? Why is not having a lemon typical?'

'It just is. Me me me. It's your whole philosophy.'

'I didn't know you were coming!'

'Exactly.'

'What?'

'You didn't know anyone was coming.'

'No one is coming.'

'That's my point: no one coming. Just you in your little world. Me me me. With your little books. At home.'

'Little books? What do you mean, "little books"? It's not little, and even if it was, I don't see what that would have to do with whether or not I've run out of lemons.'

'Well, if you don't understand, *I* can't explain.'

Gillian felt a prickle of sweat on her upper lip and swiftly dabbed at it with the side of her thumb, a nervous tic she had acquired in the last few years, as her body's thermostat had taken on a wayward and unpredictable personality.

She was feeling tense and uncomfortable, sensations which invariably manifested themselves in Gillian as aggression. She did not belong here. She had no place barging into Daniel's life like this, and with a four-hundred-mile journey behind her, she was giving him no choice but to take her in.

She had already spent half an hour in the car outside, pondering the idea of turning round and driving straight back to London. But the longer she sat there, the more confused she became, until she realised that she had lost any capacity to make a rational decision about what to do, and was no longer even thinking about the problem. She was simply sitting there, gazing into space like a mad person.

It was the desire for a cup of tea that had eventually driven her to ring his doorbell. At the moment she pressed the buzzer, she suddenly and decisively knew she was doing a bad thing. It was wrong to force herself on her son like this. But she had buzzed. Now she just had to brazen it out.

With a sigh, Daniel handed Gillian her drink. 'Is this supposed to be logical?' he said. 'Should I be following this, or are you just talking for the pleasure of hearing noises come out of your mouth?'

'Always the clever words. Trying to act like I'm the stupid one who can't make herself understood.'

'You can't make yourself understood! I'm not calling you stupid—I'd never call you stupid—but I don't understand what you're talking about or why you're here.'

'Charming! Is this how I raised you? A woman travels hundreds of miles to visit her son, and the first thing he says to her is, "What are you doing here?"'

'It's not the first thing I said to you, and that isn't even what I said.'

'OK, I'll go. You don't want me, I'll go. Get me my coat.' Gillian tipped her steaming tea into the sink and began to rinse out her mug.

'I don't want you to go. Stay. I'm just asking why you didn't ring to tell me you were coming.'

'I have to ask permission?'

'You don't have to ask permission. I'm just asking. You don't think it's normal for me to be surprised?'

'There are thousands of women in this city. Not as many as in a proper city, but you're a handsome man. She doesn't have to be Jewish. We gave up on that years ago, Daniel. You can choose anyone.'

'Oh, now you're giving *me* permission?'

'Women like Jews. They like something exotic.

42

Generations of suffering and a good university degree—it's what every sensible girl is looking for.'

'I'm really not getting dragged into this conversation.'

'You're handsome. You've always acted like you think women are going to say "no" to you, and that's a terrible mistake. I should have told you more often how good-looking you are, when you were a boy, but I didn't want to make you conceited. Maybe it's my fault.'

'You're right. It's your fault. Now how was your journey? Shall I make you another cup of tea?'

'How can you say that?'

'Say what?'

'That it's my fault!'

'I was being sarcastic, Mum.'

'You're always sarcastic. It's the modern disease. No one knows what anyone else means any more.'

'Why don't we go and sit in the living room?' said Daniel, knowing she wouldn't, since she didn't like living rooms and didn't like sitting. At home, the lounge was always under-heated and over-lit. It was a place for watching TV or entertaining visitors you didn't really like. The kitchen was where everything happened.

'You could have done so much better,' continued Gillian, not budging from her spot beside the oven. 'Even the women you did go out with, they were never much to write home about. That girl Lucy you stuck around with for years, honestly, she was lumpen. Just a solid, healthy, country girl. OK, maybe that's interesting for a while, as an experiment, but for a boy like you—an intellectual—it's totally unsuitable.'

'I'm not an intellectual, Mum.'

43

'Well, I don't know what the word for it is, but you're certainly no country boy.'

'I never said I was. And since when is "healthy" an insult?'

'And that other one. Erin. What kind of a name is Erin?' Gillian refilled the kettle and began making herself another cup of tea. 'It's like the leftovers from a Scrabble hand.'

'And that's a character flaw, is it?'

'I never liked Erin.'

Gillian wasn't quite sure how the conversation had taken this turn, and why she had chosen this moment to bully her son with a diatribe against his ex-girlfriends. Something similar often seemed to happen between the two of them. She'd begin a conversation intending to talk to him in the way she spoke to her friends, and within minutes she'd find herself hectoring him as if he was a recalcitrant teenager. Whatever good intentions she started with, she always ended up behaving like this: like—though it pained her to admit it—her own mother.

'Can we change the subject?' said Daniel, sitting down heavily at the kitchen table.

The problem was, once she had begun, Gillian found it almost impossible to backtrack. And on this particular occasion she had a good reason for pressing on, as a tactic to divert attention from her abrupt intrusion into his life. The longer she could delay an explanation, the better her chances of getting away with it, and the best way to steer him away from demanding the reason for her arrival was to find something more vexing to talk about. She had to keep him on the defensive. 'There was a vulgarity, wasn't there?' said Gillian, feeling only slightly ashamed of herself. 'She was very pushy.'

'You only met her a few times, and you barely spoke to her. You never gave her a chance.'

'Did you see the way she held her cutlery?'

'That's not something that's burned on my—'

'Like she'd never seen it before! Like she'd been raised by Chinamen! By the end of the meal, she had food on her fingers!'

'So you've come to insult my ex-girlfriend's table manners? That's why you're here?'

'Why do you keep asking me that? It's very rude.'

'Oh, and it's not rude to fling racist slurs at all the women I've ever loved.'

'You loved them?'

'I don't know.'

'You *loved* them!'

'I didn't say that.'

'You did say that! That's exactly what you said.'

'It's a turn of phrase. I was exaggerating.'

'Well, did you? Did you love them?'

'Why do you care? It was ages ago.'

'Well, if you could love *them*, why are you just sitting around mooching now? It's not like you're waiting for someone to match up to them, is it? I thought you were being choosy—and I respect that—but I think you've been shopping below your market.'

'It's not shopping. I'm not going to talk about it in these terms, Mum.'

'You've always undervalued yourself. It's probably my fault. I'm going to try and put things right again.'

'What things?'

'I'm going to help you.'

45

'Help me do what?'

'Get yourself back on your feet.'

'I am on my feet. I was never off my feet.'

'With girls, I mean.'

'With girls! How are *you* going to help *me*? And who says I need help, anyway?'

'The facts is who. A year is who. Without a girlfriend.'

'I don't need help, and I don't want help.'

'Well, you're getting help. I've brought an overnight bag. I'm going to stay here for a while and sort you out.'

'I am sorted out! I don't need sorting out!'

'How long did you live in my house?'

'What?'

'How long did you live in my house?'

'What are you talking about?'

'Eighteen years! Eighteen years! And now you're saying one week the other way round is too much to ask?'

'A week! You want to stay a week?'

'I'll go and get my bag. It's in the car.'

'You drove?'

'I told you, it was an impulse. And I like long drives. It's the only chance I get to sit still.'

Abandoning her second untouched cup of tea, Gillian strode into the hall, closely followed by Daniel.

'Does Dad know you're doing this?'

'Of course.'

'And what does he think?'

'I don't know. I didn't ask.'

'This is crazy!'

'Don't be stubborn. And I hope that by the end of this week I'll have turned you into the kind of

46

man who doesn't send his aged mother out into the street to carry her own suitcase.'

The front door slammed behind her. Checking he had keys in his pocket, Daniel followed her out. A minute later, he found himself carrying his mother's suitcase up the tenement staircase to the door of his flat. It weighed as much as a piano.

He didn't understand how this had happened. He had no recollection of agreeing to have her, or of giving even the slightest hint that she was welcome to stay. But she was staying and, judging by the size of her suitcase, which was not so much an overnight bag as a coffin with a handle, she was planning to settle in.

Although part of him thought her stay might well end in matricide, and despite the fact that his mother was possibly the most irritating human being he had ever met, Daniel was surprised to find himself pleased to see her, and flattered that she had driven so far to visit him. He somehow felt equal measures of dread and pleasure at the thought of spending time with her. Even though conversing with her sometimes made him feel like a hedgehog attempting to negotiate rights of way with a juggernaut, even though she rarely said anything to him that couldn't be read as some kind of barb or criticism, he never felt in any doubt that she loved him.

When they argued, which they usually did, the arguments were always comfortingly familiar. Even when their time together was dominated by a carefully enumerated litany of his current top ten flaws, she always gave off a warmth that somehow made him feel at home.

Talking to her was like a sauna of the ego—a

full Finnish one where they strip you naked, send you out into the snow and beat you with branches. While it was happening, you felt nothing but discomfort; once it was over, a quiet inner glow told you that you had done yourself some good. Contact with his mother was, in essence, a gruelling form of masochistic pampering.

In the six months since moving to Edinburgh, Daniel had been surprised to find that he missed her and his sister, Rose, more than he missed his friends. For a man in his mid-thirties this was clearly not healthy, but the ease with which he'd walked away from the network of London-based friendships that had sustained him since his childhood had taken him by surprise.

Almost all his old, close friends now had children, a process which, one by one, appeared to have turned them into zombies. When he saw them at weekends, attempting to do his duty to show an interest in their families, he often ended up feeling like a foreign exchange student: he tried his best to communicate, but usually found it impossible to tell what was being talked about, where the conversation was going, or whether or not everyone else in the room was secretly bored of him and desperate for him to leave so they could get on with their lives. He always felt less like a visitor, more like an interruption. When he succeeded in dragging his friends out to the pub to see them alone, they always had the glazed look in their eyes of an ageing boxer who's been punched in the head once too often. It was as if the ghosts of their children were still there in the pub with them, running invisibly round the table, destroying their father's ability to focus on one topic of conversation for more than thirty seconds.

The only friends of Daniel's who didn't have children also tended to have no girlfriend, and as a result seemed to be incapable of leaving home without going on the pull, which gave them an attention span barely any longer than the punch-drunk fathers.

As the number of Daniel's friends capable of sustaining a coherent conversation dwindled, he began to feel as if friendship as a pastime was becoming an obligation rather than a pleasure. A few hundred miles' distance, he thought, might revive these friendships over the phone, with fewer dutiful visits to drag things down. But since arriving in Edinburgh, his phone bills each month revealed more calls to the local curry house than to any London number.

This had been the strangest discovery to come out of his move to Scotland: he simply did not miss his friends. Erin, on the other hand, stabbed into his thoughts on an hourly basis.

TWO WEEKS EARLIER

MOTHER'S DAY

It was not that Mother's Day meant anything to Helen. She didn't really believe in it, and had no expectations of it. But as she walked downstairs, wrapped in her ancient padded dressing-gown, there was a brief, irrational moment when she thought that maybe, just this once, there would be a card from her son. She wasn't hoping for flowers

49

or chocolates or even a phone call, but a card—a tiny indication that he remembered who she was and what she had done for him—would have breathed life into her day.

The doormat, of course, was empty. It was Sunday. There wasn't even a delivery. A solitary pizza take-away leaflet mocked her hopes of filial devotion.

Helen crumpled the leaflet in her fist and jammed it into the kitchen bin. She was trying to give up breakfast. Bread was the fashionable thing to avoid these days, and toast was the only food she could face in the morning. She gave herself a black tea and dutifully worked her way down a banana. There was something depressing about bananas: the cloying noise they made as you chewed them; their garish, pseudo-cheerful colour; the useless spent bulk of their skin after you'd finished. The only reason for their popularity was probably that you could eat one without getting your hands sticky.

This is not healthy, she thought to herself. Here I am, a grown, intelligent woman, passing my time mentally listing to myself the pros and cons of bananas. My head should be filled with more interesting things than this. I should be doing more with my brain.

At least it was a book-group day. They called it a book group, though it wasn't really a group, and they didn't actually bother with books any more. It was just a regular social occasion: the last Sunday of each month, Gillian, Carol and Helen got together for morning coffee and a chat, the venue rotating month by month between their respective houses. This was the rump of a gathering of mums

50

that had formed around a local playgroup roughly thirty years earlier. They all had children the same age, and they'd regularly got together to relieve the boredom of early motherhood. Though some had come simply for a break in the routine, these three had genuinely liked one another, and their sons could—at a push—be persuaded to keep one another entertained without too much noise or bloodshed. There had only ever been one hospitalisation.

The group had swelled and shrunk, as various people moved in, moved away, gave birth, changed schools and got divorced. At its peak, one year there had even been a camping holiday involving more families than could ever hope to go away together without a major social catastrophe befalling them. But through everything, over more than three decades, Gillian, Carol and Helen had remained neighbours and friends.

They had stopped gathering once the children hit secondary-school age, and though they all remained more or less in touch, they didn't meet up as a group for more than ten years. Then, with their kids all in their twenties, all having left home, Carol had suggested they start up the Sunday morning coffee routine. It was Gillian, frustrated by the fact that all they seemed to talk about was their children, who suggested turning it into a book group.

This was a success for a while, not least because it got rid of some of the more irritating women, but it wasn't long before people stopped reading the books and, even if they had read the books, stopped talking about them. Eventually, all that remained was Helen, Carol and Gillian, and their

Sunday morning coffee. As far as Helen was concerned, this was more or less perfect. It was, though she could barely admit it to herself, the highlight of her month.

When Helen had first moved out from Kensington to Pinner, she had initially scorned and pitied the suburban women around her. In choosing the house, she had been far more concerned with the life she wanted to get away from than with worrying about what she was moving towards. She had only really thought about the house and the garden, not about the community she would have to fit into.

She soon realised that this short journey of a few miles up the Metropolitan line had, culturally, almost taken her back to Derby. These women had clearly never been to the kind of parties that were part of her weekly routine. They seemed about as worldly as Helen thought she must have been when she first arrived in the capital. Every one of them gave the impression of having lived through the whole of the sixties without smoking a single joint or sleeping with anyone other than their husband. They rarely even went to the centre of town; their suburban little parade of shops somehow appeared to satisfy all their needs. And the way they dressed made Helen want to grab them by the arms and shout, 'Have you not looked in a magazine for the last five years? Do you never open your eyes?'

At first Helen told herself that she only socialised with these women for Paul's sake—to provide him with friends—but as the years went by, though she never quite lost her horror at the way they dressed, and though she always clung on to a notion somewhere in her soul that she was simply passing through suburbia out of parental convenience and was at heart a genuine metropolitan, her aloofness slowly dwindled away. She never quite admitted to herself that she was the same as them, but she did gradually come to acknowledge that they had so much in common, the differences had ceased to matter.

They had watched one another's babies grow through childhood into adolescence and adulthood, while slowly seeing each other getting old. They had cajoled, advised and comforted one another through the cement mixer of parenthood. Proximity and shared experience, year by year, knitted their lives together. Outside of family, Helen had never shared an intimacy deeper than that she now had with Gillian and Carol. Her friendships, in the end, had been as important to Helen as her marriages; if nothing else, they had lasted longer.

Even so, after more than three decades, she'd still not built up the courage to give them a talking-to about their clothes.

As Helen poured the tea and handed round the plate of neatly overlapping biscuits that she had laid out a good hour before the arrival of her two guests, she pointed out that it was Mother's Day.

'Ha!' said Gillian.

Helen didn't even need to ask what that meant. Though Gillian was in the habit of talking far too much, she also had a knack of compressing complex thoughts into very small packages. 'Ha!' somehow said it all.

'Any cards?' said Helen.

'Oh, Matt buys me a weekend in Paris every Mother's Day,' said Carol, her voice heavy with wistful sarcasm.

'Nothing at all?' said Helen.

'Do people really get things?' said Carol.

'The shops are all crammed with stuff. Someone must buy it,' said Gillian.

'Nothing from Daniel?' said Helen.

Gillian rolled her eyes. 'I don't think Daniel can even remember our phone number, let alone our postcode.'

'What's wrong with them? I mean, WHAT'S WRONG WITH THEM ALL?' said Helen, her teacup rattling in her hand as a nebulous anger rose up within her. Helen didn't quite know what it was she was angry about, but since she was among close friends, she felt that the best way to find out was simply to carry on talking and see where it took her. 'They're grown men! They're not children any more. You expect them to hate you for a while when they're adolescents, but they're supposed to grow out of it, aren't they? We should be on civil, adult terms by now. They should be grown-ups. They should have children of their own. They should be going through what we went through, and realising what sheer bloody hard work it all is, and . . . I mean . . . we've waited thirty years for a bit of understanding and gratitude, and I'm sick of it.'

She sat back in her chair and sighed, feeling rather pleased with her rant, even a little flushed and exhilarated, like after a hefty spring-clean.

'You'll be waiting another thirty years if what you're after is gratitude,' said Gillian.

'Well, just some communication would be a start. Paul doesn't want to speak to me any more. He thinks I'm boring and stupid and he talks to me

54

as rarely as he thinks he can get away with, and when he does, he tells me as little as possible.'

'Children are supposed to think their parents are boring and stupid,' said Gillian. 'It's a natural cycle. It means you brought him up well and gave him higher goals in life.'

'Are you saying I *am* boring and stupid?' said Helen.

'I'm just saying it's normal,' said Gillian. 'Especially with boys. And there's no point in feeling angry about it. Is there, Carol?'

Gillian turned to Carol for support, noticing as she did so that Carol had a strange, intent look in her eye. Helen noticed it, too, and they both stared at Carol, waiting for her to speak. It was a long wait.

Though Carol didn't usually even register Mother's Day, and had never encouraged her son to mark it with cards or gifts, the previous evening she happened to have spoken to Matt on the phone, after which she had been surprised to find herself close to tears. They had not argued, Matt had not been rude, or any more dismissive of her than usual, and they had not even suffered any particularly long silences. There had simply been something in the air between them that made Carol want to grieve. The essence of it was that there had been nothing between them. Carol frequently had more satisfactory and open conversations with strangers.

After putting the phone down, she had sat and watched the news with her husband, as she always did, but as the images of global mayhem flashed in front of her eyes, not a word from the TV sank in. It had never occurred to her that grief was a sensation you could feel for a living relative, for someone you still loved. Matt was still entirely alive and healthy, but their relationship, she realised, had died. All that remained of it was the faintly humiliating one-way flow of her love. Matt, her one and only child, the focus of her life, thought of her as simply another chore, on a par with doing the laundry and emptying the dishwasher. Never before had she felt quite so old and useless.

'They've ditched us,' Carol said, eventually. 'They took everything we had to give, for years on end, and now they think the odd grumpy phone call every other week is enough to pay off the debt.'

'That's how it works,' said Gillian.

'Well, it shouldn't,' said Carol, her voice trembling with constrained emotion. Helen had given her a thought. Perhaps she was not, after all, old and useless. Perhaps, for once, she should override her natural instinct to assume that every problem was her own fault, and she should consider the idea that maybe the fault was with Matt. Maybe he was young and useless.

'No, it shouldn't,' said Helen, delighted to be backed up. She found herself smirking at Gillian, the two sharing a little worried-amused glance at Carol's strange mood.

'Of course it *shouldn't*,' said Gillian. 'But if that's how they want to behave, we just have to live with it.'

'Why?' said Carol, rounding on Gillian, as if suddenly angry with her.

'What do you mean, why?' said Gillian.

'Why do we just have to live with it?' Carol

56

snapped, waving a half-eaten biscuit sharply through the air.

'What's the alternative?' said Gillian. 'You think being eaten up with resentment is going to improve anything?'

'Well, maybe instead of just sitting here, moaning, we should do something about it,' said Carol.

'Like what?'

'Think of what we did for them. Year after year after year. They owe us.' As these words came out of her mouth, Carol realised she had never before thought about Matt in these terms. In the past, she had been angry with him about specific things he had done, and there had been times when she'd expected him to apologise and mollify her, but she had never before thought in terms of one big outstanding debt of love on which her feckless and ungrateful son was defaulting.

'What do they owe us?' said Gillian.

'Well,' said Carol, floundering for a way to express her grievance, before suddenly thinking of something that got to the heart of it all. 'Grandchildren, for a start.'

'Ha!' said Gillian.

'They're thirty-four!' continued Carol, sitting forwards in her chair and putting down her tea. 'It's time. And not one of them has married, or even settled down, let alone produced any children. We should be grandmothers by now. We should be surrounded by little people who adore us and think we're wonderful, but who never keep us awake all night, and who we can hand back when they have a full nappy. That's the payback. It's what we're owed.'

'It would be nice,' said Helen, 'but it's not going to happen.'

'Why not?' said Carol. 'Why are we being left out?'

'Maybe they just need a bit longer,' said Gillian. 'It's bound to happen eventually.'

'WHEN? Next year they'll be thirty-five. That's not even young. That's middle age. They're almost middle-aged, and they still want to live like children.'

'It's not middle age.'

'It's not young,' said Carol. 'If they were women it would almost be too late.'

'You're being hysterical,' said Gillian. 'They're not women, and it isn't too late.'

'But it's not like they're on the brink. They're not even close. Any of them.'

'That's just how it is,' said Helen, thinking to herself that in Paul's case there was a far bigger impediment than his age.

'But why?' continued Carol, still angrily waving the remnants of her biscuit. 'If they're not going to do it, I suppose that's their right, but are we just going to sit here and not even find out why? Maybe it's something we did.'

'What are you suggesting?' said Gillian.

'Let's go and find out,' said Carol. 'We can't force them to have children, but we can at least make them give us an explanation. They can't deny us *that*.'

'They can,' said Gillian. 'And they probably will.'

'Well then, maybe we're making it too easy for them. Maybe it's time to force the issue.'

'How?' said Helen.

'By not going away so easily. By not giving up.'

'Not going away?'

'Yes. What if we went? To visit. And stayed,' said Carol, the idea only popping into her head at the moment it came out of her mouth. If there had been any pause between thinking it and saying it, she would probably have dismissed the thought as ludicrous.

'*Stayed?*' said Gillian.

'Just for . . . maybe, a week.' Carol still didn't quite believe her own proposal, but now she had started, it seemed worth batting the idea around, just to see what the other two thought—to get to the core of why it was that such a simple notion should seem so outlandish.

'A week!' Helen almost spilt her tea.

'Yes. They lived with us for long enough. They ought to be able to cope with a week the other way round,' Carol said, defiantly.

'They'd never agree to it,' said Gillian.

'So we wouldn't give them the chance to say no.'

'How?' said Helen.

'By not asking permission. We'd just turn up. They wouldn't throw us out. Not if we acted tough.'

'But why?' said Gillian.

'Because we can't just let them give up on us. Even forgetting grandchildren, if there's one thing they really do owe us, it's the right to know them. And they've shut us out, which just isn't fair.'

'It wouldn't work,' said Helen.

'And it wouldn't only be about us, it would be about them,' continued Carol, her tone rising in confidence as she became alarmed and excited to discover that she was beginning to believe what she was saying. Gillian and Helen's objections—which were at heart also hers—sounded feeble and cowardly. Carol was, to her surprise, winning the argument. 'If they can't finish growing up on their own, maybe they need us to make them grow up,' she said. 'They're not too old to be told off, and they're not too sorted out to still be in need of . . . of . . . I don't know . . . mothering.'

'Mothering?' said Helen.

'Yes, mothering. We haven't finished the job. It's as simple as that.'

'A week?' said Helen.

'But . . . how?' said Gillian. 'I mean, what would we do? How would they take it?'

'We'll find out, won't we? If they think they've got the right to forget us, then we've got the right to go and remind them.'

'Like a student protest? A sit-in?' said Helen.

'No, we make it a nice visit. We just try to remind them who we are, and try to figure out who they are. I honestly don't think I know any more.'

'No,' said Helen. 'Me neither.'

'Nor me,' said Gillian.

'You are joking, though,' said Helen. 'I mean, you wouldn't actually do it, would you?'

CAROL AND MATT

WAXY PALLOR

Sitting alone in Matt's strange, soulless cavern of an apartment, Carol wondered how the other two were getting on. Perhaps she was the only one who had gone through with it. Even right up to the last

60

moment before she rang the doorbell, she had been on the brink of backing out and heading home. The chances of Helen and Gillian being as brave as her, and of getting away with it, seemed low.

She took out her mobile to ring and find out, then stopped herself. She didn't want to know; she didn't want to be put off. What her friends did was no longer the point. Now she was here, she just had to think about her and Matt. The fact that he hadn't turned her away did not, of itself, amount to a significant achievement. It was just the start. She had to focus on her objective, which was to help him.

Carol would never have thought of herself as the kind of person likely to snoop, least of all in breach of the trust that a host has placed in a guest, but Matt wasn't really a host, and she wasn't really a guest. She knew it wasn't her flat, but it was, in a sense, the next best thing. He was her son and she loved him. She'd never do anything that wasn't in his interests.

By this logic, just the fact that she wanted to look around made it justifiable, and she decided to start by looking under his bed. The first stage of the operation was research. She had to find out more about who he really was. Specifically, she had to seek out the gulf between how he presented himself to her and who he really was. Under the bed seemed like a logical place to begin.

The main thing he kept there, she discovered, was dust. Dust and sports equipment, the combination of which told her that he was the kind of man who enjoyed buying his gear more than using it. This didn't come as much of a surprise.

Throughout his childhood he'd been the same, nagging for a particular must-have Christmas present from October, only to lose interest in it by the end of Boxing Day.

A small, black, interestingly un-sporty box caught her eye just as she was about to stand up. She reached through the shag-pile of dust to claw it free from the corner in which it was wedged. The box had no lettering or logo on it, but was solidly made out of expensive cardboard. This was a woman box, not a man box.

Carol sat on the bed and opened it up. Inside, on a bed of artfully crumpled red tissue-paper, was a pair of handcuffs, two tubes of 'Lick Me Lubricant' and 'Spunky Cappuccino Chocolate Body Paint', and a small string of beads that had presumably been left in the box by accident. Tucked down the side of the crêpe paper was a tiny envelope, on the front of which was the letter 'M', written in a swirling, feminine hand.

It wasn't entirely without a pang of conscience that Carol pulled the card from the envelope. She had fallen out with Matt in the past over her slight tendency towards nosiness, but the fact is, if it is your job to empty your child's bedroom bins, you simply will stumble across things that may not have been intended for your eyes. She knew she had, on occasion, overreacted. She could see now that her reaction to his fountain pen refill kit, which really had looked startlingly like a syringe, had been a little hysterical, but she had only been trying to do the right thing. Everything she had ever done for her child had always been only for him. But the difficult thing with children was that they never forgot or forgave anything. You could get a thousand things right, but it was the one thing they objected to that would be remembered.

It occurred to Carol that, with each passing generation, parents seemed to be getting more lenient with their children, while children got stricter with their parents. How long would it be, she thought, before things went full circle, and teenagers started beating their parents when they misbehaved?

As an envelope-opening pang override, Carol asked herself what kind of person could possibly not look. What freak of self-control would stop herself reading the card? Anyone lacking that curiosity would be inhumanly self-absorbed. Such a person would be, above all else, a terrible mother. It was, therefore, in her capacity as a good mother that she opened the card and read it.

The front of the card was blank cream, textured with thin, shallow ridges. The inside said:

M
You have been a very bad boy.
I am going to have to punish you.
Mercilessly.
K
XXX

Who was K? What had Matt done? How she had punished him didn't require too much figuring out.

Carol realised that her hands had begun to tremble, and beads of moisture were prickling at her neck. Was her son a pervert? Did this count as bondage? Did people really do this? Normal people? Was this something a mother should worry

63

about? Were there self-help groups for this kind of thing?

Carol had another look at the tubes. On closer inspection, they seemed like they had been used once. Enthusiastically. Unsparingly. But only once. The lid of the box, moreover, had been just as dusty, if not even dustier, than the squash and tennis rackets. Once, on reflection, probably wasn't enough to class you as a pervert.

Carol put the tubes back in the box, her fingers working with clumsy haste as she rearranged the tissue-paper into its previous position. She felt suddenly rather hot, and began to think she might be blushing. Lurid images were now flashing into her mind, of a variety she didn't know her subconscious even housed.

She clapped the lid on the box, pushed it firmly back to a distant corner among the under-bed filth, and stood up. She walked briskly to the kitchen and swallowed down a tall glass of water, its coolness on her tongue and lips dispelling the sordid murk that had begun to cloud her mind.

She washed her hands, twice, sensing as she dried them a tiny and rather surprising upswell of maternal pride. Women wanted her son. Not just mousy, bland women, but women like 'K', who were capable of going into heaven knows what kind of shops and emerging with small black boxes of unspeakable items.

You wouldn't want your son to marry a K. You certainly wouldn't want a K as the mother of your grandchildren. But there was a certain pride in discovering that your son knew how to handle one. It was a little like mountain-climbing. You wouldn't like the idea of your child going, but you'd feel proud when he got back home safely.

The world was full of Ks, and always had been, even though they had only recently opened shops for them. Carol knew there was a K in every Tube train, every office, every supermarket, and next time she found herself near one, she resolved to feel a little less scornful, and a little less intimidated.

As for Carol's research, this was important and discouraging news. Her pursuit of an explanation for the lack of grandchildren had immediately taken a step forwards. Now she knew the scale of the task. If Matt was to produce for her the babies she so craved, he had to travel from a K to a breeder.

The idea that Carol would be able to have any effect on his taste in women at all, let alone such a radical one, suddenly struck her as ludicrously ambitious. Unless, these days, there were women like K who also wanted children. It was possible. There was no limit to the increasing demands that men felt they could make on women, and a touch of whorishness in the bedroom had quite possibly, since her day, been added to the menu. But how she would find such a woman, or persuade Matt to take an interest in her, she had no idea.

The vigour with which Carol set about cleaning Matt's apartment demonstrated that her prying into her son's secrets had not been entirely without guilt. There was something almost purgatorial in the zeal she applied to the task. By the time she had finished, everything sparkled, even things that weren't supposed to. The entire flat was transformed from sepia matt to high gloss, its odour from old cigarettes to pungent chemical slanders against pine and lemon.

Worrying that she had perhaps gone overboard on the cleaning products—it was, after all, a little difficult to breathe—Carol opened the windows and set off in search of flowers.

By the time she had finished, the flat was barely recognisable. This gave her a moment's pause, as she remembered that it was not in fact hers, but the more she thought about it, the more confident she felt that Matt wouldn't be so churlish as to resent her efforts.

She slumped into Matt's sofa, exhausted by her domestic exertions. With no one watching, she saw no reason not to give herself up to the sluttishly enveloping upholstery, and she had to admit that it was alarmingly comfortable. Furniture really wasn't supposed to do this to you. This level of physical luxuriance was almost obscene. It wasn't healthy to get this much pleasure just from sitting down. Drugs, Carol imagined, probably felt like this, only more so.

No wonder people like Matt were lazy. If sitting down was this good, standing up must seem like such an effort, and so joyless.

It wasn't a notion that entirely made sense, but Carol found herself thinking that young people these days made it very hard for themselves by making everything so easy. There were so many more things luring them into idleness. And not just idleness, either. Just about any sin you could think of had a higher billing than it used to. When she was young, if you wanted to sin, you had to make it all up for yourself. Now every advertisement hoarding and TV programme that caught your eye was an instruction manual for moral depravity.

When it was so much easier to be bad, it must surely be harder to be good.

Under the coffee table, among a heap of DVDs, Carol spotted a copy of the magazine whose title, *BALLS!*, she recognised. This was where Matt worked. She had never read it before. Matt had never actively discouraged her from reading it, but he had never sent her a copy, and had never told her where to get one. Now she could see why.

On the cover was an almost-naked girl whose expression was half gloating, half that of someone who has just sat on something unexpectedly sharp. She was holding, with almost erotic reverence, a hinged silver ingot of technology that might have been a camera, a phone, a computer, or a state-of-the-art set of cake forks. Carol wasn't really qualified to tell. Perhaps it was the object she had accidentally sat on.

BALLS! the magazine proclaimed, and underneath, in smaller type, 'DON'T FORGET YOUR BALLS!'

The magazine began with what called itself a news page, though every item was nothing more than a picture of a girl or a pair of girls, either in a bikini or topless, with a caption giving their name (Carol had no idea if she was supposed to recognise them) and a tongue-in-cheek comment about either where they were, who they were with, or what had happened to their clothes. Further on there were more articles in the same vein, mixed in with the odd piece on football, gadgets or cars, but even those were heavily illustrated with near-naked women, their crotches usually concealed by a prop (a football, say, or a tyre) relevant to the theme of the article. Carol couldn't tell whether the magazine was trying to be pornography or journalism or the mail-order catalogue for an electronic goods firm.

There were a few interviews, some with girls who were only given a first name, which Carol assumed meant they were either global megastars who didn't need a surname, or girls off the street. The interviews tended to consist of four or five questions, along the lines of 'What's the easiest way to chat you up?' and 'Have you ever flashed before?'

Even regardless of her son's involvement, just discovering that a magazine like this existed was depressing. The mental age of the intended readers looked to be about twelve. It was almost a comic. Yet it was all about sex, or rather about breasts. Carol genuinely couldn't understand what *BALLS!* was, or why it was there, or who it was for. The idea that this was her son's life made her want to cry.

Carol returned the magazine to the coffee table and wiped her hands on her skirt. She had often talked to Matt about his job—about how his career was on the up and up, and the number of people he had working under him, and how the circulation had been soaring—but the topic of what was actually in the magazine had never cropped up. She had never thought to ask, and he had never offered the information. She had simply known that it was a men's magazine, and until now she always thought she understood what that meant.

On the rare occasions that she'd pondered his reticence, she had thought it must simply stem from his fear (accurate, as it happened) that Carol thought magazines were somehow effeminate.

Men's magazines, for all their vein-busting effort to be manly, had always aroused Carol's suspicions. Real men, as she saw it, didn't need advice or help in how to be masculine.

Yes, thinking about it now, she saw that he had been actively evasive about the content of his magazine, but she had allowed him to be, thinking she understood the reason why. She had always felt they were tacitly drawing a veil, together, over the embarrassingly effete nature of his job. It had never occurred to her that he was concealing something genuinely sordid.

When she saw girls exposing themselves on advertisement hoardings, she sometimes wondered how they faced their mothers, and if their families knew what they did for a living. Now Carol asked herself how she would face her son.

She doubted that it would be advisable to let him know what she thought. If she said anything at all, her full revulsion would flood out, and before she knew it she'd be telling him his life was mired in filth. If her goal was to improve their relationship, this was possibly not the most fruitful path to pursue.

*　　　*　　　*

Matt, meanwhile, was having a frantic day, up against the monthly deadline that, as ever, caused an afternoon of panic, tipping into exhilaration as the pages were finally sent. As was the tradition, the whole staff then went to a Soho bar popular with footballers, models and people who were willing to pay five pounds a beer in order to drink with footballers and models. It did not occur to

Matt, who had for the moment forgotten about his visitor, to skip the celebration and head home.

Matt bought the first round, which came in at forty quid, including the tip he gave to Marcello, the Cuban barman, who according to one rumour was in fact Brian from Hounslow. By the time he had spent eighty pounds, his gang of colleagues was beginning to get rowdy. As the total nudged over a hundred, a flock of models swanned into the bar, which brought a touch of sobriety back to the evening as the group zeroed in on their various targets.

Matt opted for a girl who was, well, nearly identical to all the others, except with black hair, slightly blacker than the other two dark ones, and who insisted that her name was Angel.

By the time he hit the hundred and fifty mark, he and Angel were getting on extremely well, all the better for Matt giving elaborate descriptions of his importance in the *BALLS!* hierarchy. There was a moment, when she described a childhood memory of a holiday on the Orkney Islands, that he thought he'd maybe had sex with her once before, but since she showed no sign of remembering him, he felt it would be inappropriate to say anything. He decided, out of courtesy, to play along with the idea that they were new acquaintances.

In the taxi back to his flat, which took the total to just over two hundred, the foreplay began. She was in the bag. Matt, of course, had no idea how much the evening had cost him, nor that Angel had so far spent one bus fare: 80p. The maths might have unsettled him.

Thanks to a frisky little moment in the lift, Matt

70

was semi-tumescent as he entered the flat, much as he had been on the previous occasion when he greeted his mother.

'Hello, darling!' she called from the kitchen. 'I've roasted up a chicken for you. It might have gone a bit dry, cause I was expecting you back earlier, but it should be all right.'

Matt grabbed Angel by the arm and whispered hurriedly in her ear, before Carol could get within earshot, 'It's my mum. We've had a . . . a family tragedy. Don't ask her about it. I'm putting her up for a few days while she tries to pull herself together. I thought she'd be at . . . at her counselling this evening, but it must have been cancelled. Forgot to mention it.'

'Oh, that's so sweet,' said Angel, a sentence she had uttered at least forty times that evening.

'Oh!' said Carol. 'You've brought a friend.'

'Yeah,' said Matt. 'I hope you don't mind.'

He looked around his apartment, wondering for an instant if he might have got out of the lift on the wrong floor. He had never seen it so tidy, or so clean. His home had never previously struck him as particularly messy, but looking at it now, he saw that the flat he'd walked out of in the morning had looked like a vandalised version of this one.

As with the breakfast, he felt simultaneously grateful and annoyed, a mix of emotion that was proving strangely difficult to communicate. But with Angel there, he couldn't even allude to what had happened without serious risk of his maternal-cohabitation excuse being exposed as a lie.

'Don't mind? It's your flat,' said Carol. 'Is this . . . is this your girlfriend?'

'Er . . . yeah. Wanted you to meet her. Mum, this

71

is Angel; Angel, Mum.'

'Angel?'

'Yeah.'

'That's a nice name.'

'Thanks. Most people don't believe it's my real name, but it is. It's not just a modelling name. My mum says she took one look at me and thought, "Angel", so that's what I am.'

'How lovely. Matt was premature. If I'd done the same thing, he'd be called Foetus.'

For such a pretty girl, it was odd that she laughed like a camel.

'Are you hungry?' said Carol. 'That chicken really needs eating.'

Matt had slept with women like Angel many times, possibly even with Angel herself. He had not eaten dinner. Angel had slept with men like Matt many, many times, and she, too, had eaten no dinner. Neither of them had been offered fresh, home-roast chicken for a long while.

The battle between hunger and sexual thwartedness was, in both cases, a no contest. In many ways, this was the perfect outcome. The fun was more in the chase, in the conquest, than in the sex itself, which was often a tense and sweaty anticlimax. Just knowing the other person wanted you was the real goal, more than making them actually go through with it, and they had passed that point. For both of them, the evening was already a victory. To get the glow of triumph, and then be spared the efforts, pitfalls and disappointments of sexual congress by a middle-aged woman appearing from nowhere and offering you a hot meal was, in fact, perfect.

'Starving,' said Matt.

'Me too,' said Angel, who was perpetually hungry, and who was suddenly as determined to eat that chicken as she was to puke it up again afterwards.

The meat was delicious. The roast potatoes and aubergines accompanying it were stupendous. Matt and Angel gobbled with ravenous awe, barely able to speak as they ate. It reminded Carol of when Matt was sixteen, and feeding him was like shovelling coals into a furnace.

'So how long have you two been together?' said Carol.

'Couple of months.'

Angel was eating with such concentration that she barely noticed the lie.

'Where did you meet?'

'A dinner party. At a friend's house.'

'That's nice. How old are you, Angel?'

'Eighteen.'

'Eighteen?' said Matt, hamming up his half-genuine surprise.

'Next month.'

'Eighteen next month?'

'Yeah.'

'So you're seventeen,' said Carol.

'Only just. I mean, not for long.'

'That's exactly half Matt's age. How neat.'

'You never said you were seventeen!' said Matt.

'You never asked.'

'You don't look seventeen. You look twenty. At least.'

'I've looked twenty since I was fourteen.'

'Don't say that.'

'You've been together two months, and you don't even know how old she is?' said Carol.

73

'Er . . . that was a lie. I was just embarrassed. We met this evening. I haven't touched her. Honest.'

'You fingered me in the taxi,' said Angel.

'She doesn't know what she's talking about. Angel, I had no idea you're seventeen. I think maybe you should go.' Matt stood, in the hope that Angel would do the same.

'I haven't finished my chicken.'

'All right, well, eat up,' said Matt. 'And next time you should be more honest about your age.'

'What do you mean, next time? You'll be so lucky.'

'I meant with other men. It's just some general advice.'

'I don't need your advice, thank you very much, Mr High and Mighty. I'm legal.'

'Why don't you just take the chicken with you? I'll give you a bag.'

'I don't want it now, Mr Patronising. I do have some dignity.'

'I'm glad.'

'Where's the bog?'

'It's over there,' said Matt.

Angel stood and wiped her mouth with the back of her hand. 'Thank you for the chicken. It was delicious,' she said to Carol, with a pointed politeness designed, in some obscure way, to put Matt in his place.

Matt strained to think of something to say to his mother while Angel visited the toilet, anything at all that might diminish his embarrassment while also masking the sound of Angel's vomiting, but nothing came to mind, so he avoided catching her eye and pretended to be absorbed in his food, hoping she'd interpret this as appreciation for her

74

efforts in the kitchen.

'Do you think I'm fat?' shouted Angel, as she staggered noisily out of the toilet. She really hadn't appeared drunk when they left the bar, Matt thought to himself. Nor had she seemed so young. This whole scenario was not going to be easy to explain away.

'Maybe you should go down and call Angel a cab,' said Carol. Matt looked at his mother and saw that her face had taken on a waxy pallor he recognised from the very worst flashpoints of his adolescence. There was anger, a noisy, red-faced, curiously exciting place; then, beyond that, you occasionally got to visit this ominously quiet, spookily still zone of genuine dismay. It was like the difference between Las Vegas and the desert beyond it. The waxy face was the give-away: he was now right out there among the cacti, with Joe Pesci driving and a shovel in the trunk.

Matt didn't feel remotely happy leaving these two women alone together in his flat, but he had no choice. When Carol had that look in her eye, you did what she said and you did it quickly. He rushed down, praying for deliverance in the form of a black cab with an orange halo.

*　　　*　　　*

Even ten minutes after Angel had been dispatched, Matt could still think of nothing to say to Carol. He wanted to ask her what she'd talked about with Angel in his absence, but that didn't seem like a dignified question. It had certainly been ominous that Angel's last words to him before she drove away were, 'I don't really want to cut your dick off.

I'm not that kind of a girl.'

It was Carol who eventually broke the silence. 'I think I'll turn in,' she said.

'Good idea,' said Matt. 'I'll clear up.'

This was an offer he had never before made to his mother. They were both, however, a little too frazzled to appreciate the breakthrough.

AT A STROKE, HE WAS TWELVE

The evening after the Angel debacle, Matt came straight home from work for a quiet evening in with his mother. He was probably twelve years old the last time he did anything even vaguely similar, but these were exceptional circumstances. He had to explain himself.

He didn't really have any clear idea how low he might have sunk in his mother's estimation, but he knew that whatever she thought of him now was humiliatingly damning. A belligerent voice in the back of his mind still occasionally squawked out that he was too old to be frightened of his mother—that a real man isn't swayed from his chosen course in life by what other people think of him—but he knew he was doing the right thing in ignoring it.

As he walked through the front door of his flat, he immediately noticed the smell: a very particular lamb stew that instantly took him back twenty-five years to long suburban Sundays of Monopoly and Swingball, of paddling pools and daisy chains and home-made dens and pillow fights, of two-a-side football and cricket with a tennis ball, of tricycles

76

in the garden and go-carts on the pavement. This was the smell of play, of comfort, of infinite leisure, of everything being right with the world. And only one woman could produce it.

'Good day at work?' said Carol, wiping her hands on a tea towel, with a mannerism that reminded him of how she used to wipe her hands on her apron. As far as he knew, his kitchen didn't contain an apron.

'Not bad. Same old, same old.' Where had that phrase come from? Was that what his dad used to say?

'Are you hungry?'

It was a good two hours earlier than Matt usually ate, but the smell of the stew had an odd effect on him. 'Starving,' he said.

'Or would you like a gin and tonic first? I bought some this afternoon.'

Gin and tonic? This was like being in a hotel. Was there anything better in life than people offering you things you didn't even know you wanted until you heard the suggestion? 'That would be amazing,' he said, throwing himself on to the sofa like a felled tree.

The drink came, with ice and lime. Not even lemon. Lime.

'Cheers,' said Carol.

'Cheers.'

The gin and tonic slipped down oh so easily. Why was it men weren't supposed to drink this? How could anything this good possibly be forbidden? Perhaps there was a feature in it. He could commission something on 'The Drinks You're Too Cool to Order'. No, 'Why Do Girls Get the Best Drinks?' would make for a better photo shoot.

'This is good,' he said.

'I hope it's not too strong.'

'I think I can handle it.'

There didn't seem to be any discernible frost in the air. However low he'd sunk, his mother had apparently not yet written him off. Things would have to get worse before she gave up on him.

A week ago, the idea of his mother giving up on him—leaving him alone and never phoning him—would have sounded rather pleasant. Something must have changed in the course of her visit, because he now felt hugely relieved that he still had a chance to explain himself to her. He didn't know why, but he wanted her forgiveness. Failing that, at the very least, he wanted a chance to show her that he was not as bad a person as he might have appeared since her arrival. With a little effort, he felt sure he could redeem himself in the remaining days before she left.

As they sat down to eat, he said, 'I'm sorry about last night.' He should have brought her some flowers. That might have helped, but it was too late now. Besides, now he looked, the flat was already full of the flowers his mother had bought, artfully arranged in a selection of Matt's beer glasses.

'Why are you sorry?' said Carol.

For a moment, Matt was thrown. 'What do you mean? I'm just sorry. It was embarrassing.'

'For who?'

'Well, for me. And you.'

'I wasn't embarrassed,' said Carol. 'I just felt sorry for you.'

'For me? Or for her?'

'For both of you.'

'It was a freak thing, I promise. That's never happened to me before.'

'I'm not interested,' snapped Carol, suddenly averting her eyes from Matt and eating with her gaze fixed on her plate.

'What?'

'If you're going to lie, I'm not interested in talking to you. You can eat in the kitchen if that's how you're going to behave.'

Yet again, at a stroke, he was twelve. How did she do this to him?

'I'm not lying.'

Carol looked up from her food and fixed her son with an angry glare. 'Matt, I've read your magazine.'

'So?'

'So I know the truth about you.'

'What's the magazine got to do with that girl being underage? Not underage. She wasn't underage. I just mean young. Younger than I thought she was.' Matt took a large swig of gin and tonic. The glass felt slippery in his hands.

'You can't see the connection?'

'She's never modelled for the magazine.'

'But you're the editor?'

'Features editor.'

'So you're important. You have some say in the content.'

'Of course. A lot of say. I have to come up with the ideas.'

'So it reflects your tastes.'

'You can't judge me on that magazine. It's my job to tailor it to a given readership. Which is young men. And young men like young girls.'

'Right, so they like young girls and you don't?'

79

'Yeah. More or less.'

'And last night was just a one-off coincidence.'

'Pretty much.'

Carol stared at him with strange, unsettling intensity. Something powerful, either rage or disappointment, seemed to be boiling under the surface of her skin.

'Why are you looking at me like that? What is it?'

Carol said nothing.

'It's true! I swear.'

She still didn't speak, just turned up the stare.

'I'm not going to the kitchen. Mum, I'm not going to the kitchen. I'm too old for that.'

'Well, I'll go, then. I'm not interested in your lies.'

'Mum, sit down! I'm not lying!'

'I'm just very upset. Upset and angry.'

'About what? That girl?'

'About you, Matt. About how you've turned out.'

'Me? How have I turned out?'

She lunged at the *BALLS!* on the coffee table, picked it up by one corner as if it was a greasy rag, and waved it in his face. 'Like this, Matt! Like this!'

For an instant, as he grabbed the magazine and chucked it on the floor, he thought she might be about to cry.

'What are you talking about?'

'You know, Matt. Don't pretend you don't understand.'

'I *don't* understand.'

'I brought you up, Matt. I know who you are. Or who you were. The first fifteen years of your life is in there, somewhere. I know it is. You can't have forgotten it all.'

'Of course I haven't.'

'Then you understand me. You know what I mean. You're decent, Matt. I know you are. At heart. It's how I made you. You're decent.'

Then, suddenly, she was crying. Standing there, looming above him, weeping.

He stared, horrified. After a while, he stood and tried to hug her. At first, her hands stayed over her face, her stiff elbows fending him off, but gradually her body began to yield, and he found himself holding her, for the first time in many, many years, while her body shook with tears.

When she quietened down, he sat her on his La-Z-Boy and gave her a fresh gin. More in order to stay out of her way than out of any genuine desire to help, he loaded the dishwasher and tidied away the remains of the stew. He even washed up the pan, delaying the moment when he'd have to look his mother in the eye.

He did understand what she meant. In fact, he'd always known this would be her reaction to the magazine, which was why he had never shown her a copy. The surprise was not that she thought it, but that she'd said it. As he stood there, slowly rinsing the saucepan, a bizarre thought floated into his head and refused to leave. He had been brought up one way, and now he was living another way. Morally—and this was not a frame of reference he often found himself calling upon— the life he had created for himself was a betrayal of the principles his mother and father tried to teach him.

As a rule, Matt was no more interested in morals than he was in mortgage rates, but the sight of Carol standing in his living room, weeping over his lack of decency—whatever that meant—unsettled him. He hadn't been allowed just to watch, either. He'd had to hug her. And because of her tears, he hadn't had the chance to argue back.

He didn't like the way she'd been able to say these things without allowing him any response. He resented being forced to stew over her criticisms on his own, without the opportunity to fight his corner. And yet, in the absence of the argument an accusation like this would normally cause, Matt was surprised to find himself feeling the beginnings of a hint of a suggestion in the back of his mind that maybe, just maybe, she had a point.

A new thought isn't like a new possession. It's not something you go out and get. It's not something you don't have, then suddenly you do have. A new thought, more often than not, is like opening a drawer you haven't looked in for a while and finding something you thought you'd lost. It was always there, it was always yours, you just become freshly aware of it.

The idea that Matt's job was somehow wrong, perhaps even a little sordid, had been sitting in an unopened drawer for a long, long time. Now, this week, the drawer was beginning to be prised open. He was fighting it. He was doing everything he could to keep it shut. But he could no longer deny to himself that he knew where the drawer was and what was in it.

He walked back to the sofa and slumped down. He couldn't look at her. Out of the corner of his eye, he saw that she wasn't looking at him.

Eventually, after the light in the flat had shifted from dusk to orange-grey street-lit semi-darkness, he said, 'Well, what do you want me to do about it?'

'I just want you to be happy. I want you to be true to yourself.'

He stood and closed the blinds.

'I have to make a living. Your career takes you where it takes you.'

'Or where you take it.'

'It's not that easy.'

After a long silence, she added, 'It would just be so sad if, when I died, you were still living like this.'

His first instinct was to bark back at her, 'Like what?' The words almost came out, but he stopped himself. He knew what she meant.

'You're not going to die,' he said.

She ignored him.

HELEN AND PAUL

THE UNEXPLODED BOMB

'Pop in?' said Paul.

'Yes. Are you pleased to see me?'

'Er . . . yes, but I . . . wasn't expecting you.'

'Of course you weren't.'

Paul stared from his mother to Andre and back again. They had been talking. Something, clearly, had passed between them that had given away more about Paul and Andre's relationship than Helen was supposed to know. Andre would not have greeted him with a kiss unless he thought there was nothing to hide. Helen must have tricked him. As ever with his mother, nothing was

83

straightforward. It really was astonishing how this old, harmless-looking woman could exhaust and exasperate him with such effortless ease.

'Why didn't you tell me you were coming?' said Paul. 'How long have you been here?'

'Oh, it was just a spur of the moment thing. I was in the area . . .'

'What were you doing round here?'

'Oh, I wasn't that close. I was just in town, and . . . it occurred to me that I could pop by.'

'But why didn't you give me a ring?' Paul asked, though he knew the answer. The visit was an ambush. She had come to see who he lived with, and had deliberately arrived before he got home from work to see what she could discover. Poor Andre had unwittingly walked into the trap and had told her everything.

'No reason,' said Helen, a little guiltily, as she stepped forwards and enfolded him in a deep, lingering hug. In the stiffness of his back and the reluctance of his arms to return her embrace, she could feel the imbalance in their love, but she didn't care. He was her boy, and she adored him. She thought about him every day, and those rare, few days when she actually saw him, when she touched him, were days of fulfilment and joy.

As he felt his mother pull him into her koala clutch, Paul's shock at her unexpected arrival was suddenly overwhelmed by the amazed realisation that, after years of lies and evasions, his big secret, at long last, was out. He wanted to be angry about the underhand manner with which Helen had set about breaching his firewall of privacy, but instead of the righteous indignation he felt was his due, he found himself filled instead with simple relief.

With this thought, he felt his back yield, and his arms rose up to embrace her. He was, it appeared, off the hook. The main reason Paul had never come out to his mother was that he didn't want the attention. He had always been reasonably confident that she wouldn't react badly, but he never liked his mother knowing much about him. Just the fact that she wanted to know everything made him want to withhold as much information as he could. His father, who was more or less indifferent to Paul's emotional life, and who had a tendency to forget or misunderstand key details, was the parent Paul had chosen as a confidant.

On the evening, many years ago, when Paul had come out to Larry, twenty minutes later they'd been discussing Wimbledon. With Larry, nothing was difficult or unnecessarily emotional. With Helen, the tiniest, most unexpected comment could blow up in your face, requiring hours or even weeks of backtracking before you convinced her that some unintended subtext had not been a barbed criticism, or that your tone of voice had not been mocking or dismissive.

He had almost told her several times, but at any given moment, faced with the choice between breaking the news and talking about something else, he'd always found the latter a more appealing prospect.

Paul, in short, was afraid of her. Not afraid that she would upset him, or wound him, or even bully him; he was afraid of the hassle, of the time that stood to be wasted putting things right when they had gone wrong. And now, without warning, the unexploded bomb that had been sitting for years in the middle of their relationship appeared to have

85

quietly and harmlessly gone off, without any injuries. For years, he'd been trying to screw up the courage to crawl towards it on his hands and knees, armed with a magnifying glass and a tiny screwdriver, knowing that the tiniest slip could blow his head off; now the job had been done without him even having to watch.

She had been devious and manipulative; she had tricked his boyfriend, and he ought to be angry with her, but he wasn't and he knew he couldn't fake it. Better just to hug, smile and move on.

'Well, it's nice to see you,' he said, drawing the embrace to a close. Wordlessly, with an apologetic glance towards Paul, Andre slipped out of the room.

'And you,' said Helen, scrutinising Paul's face like a shopkeeper with a suspicious fifty-pound note.

'Do you want a drink?' said Paul.

'A glass of wine would be wonderful.'

'I'll see what we've got,' he said, opening the fridge. 'White?'

'Perfect. Why don't I cook you dinner. You must be tired,' said Helen.

Paul, like many men, lacked the ability to read and hear at the same time. At that moment, he was concentrating on the wine label.

'Sorry?' he said.

'Why don't I cook you dinner?'

Paul stared at her, baffled. This woman, who doesn't visit him for months on end, suddenly comes round while he's out at work, grills his boyfriend for personal information, then, as if it is he who had popped in unexpectedly on her, offers to cook a meal. There was no etiquette Paul knew

86

of for dealing with behaviour of this sort.

It was, however, a mealtime. He was hungry, and she had just arrived. They now had to spend some time together, so there were three options. Either he invited her out for a meal, or she cooked, or he cooked. From this range of choices, her bizarre offer seemed the least unpleasant. Then he remembered what day it was.

'I'm supposed to be cooking for the whole house,' he said. 'We take turns on Monday nights.'

'Well, I can do it for you. It would be my pleasure. We could do it together. How many people are there?'

'Five.'

'Plus me is six,' said Helen.

'OK,' said Paul. 'Six.' If he had to eat with Helen, five people to help dilute her could only be a good thing. They'd understand. He knew them all too well for the inevitable embarrassment to be a serious problem. He'd moaned about his mother to them for so long, they'd all be interested to meet her. There was little doubt that she'd put on a good show.

'Do you want a hand?' he said, trying (not very hard) to conceal the reluctance in his voice.

'No, no. You put your feet up. I'm sure you've had a hard day. There'll be plenty of time to talk later in the week.'

This sounded distinctly ominous, but since nothing she could say really registered for ominousness up against the vast über-ominousness of her being there at all, he decided to let it slide. 'OK,' he said. 'If you say so. I'll get some glasses.'

A shot of alcohol and a period of calm were, they both knew, exactly what was needed to prepare them for whatever was ahead.

Helen hated cooking. She was amazed that Paul had seemingly forgotten how bad she was at it. But the opportunity to have an hour or so alone in the house, to gather her thoughts and plot her next move, was priceless. There had already been so much to absorb.

As she stared vacantly into the fridge, at a loss as to what she could make, suddenly overwhelmed by a wave of tiredness, she reminded herself that the hardest bit was over. She knew she might have come across as devious or senile or both, but she was in. She had achieved what she set out to achieve. And though the situation was still a little ambiguous, it seemed to have been accepted that she was staying.

WHAT DO YOU JUST WANT?

'PAUL! DINNER!'

The feeling of those words coming out of her mouth, shouted up a staircase, took her back twenty years. She fleetingly imagined that he might walk in as a tousled, hungry teenager, followed by Larry. She had already lost count of her Larry thoughts for the day. Today was a bad one. She really, really had to cut down.

Andre and Paul arrived together, bringing with them one of those conspiratorial silences that comes off couples when they walk into a room containing the person they've just been discussing. Not far behind them was a man who introduced himself as Miles, who was neither fashionable nor young, nor thin, all of which Helen thought might be obligatory to qualify you for entrance to a gay commune. (If that's what this place was.)

'This is very *civilised*,' he said, pronouncing the word with distaste, as if he was saying the precise opposite.

'This is Miles,' said Paul.

'I'm the *éminence grise* of this establishment,' he said.

'That means landlord,' said Andre.

It was as if there was a pendulum in Helen's head that with every new piece of information swung from 'this is sordid' to 'this is actually rather normal' and back again. She tried to compose her face in such a way that it wouldn't give away the latest swing of the pendulum back to maximum sordidness. So this was how it worked. Middle-aged gay man in large house rents out spare rooms to young gay men in return for what, precisely? Or was it prejudiced even to think that some currency other than money might be in use here? Surely her son, her precious, adorable son, would not be party to such a thing.

Quite how the five men in this house interrelated was a mystery to Helen, and the more she found out, the less she understood. With straight people, you always knew who was who, and how they fitted together. If you didn't, you could ask. Here she just had to flounder, trying to piece things together from conversational scraps. It felt like swimming in heavy clothing.

Muscle Midget, who was introduced as Calvin, appeared in the room, immediately followed by another thirty-ish guy, Luke, also in expensively ill-fitting clothes. Everyone, Helen sensed, had been briefed. She had no idea what had been said, but as they all took their places there was something in the quality of the silence that had the air of a rowdy and intimate group hushed by a thin veneer of social restraint. Whether this restraint was the product of politeness, loathing or simple social tension, Helen couldn't tell.

There ought to be a word, she thought, for paranoia, but without the connotations of delusion. In a situation like this, you'd have to be delusional not to feel paranoid.

'Well, isn't this nice?' she said, wondering, even as the words came out of her mouth, what it was that had made her say the opposite of what she was thinking. 'What are you all doing here, and who's screwing who?' would have been more honest.

As if sensing her confusion, Paul said, 'We eat together on Mondays. It's a tradition.'

'That's nice,' said Helen.

'It was me and Andre's turn to cook, but since you offered . . .'

'I just hope it's up to scratch,' said Helen, suddenly struck by the fear that gay men were all epicurean aesthetes who'd be snobbishly unimpressed by her pasta bake. As she plonked her bubbling, slightly burnt offering on to the table, she felt like a hairy, stinking old dinner lady faced with a class of precocious pretty-boys holding in their smirks at her vulgarity and incompetence.

'Oooh, pasta bake!' said Miles. 'I haven't had one of those for years.'

Despite the superficial enthusiasm of his tone, this somehow didn't come across as a compliment.

'Don't be such a fucking snob,' said Andre. 'I'd rather have a pasta bake than your venison curry any day.'

'Pearls before swine. I'm wasted on you.'

'If anyone here's the swine, it's you, old man,' said Calvin.

'Have you seen what I have to put up with?' said Miles, directing his comment at Helen, in her capacity as the only other old person in the room, she assumed. Helen jumped at the invitation to join in the banter, even though her first choice would have been to go and hide in a cupboard. 'The young are ungrateful,' she said. 'It's the first thing you learn as a mother.'

In her head, this had sounded like friendly mockery, but it came out rather more bitter and heartfelt than she had intended. An awkward silence followed, everyone avoiding her eyes.

'Well, I'd like to welcome you,' said Miles, 'as the first mother to join our little Monday night soirées. And I'd like to thank Paul for inviting you. It's a lovely idea, and I hope the rest of you will do the same.'

An audible groan went round the table, as if Miles had just asked who was going to clean the oven.

'Thank you,' said Helen.

'Perhaps we should make it a tradition. Spice things up a bit,' continued Miles, who seemed to be warming to his theme, so much so that Helen began to wonder if he was mocking her. 'I'd invite my own mother next week, except that I don't think she'd appreciate being dug up. A toast! To mothers!'

'To mothers!' said Helen, enthusiastically.

'To mothers,' grunted Paul, Andre, Luke and Calvin, reluctantly.

'Not a day goes by that I don't think of my mother,' said Miles, addressing his comment only to Helen. 'I've never been the same since she died.'

'That's a very sweet sentiment,' said Helen. 'I'm sure she loved you very much, too.'

'And Paul will be the same,' said Miles. 'When you're gone. Whether he knows it now or not.'

'Miles, will you shut up,' said Paul.

'Paul!' said Helen.

'It's all right, dear,' said Miles. 'I've had far worse.'

'Do you mind me asking?' said Helen. 'You said you were very close to your mother. I was wondering when you came out to her.'

'Oh, never. It would have killed her.'

'It did kill her,' said Luke. 'He bumped her off by showing her a picture of him being fis—'

'Luke!' snapped Miles. 'Shut that filthy mouth of yours.'

'I'm joking,' said Luke, to Helen.

'And what about you?'

'Me?' said Luke.

'You have told her, haven't you?'

'Of course.'

'When? I mean, at what age?'

'You really want to know?'

'If you don't mind. I just want to know how it usually works.'

'I came out at university, then one weekend I came home for my dad's fiftieth birthday. He was having a big party, with lots of family and friends coming over, and I thought I'd tell them that weekend, the day after. But I got a bit excited and I couldn't hold it in, and I ended up saying it on the day, about five minutes before the first guests

92

arrived. Which made for a strange party. I didn't mean to. It just came out.'

'And did they make a fuss?' said Helen.

'They couldn't. They had thirty guests in the house.'

'I mean after that.'

'It took them a while to get used to it, but they were fine in the end. Good, actually.'

'So it's normal to tell your parents quite soon?'

'Who gives a shit what's normal?' said Calvin. 'Who wants to be normal?'

Helen took a gulp of wine. 'It's just that Paul's never come out to me. I'm still waiting.'

Paul's face fell. This meal had been a terrible idea. The opportunity to escape from the cooking rota had fatally clouded his judgement.

'Oh, Paul!' said Miles. 'I'm very disappointed in you.'

'No time like the present,' said Luke.

'What are you talking about?'

'Come on,' said Miles. 'Tell your mother about your sordid little habits.'

'What is all this crap about coming out, anyway?' said Paul. 'I mean, it's not as if straight people have to gather their parents round the kitchen table when they're eighteen and find a way of carefully breaking it to them that they've decided they're heterosexual. Why should it be any different for us? Why can't they just be expected to see what they see and figure it out for themselves? It's not a sin. It's not something I have to confess. It's just one of the things that makes me what I am, and that if you've got any sense you'll figure out for yourself.'

'It would just be nice,' said Helen, 'to have a bit

of openness. I can't be accepting and loving if you won't be open.'

'Do it!' said Luke. 'Do it now.'

'What a lovely idea,' said Miles. 'Come on, Paul. Spit it out.'

Gradually, the momentum behind this suggestion built until everyone round the table was jeering at Paul to come out to Helen, laughing and brandishing wine glasses. Eventually, Paul lifted his glass. Somehow, the impending declaration had been turned into a toast.

'Waitwaitwait,' said Miles, topping up everyone's glasses. 'OK.'

'Mum,' said Paul. 'I'm queer.'

A huge cheer went up round the table.

'Thank you, and I would never want you to be anything other than how you want to be,' said Helen, a line she had been pondering, honing and rehearsing for almost a decade.

'Give her a kiss!' said Luke.

Paul stood and gave Helen a kiss, which turned into a hug. When the excitement subsided, and they were back in their seats, Helen said, 'Well, that's fabulous. I'm very pleased. All you have to do now is tell your father.' The idea of it filled her with a warm glow of *schadenfreude*. The discovery that his one and only son was gay would drive Larry crazy. He'd take it as a personal affront to his own machismo. It would puncture his ego in a way that Helen, through all their years of arguing, had never once managed.

'I told him ages ago,' said Paul, without thinking.

Helen's face didn't just fall, it plummeted. It was as if he had turned round and slapped her.

'When?' said Helen, her voice faltering,

94

seemingly on the brink of tears.

Paul suddenly felt as if his legs had filled with lead. This was one of those moments with his mother where the wrong thing slips out of your mouth, and suddenly the ground falls away beneath you. What was a pleasant and friendly conversation suddenly becomes a tense and deathly stand-off. If he could only unsay it, take back this tiny, unimportant piece of information that he had successfully concealed for several years; if only he had been a little more alert and hadn't allowed himself, buoyed up by all the laughter, to relax his guard.

'Oh . . . a while ago.'

'When?'

'I don't know. A few years.'

'A few *years*?'

'I think so.'

'How many years?'

'Does it matter?'

'How many years?'

'I can't remember.'

'How many? Two? Five? Ten?'

'Mum, why does it make any difference?'

'HOW MANY?'

'I think maybe we'll leave you two to catch up in private,' said Miles, standing and walking to the stairs with his plate. Within seconds, Helen and Paul were alone in the room.

'I don't know. Three-ish.'

'Why?'

'Why what?'

'Why did you tell him and not me?'

'It just happened. It doesn't mean anything.'

'Of course it means something. It means

everything. And I want to know why.'

'There's no reason.'

'Of course there's a reason.'

'Well, maybe it's private.'

'What's private?'

'Maybe this is the reason, Mum. Because I never know when you're going to fly off the handle. I never know what you want from me. I never know when you're going to throw a big emotional scene and when you're going to ignore me. Maybe I didn't want the grief. Maybe what I didn't want was exactly this, exactly what's happening right now.'

'That's very unfair. That's cruel, Paul. This has nothing to do with you coming out to me. This isn't about that. This is about me and your father.'

'THERE IS NO YOU AND MY FATHER. YOU'RE DIVORCED! There's me and him, and there's me and you, but there's no you and him. And I'm not willing to be the you and him, which is what you always want me to be, which is why you're blowing up now. If you want to speak to him, ring him up. But what goes on between me and him is none of your business.'

'How often do you see him?'

'Mum, stop it.'

'But . . . I just want . . .' She couldn't continue. What she wanted was Paul's love; she wanted him to love her more than he loved Larry. For him to favour Larry was such an outrage, such an injustice. Did Paul not even realise that, for the first five years of his life, she had done everything? She had been his universe, while Larry barely changed a nappy and, she was sure, delayed his return from work until bath and bedtime were over, professing to be upset to have missed a goodnight story while walking into the house smelling of the pub. He had been so offhand, and so lazy. Even after that, he had barely done any more than the minimum. Helen had poured years of her life into Paul. She had sacrificed as much of her time and energy and love as any human being could sacrifice for another, while Larry had treated fatherhood as a hobby he might turn to after he'd read the paper. For him to be favoured over her now was simply intolerable. But what could she do? What could she say? That she deserved more love? More gratitude? That Paul ought to be fair?

'What?' said Paul, impatiently. 'What do you just want?'

'I don't know. I want some more wine.'

Paul topped up her glass, and his own. He put an apologetic hand on her shoulder.

'And I'd like to stay for a few days.'

'I'm sorry?'

'I brought an overnight bag. I thought it might be fun to stay.'

'Er . . .' Paul's mouth went dry, his brain blank. 'Fun?'

'Yes, where can I sleep?'

Helen wasn't going to give up. Much as she wanted to slope home, defeated, back to Clive, she resolved not to allow herself to cave in. She wouldn't leave until there was some kind of positive outcome. This visit was a drastic measure: kill or cure. If she allowed herself to walk away from Paul without a remedy for their faltering relationship, she'd regret it for ever. This was her last chance to claw back for herself any meaningful role in his life. If she left now, that would be it. He'd just think of her as a peripheral,

97

unpredictable, over-emotional annoyance, until she let him off the hook by dying.

'Why didn't you mention this when you arrived?'

'Did I forget? I'm sorry.'

'Are you sure it's a good idea?' said Paul, so taken aback by her proposal that he found himself unable to mount a decent defence against it.

'Unless you refuse to have me. If it's too much to ask . . .'

Helen let her voice tail away. She watched her son squirm, with something that looked like panic spreading over his features as he rifled through his mental filing cabinet of family etiquette, searching for the folder labelled POLITE WAYS TO FORCIBLY EJECT YOUR MOTHER FROM YOUR HOUSE and finding it empty.

Paul eventually sighed and stood. 'I can sleep in Andre's room. I'll change the sheets on my bed.'

With slow, heavy footsteps, he walked out of the room and up the stairs, wondering as he did so why it was that being with his mother always felt like losing at chess.

GILLIAN AND DANIEL

WE'RE SPLITTING UP AND YOU'RE THINKING ABOUT SEX

It wasn't just his mother's snoring, resonantly audible through the bedroom wall, that kept Daniel awake. In the last few weeks, he had woken almost every night at around four in the morning and been unable to get back to sleep. More often than not, according to his bedside clock, it was precisely 3:53 when his eyes opened, as if some internal alarm had been set for this exact time.

Now, at 4:11, he began the nightly ritual that kept him occupied for the remaining hours until dawn. It had become a compulsion. The more he tried to resist, the less he could stop himself doing it. He even thought his brain might be deliberately waking him up to make him do it, over and over again, in the hope that eventually, with enough repetition, the outcome would be different.

The ritual was simple. He rehearsed in his mind, night after night, his final argument with Erin.

*   *   *

'Why?' said Daniel.

'I've told you why,' said Erin.

'Say it again.'

'Why do you want me to say it again?'

'So I can understand.'

'What don't you understand?'

'Anything. Everything.'

'It's simple. I want you to leave,' said Erin.

They had been arguing from the moment they sat down to Sunday lunch, and it was now late afternoon. It felt as if they had been arguing for weeks. Neither of them could remember what kicked off this particular bout, but the pattern was familiar enough. It was probably something Daniel had done, or had forgotten to do: something domestic, something trivial, but a convenient launch pad, nonetheless, for another trawl through everything that was wrong with Daniel's behaviour and with Daniel and Erin's relationship.

Their arguments were like a favourite CD played on shuffle. Each individual track was familiar, but Daniel never quite knew which one was coming up next. Increasingly, though, it came back again and again to the title track: 'When Can We Have a Baby?'

Daniel thought he knew the whole CD by heart, but on this occasion he'd been amazed to find Erin introducing a hidden bonus song he had never heard before: 'I Want You to Leave'.

'But why?' he said.

'I've *told* you.'

'Tell me properly.'

'What do you mean, properly? We've been over it a hundred times and I'm sick of it, and you never budge an inch, and now I'm telling you to go away and not come back until you've decided.'

'This is ridiculous, why can't we just talk about this like adults?'

'This is adult. I'm asking you to move out. It doesn't get more adult than that, Daniel.'

'Calmly, I mean. Talk it through calmly. Instead of these . . . ultimatums.'

'I AM CALM. I'M PERFECTLY CALM. AND I WANT YOU TO LEAVE!'

'You don't sound calm. You sound angry.'

'OF COURSE I'M ANGRY. I CAN BE ANGRY AND CALM. IT'S PERFECTLY POSSIBLE TO BE ANGRY AND CALM!'

'So why are you shouting?'

Erin stood up sharply from the kitchen table, her chair clattering to the floor behind her, and, without picking it up, walked out of the room. Daniel righted the chair and followed her into the sitting room, where he found Erin curled on the sofa, her feet tucked under her and her arms wrapped around a cushion.

The moment he entered the room, she began speaking. 'That's typical. That is just so 100 per cent typical. I'm telling you that unless you change your mind, our relationship is over, that you have to move out, that I don't want to see you, that from today nothing is ever going to be the same again, and do you want to talk about that? No. You want to discuss whether or not I'm shouting. Brilliant.'

'I don't want to discuss whether or not you're shouting. I'm just trying to get you to stop shouting so we can talk about all those things. But you don't want to talk about them. You just want to shout.'

'I'm not shouting. I'm talking, quietly, and I'm asking you to go.'

Daniel sat beside her on the sofa, as close as he could get, but her knees and elbows were angled to keep him at a distance. He tried to catch her eye, but her gaze was fixed rigidly on her own hands. 'What do you mean, you don't want to see me?' he said. 'You never said that.'

'Well, I don't! Not if you're going to be like this.'

'But if I'm not like this you do want to see me?'

'I don't know.'

'Well, how do you want me to be? What's the "this"? I don't understand what I'm doing.'

'The this is this. It's *this*. It's arguing the toss. About everything. Just . . . missing the point about everything and arguing on and on about some tiny thing that isn't the thing. That's what it is!'

'What—so the thing that's annoying is asking questions to try and understand what you mean?'

'No!'

'But that's what you just said.'

101

'It isn't, Daniel. It isn't.'

'I'm not arguing, I'm asking. I'm trying to understand what you want. I'm asking you to explain. Just . . . tell me what it is.'

'Oh, Daniel. I've been trying all afternoon. I'm so tired. I'm so tired of all this.'

'Well so am I! You're chucking me out of my home and all I want is an explanation. It's not a lot to ask. I'm not running around smashing things. I'm not weeping and wailing. I'm not bullying you. I'm just asking to know why.'

'You are, though.'

'I am what?'

'Bullying me.'

'*Bullying you?* I've never laid a finger on you!'

'This! All this! It's bullying! On and on, talking and talking, arguing and arguing, never giving me a chance to say in a normal way what I'm trying to say. You never let me say anything. It's always you, bullying and bullying.'

Tossing her cushion aside, Erin stood and walked to the window, where she stood, looking down at the bus stop below their flat.

Daniel leapt up and stood behind her, addressing the back of her head. 'What was the last thing I said? I said, "Tell me what it is." I didn't interrupt you. I'm not shouting at you. I'm asking you to tell me. All afternoon I've been asking you to tell me. It's all I want. I just want a proper explanation, and now you're telling me that I don't let you speak! It's ridiculous!'

'You don't let me speak normally. You don't let me explain.'

'SO SPEAK! EXPLAIN!' said Daniel.

'I can't.'

'Why?'

'Not like this. Not with you shouting at me,' said Erin, spinning round, glaring at Daniel, her eyes glossy with tears.

'I'M NOT SHOUTING!'

'You are. You're shouting. That was a shout.'

'OK! THAT WAS A SHOUT! BUT THE ONLY REASON I'M SHOUTING IS BECAUSE I'VE BEEN TALKING FOR HOURS AND HOURS, SOFTLY SOFTLY, ASKING YOU AGAIN AND AGAIN TO EXPLAIN TO ME WHY IT IS YOU'RE CHUCKING ME OUT OF MY HOME, AND THEN, FINALLY, AFTER A WHOLE AFTERNOON OF TRYING TO BE REASONABLE, I RAISE MY VOICE FOR TWO SECONDS AND YOU TELL ME THAT YOU WERE ON THE BRINK OF EXPLAINING, BUT NOW YOU CAN'T BECAUSE I'VE SHOUTED. YOU'RE CRAZY. YOU'RE FUCKING CRAZY!'

'See? This is it. This is exactly it. You don't want to hear. You act all reasonable, but somehow you make sure that when it comes down to it you never have to listen to me saying what I want to say.'

'This is amazing. Now I'm the unreasonable one.'

'I'm so tired, Daniel. I'm so tired of all this.' Erin dropped her head, raised her hands and covered her face, as if she was crying, but no sound came out and her body remained still. He was close enough to reach out and hold her, but he remained motionless, staring at the back of her hands.

Eventually, Erin spoke again, her voice muffled by her palms. 'There's no point,' she said.

Daniel put an arm on her back and gave a gentle

rub with his thumb. 'No point in what?'

'Why are we doing this?'

'I don't know,' said Daniel, pulling her into an embrace. 'And you're not the only one who's tired.'

Reluctantly, Erin removed her hands from her face and draped her arms limply around Daniel. They held one another, still and silent. He listened to Erin's breath close by his ear, as it slowed from short, shallow gasps of air to deep, slow waves of inhalation and exhalation. Out of the window, he saw a bus disgorge a boisterous herd of teenagers: a group of boys and a group of girls, engaged in a noisy, flirtatious row, which continued as they walked away in different directions. The bus shelter slowly accumulated more people; another bus came and went; and still Daniel and Erin stood by the window, holding one another, not speaking.

Daniel drew back his head to catch Erin's eye. She blinked at him, her huge green eyes, even now, after all these years, surprising him with their beauty. He still could not quite believe that she was his, that he was the one she wanted to hug, that those stunning eyes never gave out to anyone else the flashes of love that occasionally came his way.

A corner of her mouth lifted: part grimace, part smile.

'Let's have a nap,' said Daniel. 'Let's go upstairs and have a nap.'

'A nap?'

'Yeah.'

Erin took a step back and brushed away a strand of hair that had stuck to her wet cheek. 'Daniel, are you trying to have sex with me?'

'A nap! A nap, I said.'

'I can't believe you're thinking about sex. We're splitting up and you're thinking about sex.'

'You're the one who's talking about sex.'

'You're ridiculous.'

'It might be nice, though,' said Daniel. 'Now you're suggesting it.'

'Was I suggesting it?'

'Come upstairs.'

'Daniel . . .'

'Come upstairs. I love you.'

Daniel reached for her waist.

'Stop that. Get off me.'

'Post-argument. It's always the best. And it was a big argument. Think about it.'

'Daniel—you're the most exhausting man in the world.'

'So take the weight off your feet. Have a lie-down.'

With one arm around her back, and the other under her knees, Daniel scooped Erin into the air and began carrying her towards the bedroom. She shrieked and pinched him on the arm, but did nothing to wriggle free.

'Daniel, you're going to drop me.'

'It's fine.'

'Ohh . . . this is so stupid.'

'I love you,' said Daniel.

'Why am I such an idiot?'

'I'll tell you after.'

Daniel tossed her on to the bed, unbuttoned her jeans and pulled them off. She lay still, watching him throw her trousers aside, an unreadable expression on her face. Daniel took off his own jeans, holding her gaze, then knelt on the bed and crawled towards her. Just as his lips were about to touch hers, she pushed him on to his back, pinned him down by the wrists, and began to kiss and bite his neck.

Soon, they were naked under the duvet. 'Get a condom,' whispered Erin into Daniel's ear, her hair falling across his face.

'What if we don't?' he mumbled, taking her head in his hands and kissing her once, gently, on the lips.

'You serious?'

'Let's not,' said Daniel.

Erin pulled away. 'You mean that?'

'Absolutely.'

'You want a baby? You've changed your mind?'

'I do know what happens . . .'

'We've been arguing about this all afternoon. Are you just giving up?'

'It's not a competition.'

'I didn't mean it like that. I just . . .'

'What?'

'I just . . . want to know why. What's different now, compared to an hour ago? Compared to all the times we've talked about this?'

'Can we have this conversation after? My brain isn't getting much blood at the moment.'

'This is important, Daniel. I need to know.'

'Er . . . there's this. This is different.'

'Your *erection?*'

Erin suddenly leapt from the bed and began searching the bedroom floor for her knickers.

'Don't say it like that. It's not a disease. Erin? What are you doing? Come back. What have I said? It was a joke.'

Erin stood, and roughly pulled on her underwear. 'It wasn't a joke. That's the amazing

106

thing. It's amazing enough that you could think it, but that you could *say* it!'

'Say what? It's just a joke. It didn't mean anything! Why are you so touchy?'

'It's incredible. It really is. I just . . . I mean . . . people say men are shallow, and sometimes you think it's just a stupid cliché, then suddenly you'll say something and I'll realise that your brain isn't . . . it isn't connected up like a proper brain. It's like half of it has been unplugged.'

'Are you going to tell me what you're talking about?'

'For you, conceiving a baby isn't about creating a person you're going to love and care for and look after for the rest of your life, day in day out; for you, it's . . . it's about fucking without a condom.'

'That's ridiculous.'

'There we are, on the point of making the most important decision you can ever make, and you'd think we'd be going through the same kind of thought process, but it turns out that actually I'm thinking about the next thirty years and you're thinking about the next five minutes. That was your profound insight into the future.'

'Erin, I'm so tired of this.'

'Oh, so you've got the energy to take on being a father for the rest of your life, but it's too much to ask that you might talk about the decision for a couple of minutes.'

Now fully dressed, Erin strode out of the room and into the toilet. Daniel, naked, followed her. She sat and peed.

'It was a joke, Erin,' said Daniel. 'I know it was a joke, you know it was a joke, and what I'm tired of is your hysterical arguments that just come out of nowhere, over some tiny, meaningless comment.'

'You're right. I'm hysterical. I mean, it's no big thing, is it? Coming within five minutes of having a baby with the world's biggest arsehole.' Erin stood, pulled up her trousers and flushed. 'I'm making a fuss about nothing. I shouldn't have opened my mouth, really.'

Erin pushed past and stamped downstairs towards the kitchen. Daniel threw on some underpants and a sweatshirt and followed. He found her filling the kettle in the kitchen.

'Why did you change your mind, Daniel?' she said. 'We talk all afternoon and you don't budge, then you get me into bed and suddenly you're ready to be a dad. While you were ripping my clothes off, you were mainly concentrating on thinking about parental responsibility, were you? Is that how your mind works?'

'It's not like that.'

'So what is it like? Tell me.'

'I just felt . . . in love. I felt love. It wasn't a thought. It was a feeling.'

The kettle boiled and clicked off. Erin, arms folded in front of her, didn't move.

'It was from the heart,' continued Daniel. 'That's all. If that makes me a monster . . . I'm sorry.'

Erin stepped towards Daniel and hit him on the chest with the ball of her hand, not quite hard enough to hurt, a gesture somehow both loving and aggressive, angry and forgiving. She then turned, snatched a sheet of kitchen towel from a holder behind Daniel's head, and walked away, dabbing at her eyes.

Daniel hoisted himself up on to the kitchen

surface, which was cold against his bare legs, and stared towards Erin, who was visible now only in outline against the window. A light drizzle had begun to fall, flecking the pane with needles of rain. He had no idea what she might be thinking.

'Why do we do this?' said Erin, eventually.

'I don't know.'

'Why can't we make each other happy?'

'We do. You do make me happy,' said Daniel, his voice heavy and unconvincing.

'I don't. You think I'm a hysterical, shrieking maniac.'

'I love you. I love hysterical, shrieking maniacs.'

'That's not funny.'

'You're laughing.'

'That doesn't mean it's funny,' said Erin with a smirk, turning back towards Daniel, gesturing with her crumpled kitchen towel.

'I love your rules. Are you going to explain them to our baby?'

'Daniel, I love you, but I do want you to leave. I want you to come back when you've decided, when you can convince me that you really know what you're taking on and you genuinely want to do it, day in, day out; day and night; year after year.'

Erin walked towards Daniel and stood between his knees. She stared intently into his eyes, which were cast down towards the floor.

'I don't mean leave leave,' she continued. 'Not end-it leave. Just, take some time. Come back when you're ready. And if you're not ready, don't come back. I won't want to see you again.'

'You mean that?'

'I do.'

'Are you talking, like, an hour or a day or a week

109

or what?'

'A month. Maybe we shouldn't see each other for a month. No contact, no phone calls, no nothing. Proper thinking time. Then we'll know. Me, too. We need to both know.'

'What, you're saying you're not sure, either?'

'I'm just saying, let's think. One month.'

ONE LAST LAP OF HONOUR

Daniel's mistake, perhaps, was that he allowed himself a shade more than one single month. By the end of the month, he had definitely reached his decision. He did want children, and he wanted them with Erin. She had been right, he realised, to make him think about it harder, and reflect on the sacrifices it would entail. A rush of love, or lust, or whatever it was, didn't constitute a solid enough base for a decision of this magnitude. From the moment of conception there was no going back. From that instant, a life's work lay ahead of you. But he was ready for it.

Though with that in mind, a month seemed like a very short time, and as it came to an end, he realised he had wasted most of it fretting over his big decision. Having made up his mind, it dawned on him that this month was a precious resource that he had squandered. It was his last chance to be truly free. So he decided to allow himself an extra week or so that he'd use properly, for bachelor pleasures.

Not sex. He had no intention of cheating on Erin. But she had given him some time to himself,

110

and it was his duty to use it. There were certain kinds of fun that just wouldn't be available once he went back to her, and he now had one last chance to do it all, and get a certain hard-to-define set of urges out of his system for good. Once you have a baby, your youth is over. But before he left it behind, he'd take one last lap of honour.

He picked up his mobile phone and scrolled through the semi-dormant recesses of his address book. Just a couple of phone calls and the sleeping monster of his single social life could be re-awakened and back in the pub. He had a few key friends left who were still living that life, and they'd be pleased to hear from him.

One of the slightly tragic things about single friends in their thirties was that they were always happy to have you back, no matter how long you'd been ignoring them. Like happy-clappy churches, they were openly desperate for more recruits. They didn't care who you were or how long you were staying or what your motives were, they just wanted extra people to help make more noise.

As soon as Daniel got to the letter 'M', he knew what to do. Matt was his oldest (though by no means his closest) friend, and Daniel knew he'd almost certainly be out, and drinking, probably in some kind of gang, which he'd immediately and happily invite Daniel to join, even though they'd only spoken once in the previous year.

'Danny Boooooooooooooooy! Good to hear from you!'

'Sorry it's been so long. I've been busy.'

'Whatever. How's things?' Matt never played the why-haven't-you-called-me game. Whether this was to preserve his dignity, or because he genuinely didn't care, Daniel never knew.

'Good. Good. What are you up to tonight?'

'You coming out to play? You been let off the leash?' said Matt.

'Sort of.'

'You split up?' There was definitely a hint of relish in Matt's voice as he said this.

'No, no. Just . . . trial separation. Very brief. Bit of thinking time. We're getting back together. Definitely.'

'Trial separation. I love it! So you came to me! Your trial separation master of ceremonies, eh? Show you what you're missing.'

'No, it's not that.'

'Course it isn't. OK. Scrabble and herbal tea for two, then, is it? Seven-thirtyish, and we can be finished in time for a nice early night.'

'Er . . . if that's what you're doing.'

'Don't be a dick. Get in a cab and get over here, you loser.'

'Where are you?'

'Don't even know. Some bar. Hang on, here's a matchbox with the address on it. If you're dressed like a student, don't bother.'

'I'm not dressed like a student!'

'You're always dressed like a student. Go home and put something decent on before you come. And I don't mean a suit. If you're wearing a suit, I don't know you.'

'I'm not an idiot.'

'I'm wearing a suit, but I have good suits. You'll just look like you're at a job interview.'

'I'm not going to wear a suit.'

'You probably don't even have one.'

The conversation continued in this vein for

112

some time, with Matt's usual mix of being both extremely friendly and phenomenally insulting at the same time. This was how their relationship had always worked, for almost thirty years.

Daniel carefully selected his least unfashionable outfit and went to join Matt at the bar, stopping at a cash machine on the way to take out a stack of notes: as much cash as would usually last him a week. He knew it would barely get him through the evening.

The address was a bar in Knightsbridge. It was years since Daniel had been to this part of London, and he was a little surprised to find it still there, and still so full of rich people and their shops. When he was travelling, he felt quite at ease sitting in cafés, watching foreign rich people and foreign rich people's shops, but there was something about English rich people and English rich people's shops that he found distasteful and depressing. It wasn't that he coveted the money, it was just that he didn't want these particular people to have it, either. If nothing else, none of them ever looked like they were enjoying it.

Daniel put on a smile and tried to give himself a mental enema as he walked down the stairs, past the bodybuilder/undertaker tableau of bouncers at the door. He'd never quite mastered the etiquette of bouncer eye-contact, and his intentions of a casual breeze-past always evaporated at the last minute, replaced by a shy smile and an ingratiating, coquettish simper.

Daniel handed over his coat to an aggravatingly beautiful coat-check girl and stepped in. To see someone so unreachably gorgeous in such a lowly job gave Daniel the feeling not just that he was too

113

ugly and poor for this place, but that he lived his life in a lower circle of existence. Perhaps this was why they employed women like her at the door: to give you the feeling that you were not just entering a bar, but being allowed access to a better world.

The bar was lit with a curious blue glow, not by any discernible bulbs, but by cubes of wall that emanated a coloured radiance which vaguely approximated to light while somehow not giving enough information to let you know where the floor was. Daniel could dimly make out that there were strange, semi-circular staircases all over the cavernous but labyrinthine room, leading up and down into little nooks and dens, containing shin-high tables, low leather stools and curved banquettes. The bar itself, which looked as if it was designed not only to serve drinks but also to monitor satellite activity over Europe, was in the most distant corner, but Daniel found it impossible to gauge how far away this was, or whether getting there involved walking up or down. Hundreds of thousands of pounds had been spent on this design, specifically in order to give people like Daniel this sensation of utter disorientation and abject fear.

The barmen and waitresses looked like the kind of people Daniel thought only existed in magazines. Most of the female customers in the bar also looked as if they'd be more comfortable in two dimensions, and all seemed to be in their early twenties. The male drinkers, by contrast, were all over thirty and generally as photogenic as eczema.

People were scattered around the booths, plinths and dens as if recovering from some terrible exertion, huddled together for comfort, but too exhausted to speak. This effect was probably due to the volume of the music, which was too loud to talk over, though no one was dancing, and there didn't appear to be any space in which dancing was possible, should anyone be struck by the urge. This was dance music in name only, designed neither for listening nor dancing, but simply to make a noise that sounded like the room looked, at a level high enough to rid you of any obligation to speak.

Daniel spotted Matt in a corner near the bar, deep in conversation with a girl in possession of a face of implausibly radiant perfection, and a physique Daniel thought only existed in the imagination of teenage boys. She looked like the type of woman you'd see drawn in lurid ink on the cover of a fantasy novel, wearing a fur bikini and carrying a lime-green stun gun.

In order to hear one another, Matt and the girl had to take turns bending forwards and shouting directly into the other's ear, a little like conversing through an apartment block entryphone, but given the physical proximity this necessitated, Daniel could see the appeal. He approached tentatively, not wanting to interrupt or fall over.

When Matt spotted him, Daniel did a will-I-be-getting-in-the-way hand gesture, but Matt waved him over and introduced him to the girl, though the introduction amounted to no more than telling each other, inaudibly, what the other one was called. They stood smiling at one another for a while. A three-way intercom-type conversation really wasn't possible unless you said everything twice, and Daniel didn't feel he knew this woman sufficiently well to go close enough to her to say anything audible. Saying anything to Matt, however, without repeating it to her, would also have seemed oddly rude. Silence seemed like the only polite course of action.

Matt then shouted something private in her ear and dragged Daniel away to the toilets.

Walking into the gents felt like waking from a disability nightmare. Daniel could see and hear again. He knew where the floor was. Never had urine smelled so sweet.

'How are you, man?' said Matt, giving him a hug.

'Good, good. This is quite a place.'

'I know. The women! Isn't it amazing?'

'Er . . . yeah.'

'Isn't she fucking hot? Isn't she? Isn't she? I've been working on her for two hours,' he said, in a tone of voice that seemed to imply this was a gruellingly long time to sustain a relationship with a female.

'And?'

'It's looking good, my friend. Very good.' Matt turned to a urinal and pissed, with noisy authority. 'Good to see you, bro. Really good to see you.'

'Are you talking to me or to your penis?' said Daniel.

'Both of you.' Matt zipped, turned and clapped Daniel on the shoulder. 'You're my two beauties.'

'Maybe wash your hands before you fondle me.'

'So fastidious.'

Still without washing his hands, Matt took a wrap of coke out of his pocket, formed it into two neat lines beside a basin with his credit card, and rolled up a banknote.

'After you,' he said.

'Not really in the mood,' said Daniel.

'You're never in the mood.' Matt stooped and sniffed, wiped his nose with manic fury, as if it had just filled with ants, then sighed and grinned broadly at Daniel. 'Your loss.'

'I realise that.'

'So—you and Erin.' Matt made a ratcheting sound in his throat and drew an imaginary razor across his neck.

'Er . . . not exactly. But thanks for your sympathy.'

'Am I supposed to be sympathising that you have split up or that you haven't? You're confusing me.'

'Just anything vaguely human would be a start.'

Matt cupped Daniel's cheeks in his hands. 'You're a beautiful man, my friend, and it's time to get you laid.'

Matt pushed Daniel's shoulders back, gave his arse a squeeze and marched out of the room. In the doorway, he stopped and turned. 'How's Gillian?' he asked.

Matt always asked after Daniel's mother. Daniel had no idea why. He thought it might be Matt's way of reminding him that they were childhood friends, that they shared something old and deep, but he wasn't sure. The other possibility was that Matt couldn't resist sharing his amazement that by some synaptic fluke he remembered her name. The cynic in Daniel even suspected that Matt perhaps forced himself to remember one obscure detail about the lives of everyone he met, to which he would refer during each encounter in the hope that it gave the impression he listened to what they said.

'She's fine,' said Daniel, as he always did.

117

'Good,' said Matt.

With that, he strode out of the room, leading Daniel back into the din. It was odd, Daniel thought, that this was where they had come to talk, that there was a separate room for unsanitary and vaguely shameful acts such as urination, defecation and conversation.

Matt failed to get Daniel laid. In fact, Daniel left within the hour, not having spoken to anyone. The art of standing alone in public with a drink, without looking pitiful, was not one he had ever mastered.

He gave Matt, who was deep in an intimate shout with the girl he'd been pursuing, a wave and an I'll-phone-you hand gesture as he left. In fact, he had no intention of phoning him for at least another six months, and Matt knew that, but he smiled and made the gesture in return anyway.

The remainder of Daniel's bachelor fortnight was not much better. Having realised that he was not a bar person, he called Andy, an old friend who was very much a pub man and who was perpetually single. Since they had last seen each other, Andy's capacity to hold his drink had shot up, while Daniel's had plummeted. It was a question of practice.

Daniel was a rubber-limbed, thick-tongued wreck before Andy had even really started. Andy drank so fast there was barely time to talk, and when they did talk, Andy seemed to talk mainly about drink. Daniel didn't have any drink stories to share, and he was almost immediately too drunk to think his way round the problem of how to change the subject. Then, suddenly, it was the next morning and Daniel was waking up fully clothed on Andy's sofa, peeling a sticky cheek off upholstery so dirty it looked like pizza.

For two days, Daniel had a headache, a sore neck and loose bowels. Getting drunk had never been Daniel's first choice for a night out, but it was depressing to discover that he was now effectively allergic to it. He was clearly just too old. He never even found out how much he had drunk, or what he had done that night, since Andy couldn't remember, either.

He decided to try Nick next, who was from the single-by-necessity-rather-than-choice camp. Daniel insisted on meeting in a café. Nick gave such a thorough account of every last detail of his disastrous and almost entirely asexual attempt at a love life that Daniel passed successively through sympathy, impatience, boredom and depression, and ultimately got to the point where he was just watching Nick's lips move, wondering if enough time had elapsed for another glance at his watch.

Nick, over the years, had worked his way down the Darwinian chain, but he still hadn't found his level. However low he went, it just never seemed to be low enough. He had tried ugly women, he had tried boring women, he had even tried ugly and boring women, but still with no success. The latest stage, it appeared, as Daniel's capacity to listen dwindled away, was Nick wrestling with the dilemma of whether to pursue women he found actively unpleasant. It appeared to be the only place left to go.

Eventually Daniel resorted to the old trick of taking his mobile to the toilet, phoning Andy, and requesting a ring-back five minutes later, which he'd be able to pass off as an emergency.

The ruse worked, with Daniel just managing to say, 'Locked out? . . . You're joking . . . OK, I'll be right there,' with a straight face, while Andy sang into his ear an impromptu song about Nick's designs on Daniel's body.

Within four days, Daniel had concluded that Matt, Andy and Nick, in their own different ways, were all somehow pitiable. Though Matt and Andy were doing what they wanted to be doing—in fact, doing what they had always done—the fun now seemed to have gone out of it. What had been exciting in their twenties, and what Daniel had often feared leaving behind too early, suddenly had overtones of habit and compulsion. All three guys had a drug of choice—casual sex, alcohol or self-pity—that had once been a hobby but was now a crutch. Though they would never admit it, Daniel suspected they were all a little bored, but had got so used to pursuing their respective passions that they could no longer remember how to do anything else.

Daniel had been afraid that making the final commitment to a woman—agreeing to have a baby—would condemn him to a life ruled by routine and habit. He now saw that perhaps this was what happened anyway, regardless of whether you were alone or in a couple. The choice was between your own habits and negotiated joint habits. The latter might have its frustrations, but at least it kept you alive, kept you sane, and kept you moving forwards.

Daniel suddenly saw how the choice was easier than he thought. He didn't need any more time. He wanted to be with Erin, right then. He didn't want to wait another minute. He loved her, he

120

needed her, he wanted to have children with her, he wanted to grow old with her. Life without Erin would be empty and pointless. There was nothing further to think about.

It was after eleven o'clock. Erin would be in bed. But for this, she wouldn't mind being woken up. She had waited years for him to reach this point; he shouldn't make her wait a moment longer. He'd get straight in a cab.

There are moments in life when a mist lifts, and the future suddenly seems navigable and habitable and clear and good. He had to share this feeling with her while it was fresh. She'd understand. She'd look in his eyes, and she'd see that all reservations and doubts had evaporated. He wouldn't even have to explain. It had taken him more than a month of thought to reach this point, but she'd understand what had happened in an instant. She knew him, she really knew him, so she'd know this. He'd go through the door, run up the stairs and slip straight into bed with her, up against the hot, private warmth of her skin. It was time for babies. It was time for the next thing. Together.

CAROL AND MATT

ONE WHO'D TURN UP IN A PUBLIC PLACE

Matt was having difficulty concentrating. He was supposed to be coming up with ideas for the Torquay Tit-a-thon piece, but his heart wasn't in it. All he'd done in the two hours he'd been sitting at his desk was tinker with his email, without actually sending or receiving anything of any importance or interest. Someone sitting ten yards away had sent him a jibe about the not entirely heterosexual cut of the T-shirt he was wearing, and he had passed a good half-hour trying to think of a riposte. In the end he resorted to 'I can see you picking your nose', which compensated with accuracy for what it lacked in wit. Feeling pleased with himself, he then sent it again, copied to everyone in the office. That would teach people to criticise his clothes.

The sudden piercing buzz from his phone gave him a start. He had temporarily forgotten who he was, where he was and what he was supposed to be doing. More than an hour had passed since the nose-picking email, but he had no awareness of how he had filled the time. His mind was utterly blank, in a manner that can only be achieved by office workers and zen masters.

'It's your mother,' said Yvonne, the receptionist. 'You want the call?'

'I'm busy,' said Matt. 'Say I'm in a meeting. Actually, no. I'll take it.'

'That's the spirit,' said Yvonne, which Matt assumed constituted mockery of some kind, but he didn't quite know how. He didn't really know why he was taking the call, either. He had a vague inkling it might be because he was curious to hear what she had to say, but that seemed unlikely. Surely things couldn't have come so far.

'Hello, darling!' trilled Carol. She sounded happy. She sounded as if she liked him. Matt was stumped. Everything she had done since arriving at his apartment had taken him by surprise.

'How are you?' she said.

'Fine. Fine.'

'What are you up to today?'

'Just working.'

'Of course. Of course. What about this evening?'

'Oh, there's a party I have to go to. It's the launch of a new aftershave.'

'The what?'

'The launch of a new aftershave.'

'The what of a new aftershave?'

'The launch. Of a new aftershave.'

'You've lost me.' Carol often found with Matt that his words individually all had a comprehensible meaning, but he put them together in an order that simply baffled her. She must have been mishearing him. The launch? Of an aftershave?

'What do you mean, I've lost you?'

'I don't understand what you're saying.'

'How many times do you want me to say it?'

'Did you really say, "launch"?'

'Yes.'

'What does that mean?'

'It's a party. A PR thing. When there's a new product, they have PR launches where press people are invited.'

'Why?'

'For publicity. Mum, I'm busy. I don't have time to explain the twenty-first century to you right now.'

'Well, can I come?'

'Come where?'

'To the party.'

'Er, no. That's not really how it works.'

'Where's it happening?'

123

'At a club on Leicester Square.'

'I can get to Leicester Square. It's on the Tube.'

'I know you can get there, Mum, but you're not invited. This isn't like a normal party. You don't just turn up with your friends and family. There's a guest list, and you have to reply, and they tick your name off as you go in. You'd hate it anyway. It isn't really a party. It's just work. I shouldn't have said it was a party.'

'So are you going for fun, or because you have to?'

'Because I have to.'

'What—you'll be in trouble if you don't go? With your boss?'

'Mum, I'm busy. There are things you just have to do. I'll see you later. I'll be late. Don't make dinner for me.'

'OK.'

'Bye.'

'Bye.'

He had to get rid of her. This wasn't healthy. The most worrying aspect of all was that he was beginning to get used to her. If he reached the point where it felt normal to be living with his mother, he'd have to either kill himself or grow a beard and take up bird-watching.

*   *   *

Carol put down the phone and looked dolefully around the flat. She was feeling at something of a loose end. Then she caught sight of the skirting-boards.

She filled a bucket with soapy water and plucked a fresh J-cloth from the ten-pack she had bought

124

on her first day at the flat. She put on her rubber gloves, knelt and began work beside the front door. While scrubbing the grey skirting-boards, which turned out to be white, as she had suspected, she found that she could not get her mind off Matt's party. She had learnt more about him in the last two days than she had in the previous decade, but there was still some way to go. A party, where she'd be able to watch him unobserved, and see how he interacted with women, presented a fascinating opportunity.

If she went, if she just turned up at Leicester Square, what was the worst thing that could happen? Maybe she wouldn't find the place. Maybe they wouldn't let her in. Neither of those was so bad. It would make for a fun trip. It would be better than sitting alone all evening in Matt's soulless, bookless flat, with its TV so big and complicated that it took three remote controls to operate it. By the time Matt had finished explaining to her how to change the channel, she'd already forgotten how to switch it on. Certain kinds of information simply refused to take root in her brain. Besides, the screen was so large, she felt sure it would give her a headache.

She tried to think of an excuse for why she might just happen to be passing through Leicester Square at the appropriate time. Nothing plausible came to mind, but how she explained it away to Matt was not yet the issue. She could worry about that later. The priority now was finding the party, and trying to get in.

Normally, she would never have dreamt of doing such a thing, but this week, the notion of normality didn't apply. Her job for the week was to find out more about her son, and this was a precious opportunity. The only reason for not going was fear.

She had never tried to gatecrash a party in her whole life, and she could only think of one person who might have done. She picked up her phone and scrolled to Helen's number. She had promised herself she wouldn't phone the others, but this wasn't about encouragement or moral support, or for any comparisons of success and failure—this was for practical advice. She needed help.

'Helen? It's Carol,' she said, her voice high and hesitant.

'Carol! Are you in?'

'I'm in. It was easy. What about you?'

'Not so easy,' said Helen. 'But I'm here. He hasn't kicked me out yet.'

'Have you heard from Gillian?'

'I texted her. She's in, too.'

'Three out of three!' said Carol. 'How amazing! And are things going well with you?'

'Turns out he lives in a gay commune, and told Larry about it years ago. So I haven't been bored.'

'Heavens! Are you OK?'

'I'm fine,' said Helen. 'How are things going with you?'

'Strange. Matt's how I always knew he was, but up close it all seems a lot worse.'

'I know what you mean.'

'His flat's filthy. You should see the skirting-boards.'

'If Paul's skirting-boards were my biggest worry, I'd be a happy woman.'

'I was ringing to ask your advice. I'm anxious about Matt's . . . well, his taste in women seems a bit . . . sordid. How bad would it be for me to follow him to a party tonight? Without him knowing. To see how he behaves. To find out . . . you know . . . the scale of the problem.'

'Do it.'

'You think?'

'You have to go. We're never going to do this again, are we?'

'I doubt it.'

'So we might as well do it properly. We've come this far—there's no point in being half-hearted, is there?'

'Maybe not.'

'Of course not. Do it, Carol. You have to go.'

'Maybe.'

'I've got to dash. Paul's taking me for lunch.'

'How lovely.'

'Mmm. We'll see.'

'Helen? Before you go . . .'

'What?'

'I was hoping you could tell me . . . how to get in.'

'Get in where?'

'To the party. Matt's party.'

'Just go.'

'But I'm not invited.'

'Oh! You're asking me how to gatecrash?'

'I mean . . . I'm sure you've never . . . I don't mean to be rude . . . I just thought you might know how.'

'Of course I have. Who hasn't?'

'Er . . . me.'

'Carol. You're a woman. It's the easiest thing in the world. You smile; you flutter your eyelashes; you walk in. That's all there is to it.'

'Are you sure?'

'I promise. Have to go. Bye.'

'Bye.'

Carol hung up and immediately phoned Gillian, who was even more adamant that Carol should follow Matt to the party. 'If he's a pervert, you need to know about it,' was how she summed up the issue, which wasn't exactly soothing but did help ginger her into action.

Carol looked through her clothes for a vaguely celebratory outfit, but was surprised to discover that she had barely brought a single thing with her that wasn't brown or beige. Her wardrobe for the week wasn't so much autumnal as positively muddy. After several attempts, checking herself each time in a huge full-length mirror that she found in Matt's bedroom, she finally settled on a biscuit-coloured linen suit jazzed up with a lilac scarf.

*　　　*　　　*

It was many years since Carol had been to Leicester Square. The area had become far glitzier and cleaner since her last visit, but at the cost of no longer seeming real. The buildings looked more like lurid façades designed to hide something than actual three-dimensional structures. The place reminded her of women who react to getting older by slapping on more and more make-up.

Tourists surged around in waves, mostly looking a little bemused, perhaps wondering what it was they were supposed to be looking at. Carol did a circuit of the square and was surprised to find there was only one place that appeared to be a

128

nightclub. A vertical banner hung over the entrance, saying DYNAMITE. Huddles of smartly dressed people were arriving, being ticked off a list at the door by a primly pretty girl wearing a tight black T-shirt bearing the slogan, 'It's Dynamite'.

This was clearly the venue. It had never occurred to her that finding the party would be so easy. As she had set off from Matt's home, she hadn't really thought she'd find what she was looking for. The trip was only really intended as a harmless jaunt to get her out of the flat. Now here she was, faced with the opportunity of actually going in.

Her first instinct was to turn round and head straight back, but she reminded herself that this was a special week. For the moment, she was not really herself. Just temporarily, she was a stronger, braver self, in pursuit of a higher purpose for which the usual niceties and weaknesses had to be laid aside.

She smiled at the bouncers, who didn't smile back—they looked as if they didn't know how—and strode with her best impersonation of self-confidence towards the woman with the clipboard.

'I'm here with Matt Walker,' said Carol. 'I'm his guest. He's the editor of . . .' (she had trouble making herself say it) 'of . . . BALLS! magazine.'

The woman ran her finger down her list and stopped at Matt's name.

'There's no plus one,' she said.

Carol had to think on her feet. She had no idea what this meant, but the word 'no' in the woman's answer seemed like a good enough clue.

'Well there should be. That's the thing. His PR—or his PA—his P-something was supposed to ring up today and do that. I was promised that there would definitely be a plus with the one and that it would be me. I'm his mother. Carol Walker. I can show you some identification. I've got a library card in here somewhere. It's the same surname. It's very important. Because I'm supposed to be writing an article. It's for publicity. It's a publicity article. About the aftershave. About Dynamite. And I'm supposed to come here and write about how the aftershave is . . . is setting sail. An older woman's perspective. Comparing aftershave now to what men used to wear when I was young. How men impress women through the ages. That kind of thing. And it's going to be illustrated with lots of publicity pictures of the aftershave. And lots of . . . of . . . young girls with big bosoms . . . holding the aftershave.'

The woman appeared to be having difficulty keeping a straight face. Carol, who felt confident she was demonstrating considerable expertise on the subject of contemporary journalism, had no idea why.

'In you go,' said the woman, with a wave of her clipboard.

'Oh, thank you so much. You're very kind.'

'Enjoy it.'

'I'm sure I will.'

As Carol walked away, she heard what sounded a little like an eruption of laughter behind her, but she thought it was only dignified to walk away without looking back.

She went through a pair of double doors and down a short staircase with leather-covered banisters, lights embedded in the floor and no carpet. Through another pair of doors, she walked

130

into a cacophony of sound that hit her like a bucket of water in the face. The room was filled with people who were all, self-evidently, from the same tribe, a tribe that Carol had never previously come across. These were people whose clothes shrieked MONEY! or POWER! or BREASTS!, or all three. Even the hair (male and female) looked expensive, swirled and sculpted in ways that weren't designed to survive a night in bed. If anyone in this room suffered from self-doubt, they had checked it in at the door with their coat.

These were Matt's people. This was his world. Carol had never seen anything like it. Her efforts to dig out her very best outfit and blow dry her hair so carefully suddenly seemed a little futile. She didn't feel intimidated, though. In fact, she felt comfortably invisible. The place was so strange that she had the sensation of walking through a sort of televisual hologram. These people just did not seem real. The idea of one of them noticing her or talking to her seemed as unlikely as someone in *EastEnders* poking their head out of the TV to demand that Carol put on the kettle.

In an attempt to dispel this unsettling sensation, Carol took a glass from the laden tray of a passing waiter. The waiter didn't look at her or say anything, but the drink was real enough. She could feel it in her hand, cold and moist with condensation. She tasted it, and it really was a drink, a genuine liquid that she could taste and swallow, but of what sort she had no idea. It was sweet and alcoholic, though the ingredients were unfathomable. Even the colour was impossible to discern in the dim swirl of blue-tinted half-light.

In a contented state of dream-like curiosity,

Carol wandered happily around the party, watching the show. Whatever this drink was, it was good. Before she knew it, she was lunging at another waiter, trading her empty glass for a full one.

Then she saw Matt, chatting animatedly in the midst of a group of people, looking as relaxed and content as if this was an ordinary pub or café filled with normal people who had normal jobs. Carol positioned herself where she could watch without any risk of Matt seeing her.

She couldn't remember the last time she had seen him from far away. For many years now, they had only ever been in the same room or apart. There had been no situation in which she'd been able simply to watch him being himself, unaware that he was being observed, his behaviour not tailored to her company.

She was at first primarily struck by his handsomeness. He was a fine specimen, and he carried himself well. Having watched the subtle shifts in her own husband's body over the previous forty years, she could see now that Matt was in his physical prime. She knew what the next stages would be in the decades to come, as the hair greyed and thinned, the stomach swelled, and the taut ripple of muscle under his clothes softened and sagged. But for now, he looked just fine. She knew she was biased, but she felt sure he was one of the most attractive men in the room, even in this room full of people whose primary goal in life seemed to be to look good.

And Carol had made him. He was hers. The thought of it made her tingle.

Matt was talking to a group of people, all of

132

whom were wearing the kind of clothes Carol simply didn't understand. Everything, to her eyes, was either too long or too short or simply the wrong shape, but from the way they stood and moved, Carol could see that every element of how they looked had been thought out, and was just how they wanted it. They all looked attractive, not because their outfits had any aesthetic merit, but simply because they looked as if they liked how they looked, giving off an aura somewhere between confidence and smugness.

Matt's attention was principally focused on a man with rectangular glasses dressed in a curiously tight suit, and an Asian woman with a crew cut whose T-shirt appeared to have shrunk in the wash. Matt was telling them a story that was making them both laugh. The woman interrupted Matt a couple of times, as if jokingly disbelieving him, and touched Matt lightly on the upper arm each time she spoke.

Watching Matt hold his own among these people, she felt a swell of pride. The shame she had felt only the previous day, reading his magazine, had not been dispelled, but had somehow found a way to coexist with its exact opposite. Her initial ideas of him as a seedy pornographer working among unsavoury men in a fetid Soho basement were now growing into something a little more ambiguous. Perhaps the world had changed more than she realised. Even if she thought his work was disgusting, these people appeared to find it acceptable. He clearly fitted in among this clique who looked, well, not exactly pleasant, and certainly not generous or kind, but who were obviously, in their own way, successful.

Perhaps it was a failing in her, a sign of moral weakness, but she found she couldn't remain indifferent to her son's achievement in becoming someone who could hold his own in this kind of company. She absolutely did not want Matt to do his current job, but at the same time she was glad he was succeeding at it. For all his faults, her precious little boy had at least grown into a somebody, a man who felt confident among the confident. Whatever mistakes she may have made, for this, at least, she knew she could take the credit. If you have given your child the strength to believe in himself, you haven't failed.

As the alcohol began to percolate into Carol's brain, she felt a surge of contentment and sociability begin to prickle inside her. She had done enough watching. She was ready to chat. So what if everyone else there was young, beautiful and rich. None of those attributes was anything a woman of her age ought to be intimidated by. She had nothing to be afraid of, least of all Matt.

He'd be annoyed to see her there, and she had at first intended only to watch him from a distance, but among all these fancy-looking people, Matt would be forced into putting a brave face on it. He'd accuse her of embarrassing him in front of his friends, but she felt reasonably sure she'd be able to win them over and have a pleasant talk. People made much too big a fuss about the generation gap. Surely the mere fact of her being a little older than the other guests was no reason for Matt to feel ashamed of her. There really was nothing for her to fear. All she had to do was walk over and say hello.

Carol waited for another waiter to pass, took a

134

few gulps of a fresh drink and, clutching her glass for courage, sidled towards her son.

The closer she got, the more her confidence ebbed away. Beyond 'Hello, I'm Matt's mum', she couldn't think of a single thing to say. These people didn't live in her world. They barely spoke her language. There was a significant chance she'd make an utter fool of herself by being unable to comprehend what they were talking about.

She was close now, close enough to reach out and touch Matt's back, and she suddenly wished she was at home with a cup of tea, not in this dismal cellar filled with ludicrously dressed, self-satisfied pipsqueaks braying to one another over a din that bore more resemblance to the sound of a cash machine having a nervous breakdown than to anything that could honestly be called music. It occurred to her that she appeared to be having a mood swing, and might perhaps be a little inebriated.

Matt's feet shifted and Carol realised he was about to turn towards her. She immediately spun on her heel and darted for a nearby pillar, behind which she barged, drink first, straight into a woman. It was a messy collision that somehow left Carol dry, and the unfortunate woman heavily cocktailed.

'Oh my God!' shrieked Carol. 'I'm so sorry. Really. I'm so embarrassed.'

The woman, now Carol looked at her, was the first person she had seen who didn't look like she belonged to the Dynamite fashion crowd. She was young and pretty, but was dressed in the kind of clothes you might see beyond the Circle line. It wasn't that she looked exactly unfashionable, it was rather that she seemed to be the only person in the room, other than Carol and the waiting staff, whose clothes weren't in some way showing off.

'Don't worry,' she said. 'It's OK. I didn't see you coming.'

'It was all my fault,' said Carol.

'It wasn't. I shouldn't really have been hiding behind a pillar. It was stupid of me.'

Anyone else in the room would probably have tried to sue Carol for dry-cleaning bills and emotional distress. This woman seemed curiously human.

'Can I . . . let me get you a napkin. I'll get some napkins. Don't move.'

Carol scurried away, returning at a trot with a fistful of paper napkins and two fresh cocktails. The woman dabbed at her clothes and accepted the drink.

'I didn't catch your name,' said Carol.

'Julia.'

'I'm Carol. Matt's mum.'

'Matt?'

'Sorry. I don't know why I said that. I was just trying to explain why I'm here.'

'And you're here because you're Matt's mum?'

'Yes.'

'I'm afraid I don't know who Matt is.'

'No. No. Of course you don't. There's no reason why you would. He's . . . he's a journalist. He's here for work and . . . I was supposed to be meeting him afterwards, but . . . there was a confusion. So I've come in with him for a little while.'

'Oh. OK. It's funny, because the way you jumped behind the pillar, it was like you were running away from someone.'

'Oh, no! Don't be ridiculous. Absolutely not. I don't even know anyone here, so who could I be running away from?'

'Well, if your son's the only person here you know, it would have to be him, wouldn't it?'

'You're . . . you're a very sharp young lady. I can hardly keep up. And what is it you do? What brings you here?'

'I'm not really supposed to be here, either. I'm just temping at the PR firm that set up the event, and everyone from the office is supposed to come, so the room doesn't look too empty at the start.'

'Are there lots of other people here who are doing the same? Pretending to be guests?'

'It's not pretending. It's just something you're supposed to do. I can probably go now. I've got lots of work to do.'

'More work? They keep you going round the clock?'

'No, no. It's my master's. I'm studying.'

'What subject?' said Carol, relieved to be at last engaged in a conversation, the parameters of which appeared recognisable. Perhaps all parties, at heart, were the same. Wherever the venue, whatever the guests were wearing or drinking, perhaps it always just came down to the same thing: people standing in a room asking one another what they did. If you knew how to do that, you'd be all right. Maybe there was nothing to be afraid of after all.

'It's OK,' said Julia. 'You really don't have to ask me lots of polite questions. I don't belong here. I'm nobody.'

'Young lady!' snapped Carol, her face suddenly pinched and angry. 'Nobody is nobody. I don't ever

137

want to hear you say that again.'

'Oh. Sorry.'

'And politeness is not insincerity.'

'No. I suppose it isn't. Sorry.'

'There's nothing to apologise for,' said Carol.

'OK.'

'Are you going to answer the question?'

'You really want to know what my MSc is?'

'I asked, which means I want to know,' said Carol, sternly.

'Well, it's on development. I'm writing a paper on nutrition, about the Masai in Kenya.'

'How fascinating! I could tell just by looking at you that you're an interesting person,' said Carol, a surge of cocktail-induced garrulousness flowing through her once more. Now she had something to distract her from the confrontation with Matt and his friends, Carol felt happy again, and she realised she definitely was drunk. There was one sure sign: she felt liberated from all worry.

The liberation-from-worry litmus test usually had one immediate effect. She'd begin to worry about being drunk. The only time Carol was ever entirely free of anxiety was in the gap between getting drunk and becoming aware of it. On this occasion, it hadn't lasted long.

'Thank you,' said Julia. 'Tell me, do you often come to parties with your son?'

'Oh, no. Never.'

'Why did he bring you to this one?'

'I didn't actually come with him. He doesn't even know I'm here. I just made up a story at the door about me being a journalist and they let me in.'

'Why?'

'Well, I had to make up something. That's what came to mind.'

'What, he isn't your son?'

'No, he is.'

'And you came because of him, but he doesn't know you're here?'

'It does sound a bit odd, I admit.'

'Just a bit.'

'I was just feeling curious about how he spends his time.'

'So it *was* him you were running away from?'

'Er . . . yes. Funnily enough.'

'God, I hope my mum's not here.'

'If she was, I'd love to meet her.'

'I think you're probably the only mum that's turned up.'

'Yes, I realised that when I walked in. And I still don't understand. Matt explained it very badly. Is this a party or not? Are people here for fun?'

'That's the big question. Nobody even knows.'

'They don't know why they're here?'

'No. No one does. But I don't think anyone's reason is as weird as yours.'

'What do you mean?'

'You think it's normal behaviour to come to a party to spy on your son?'

'I never said it was normal. And it's hardly spying. I'm just having trouble plucking up the courage to go over and tell him I'm here. Perhaps you could help.'

'How?'

'Would you mind awfully if I asked you to come with me? I could introduce you to him.'

'Why do you need help going to talk to him? He's your son.'

'Well he may be angry that I'm here.'

'Spying on him.'

'He might see it that way. That's what I'm hoping to avoid.'

'By introducing him to me?'

'Exactly.'

Julia looked at this woman who she had only met a few minutes ago, who had begun their interaction by throwing a drink all over her most expensive dress, and felt a sudden, strangely sad fondness for her.

Julia spoke to her own mother once a week, on a Sunday evening, never more, rarely less. Their relationship was easy, cordial and neutral, heartbreakingly so. Julia sometimes felt orphaned by her mother's politeness and reticence, by her brand of courtesy that was hard to distinguish from disinterest. Julia's mother certainly didn't suffer from curiosity about how Julia spent her time. The idea that she might actually pursue her to a nightclub to get an answer to this question was preposterous.

This Carol, however nuts she seemed to be, deserved Julia's help. Julia liked her, and even if her method was a little eccentric, a little wayward, her cause was admirable, and Julia would be pleased to play a part in it.

Her pang of sadness, Julia suddenly realised, was for herself, for what she was missing. It was a twinge of grief, almost, for the mother-love that was missing from her life. Everyone deserved to be loved how this man, Carol's son, was loved. Everyone ought to know there was a mother somewhere who was wondering what you were doing with your time, and if you were safe and happy. But you just had to take what you were given. Some were lucky; others, like Julia, weren't.

'Maybe I should just go home,' said Carol.

'You can't do that,' said Julia.

'Why?'

'He might have seen you. How will you explain that? To come here and not talk to him is even weirder than coming and owning up to it.'

'Is it?'

'Yes.'

'You think I should just go up to him and tell the truth.'

'Probably. Even if his first reaction is bad, in the long run he'll be pleased you came.'

'You think?'

'He'll be touched. To know you care. When he's had time to think about it. But he might be kind of freaked out at first.'

'Will you come with me?' said Carol. 'He's a lovely boy. And he's a very successful journalist. Actually, he's working for a frightful magazine at the moment, but he's looking for a job elsewhere. I mean, he hates it. He's a very intelligent and sophisticated boy, and he's found himself working in an area that's quite frankly beneath him. And he's single. Still holding out for Miss Right.'

'I'm not sure,' said Julia, her tone of voice disguising the fact that her curiosity had now been piqued.

'You'll like him. I promise. Then you can go and do your homework, and you'll know you haven't wasted your evening because you've made two new friends.'

'Two new friends?'

'Yes. Me and him.'

'This is kind of strange.'

'It's what you do at parties. You meet people. It's perfectly normal. Come with me.'

With that, Carol took Julia by the arm and marched, with only slightly faltering confidence, towards Matt, who was still in the same spot, chatting to what looked like a different group of people.

Carol tapped Matt on the shoulder. 'Hi,' she said. 'Decided to come along anyway.'

Matt turned and gaped at his mother, aghast, speechless.

'This is Julia,' said Carol. 'I spilt my drink on her, but it's already blossomed into a friendship. I thought you'd like to meet her.'

'Er . . . hi,' said Matt.

Julia gave an embarrassed nod. Matt was certainly handsome, but he looked off-puttingly aware of it. Perhaps this was what excessive mother-love did to you: turned you into the kind of person who spent that little bit too long each day looking in the mirror.

'Sorry for interrupting,' said Carol to the group around Matt. 'I'm Matt's mum. I'm staying with him for a few days.'

'What are you doing here?' spat Matt.

'I came to see you.'

Matt turned his body to screen his mother from the group and bent to talk sharply into her ear. 'Why? How did you get in?' He could feel a cold sweat beginning to leak through his back. The strangest thing of all about his mother was that, though she was a deeply anxious person, cautious to the point of paranoia, you could never predict which bizarre things she'd be unafraid of. Matt was

142

astonished and at the same time wearily unsurprised by the fact that she had taken the psychotic decision to follow him to this party.

'They just let me in,' said Carol. 'It was no problem. I don't know why you said it would be.'

'But why are you here?'

'I just felt like it.'

'That's not a reason. You're freaking me out.'

'Don't be so sensitive. Aren't you going to introduce me?' she said, stepping around Matt to put herself back within sight of his friends, who were all still staring at her blankly, seemingly struck dumb by the horror of Matt's plight.

As if in a punch-drunk stupor, Matt went round the group, introducing his mother, telling them all, for a reason Carol couldn't fathom, that her visit had been prompted by a 'family tragedy'. The last person was introduced as 'Tony, from *Stuff*'. He had the smallest beard Carol had ever seen, the size of a bit of carpet fluff. She had the urge to turn a Hoover on him, to see if it came loose.

'You're from stuff?' said Carol, rather at a loss, fishing for an explanation.

'Yeah, I've been there for a couple of years.'

'Right,' she said. 'And is it a nice place?'

'It's an OK job. I like it.'

'Oh, it's a job! You *work* at stuff.'

'Yeah.'

'What kind of stuff?'

'*Stuff*, the magazine.'

'Stuff what magazine?'

'The magazine. The magazine called *Stuff*,' barked Matt.

'Oh,' said Carol, beginning to worry that she might be making a fool of herself. 'Is that a cookery magazine?'

'Er . . . no,' said Tony. 'Technology. Gadgets. That kind of thing.'

'Oh. I see.'

This was going badly. Carol wasn't doing quite as good a job of charming Matt's friends as she had hoped. 'This is Julia,' she said, in desperation. 'She's doing an MSc on nutrition in the Third World. She's an expert on Kenya.'

'Actually,' said Julia, 'I'm off. It was very nice to meet you.'

With a small wave and a sympathetic smile, Julia walked away through the crowd, leaving Carol to her fate.

'Well, isn't this lovely?' Carol said, clapping her hands together. 'I do enjoy a good party.'

Everyone seemed to be staring at her as if she was deranged.

'Maybe we should go,' said Matt.

'OK, dear,' said Carol.

'I'm really sorry,' said Matt, to his group of friends, in the tone of voice you might use if your child had peed on a wedding cake.

None of them spoke. They all seemed lost in private nightmares about their own mothers arriving unannounced at a party. If it could happen to Matt, it could happen to anyone. Matt was the kind of person you didn't imagine having a mother at all, let alone one he'd see, or one who'd turn up in a public place.

Matt grabbed Carol's upper arm, citizen's-arrest style, and walked her to the exit. Just short of the door, Matt froze, jolting Carol to a halt. 'Fuck!' he said. 'It's Mitzi Badminton.'

'Sorry?'

144

'Mitzi Badminton! Over there! Looking right at us.'

'I don't understand what you're saying.'

'Have you never read the fucking *Evening Standard*?'

'I don't believe I have.'

'The gossip column! Mitzi Badminton!'

'Is that a woman's name?'

'She's coming towards us. Turn round. There must be a fire escape somewhere.'

'What are you doing?'

'Just come with me.'

Matt tried to force them through the press of bodies, but progress was slow and circuitous. The second they hit a patch of clear space, Matt froze again. The permed and primped woman they seemed to be fleeing was again in front of them, approaching fast.

In their last remaining private second, Matt whisper-shouted in Carol's ear, 'Don't say ANYTHING!' Then, almost seamlessly, his face contorted itself into a grin. 'Mitzi!' he said. 'How lovely to see you!'

They kissed, cheek on cheek, like old friends.

'I could have sworn you were running away from me, Matt, you naughty boy.'

'Now why on earth would I run away from a beauty like you, Mitzi?'

'Search me. And who's your friend?'

'I'm Ca—'

'She's Carol. High-powered lawyer who's doing some work for us. Very hush-hush. Dynamite are involved, so I thought I'd bring her here to introduce her to some of the key players. But she's not feeling well, so I was just showing her out.'

'That's funny,' said Mizti, 'cause I just got a little tip-off from Jemma at the door. Said that a woman had blagged her way in claiming to be your mother.'

'Really? Well—people will say anything, won't they? Amazing, isn't it? Maybe I've got a stalker.'

Mitzi turned to Carol.

'Mrs Walker?'

'Yes?'

'Are you Matt's mother?'

'Oh, no. I'm a very high-powered lawyer. All my work is extremely hush-hush.'

'So it's just a coincidence that you've got the same surname?'

'What? Oh, dammit. Blast.'

'Mitzi,' said Matt. 'We're old friends, aren't we? Aren't we? You wouldn't print this, would you? I mean, who's interested in this? She's my mum. She's staying over. She's a little *confused*, if you know what I mean.' Matt tapped his temple with an index finger. 'I'm just doing what any loving son would do. You could damage my reputation. I'm just asking you to have a heart. Don't trash me for trying to be decent.'

'Bye, Matt. Lovely to see you,' said Mitzi, blowing him a kiss and slipping away into the crowd.

'What do you mean, confused?' said Carol. 'That's very rude.'

'Don't. Say. Anything. That's all I asked. I can't believe what you've done. This is the worst night of my life.'

'It's not my fault you find me embarrassing.'

'It is your fault. It's your fault because you're here when I told you not to come, for a very good

146

reason, which is that this is my work. If I was a . . . brain surgeon, would you feel you could just barge into the operating theatre for a chat with my patients?'

'But you're not a brain surgeon. If you were a brain surgeon I wouldn't be worried about you.'

'I'm just saying it's my work, and it's not right for you to be here.'

'You said it was a party.'

'A party can be work. Why can't you understand that?'

'Because it doesn't make sense. A party is a party and work is work. They're opposites.'

'People are watching. People are watching me argue with my mother like a child. How are you doing this to me? I'm going. If you want to share a cab, come now.'

'I came on the bus. It's very easy.'

'Then get the bus. I'm going by cab.'

'That's a terrible waste of money.'

'I'm leaving. Come if you want.'

He left. She followed. The cab journey passed in silence.

HELEN AND PAUL

NOW WE'RE ARGUING ABOUT IT

Helen woke late. By the time she had showered and dressed, the house appeared to be empty, though down in the kitchen she came across Andre in his dressing-gown, munching slowly through a bowl of muesli while reading the back of the

147

packet with evident concentration.

'Morning,' he said, reluctantly drawing his eyes away from the finer points of Alpen's heritage napkin-ring set offer.

'Hi.'

'Cereal's there, bread and toaster's there, jam, honey and stuff there, butter here. Cup of tea?'

'Mmm. Thanks.'

'There's a note for you from Paul.'

Andre peeled a Post-it off the kitchen table and handed it to Helen.

Sorry we argued. Come to lunch.
My office. 1ish. I'll take you somewhere nice.
Paul
xxx

'He's taking me to lunch,' said Helen.

'I know.'

'Somewhere nice,' said Helen.

'Good,' said Andre. 'Good. I have to dash. Sorry.'

With that, he clattered up the stairs and disappeared. All the warmth she had created between them the day before seemed to have vanished. Helen had the distinct impression that Andre had been put under orders not to associate with her.

*   *   *

'So,' said Paul, as the waiter walked them to their table deep inside the ultra-fashionable City restaurant, which Paul had proudly told her was a converted abattoir, 'how's Clive?'

148

This was a first. Helen wasn't sure she had ever heard her husband's name pass Paul's lips. She would have liked to acknowledge this breakthrough with some effusive or fascinating response that would point out to Paul what he had been missing in the intervening years by not asking, but after a long think she failed to come up with anything better than, 'He's fine. Very well, actually.'

'Good. And things are good at home?'

'I'm very happy with him,' said Helen, answering the question that Paul was obviously driving at but didn't feel he could ask; the mutually understood subtext of her response being, 'I'm not nearly as bored as you think I am.'

'I'm glad,' said Paul, in a tone of voice that immediately angered Helen. His insincerity was badly disguised, as if he was declaring himself not so much pleased that she was happy, but relieved that she was choosing to remain in denial about her husband's failings.

Paul, it had always been clear, found Clive unforgivably dull, and he rarely made any effort to conceal his dislike. Helen was never quite sure to what extent this was a natural oedipal reaction to a beloved mother's second marriage, and to what extent it stemmed from the fact that Clive actually was, in all honesty, quite bland.

'There's more to him than meets the eye. He's a very decent man.'

'I'm sure he is.'

'I'm happier now than I have been for years.'

'Good. You seem it.'

'Do I?' Helen felt herself flushing. She loved compliments, was perhaps mildly addicted to them,

149

and to get one from her son, of all people, was a delicious treat.

'Don't sound so surprised.'

'I'm not. I . . . I don't know. It's just nice to hear.'

Their starters arrived, and they ate for a while in silence before asking one another how their food was, each offering and declining a taste, then lapsing into silence again.

'I'm sorry I attacked you last night,' said Paul, eventually. 'About Larry.'

'Oh.'

'I shouldn't have. I was talking to Andre about it after, and . . . you know . . . he got me thinking, and I reckon I was probably a bit unfair.'

'Well. Thank you.'

This was unprecedented. A compliment *and* an apology. She wanted to fold her arms around him and kiss his neck. Was this really all it took? Was her visit already beginning to repair their relationship? Could she perhaps now dare to believe that the long-yearned-for détente between them might be on the brink of taking place? She had wanted this, ached for this, for so long that she had almost stopped believing it might actually be possible.

'I mean, I can't expect you to be neutral about him,' said Paul.

'No.'

'And it's really not my problem if you can't let go. I have to just let you feel what you feel.'

'What do you mean I can't let go?' said Helen, blinking as she tucked a loose strand of hair behind her ear.

'I'm just saying that's the problem. That's why it

always turns into such an emotional issue.'

'What are you talking about? I'm happily married to someone else.'

'Er . . . OK.'

'What do you mean, "OK"?'

'Just OK. It doesn't mean anything. If that's the way you want to have it, fine.'

' "If that's the way I want to have it"? Why are you talking to me as if I'm some deluded imbecile?'

'What do you want me to say?'

'I don't want you to *say* anything. I do want you to stop patronising me.' Helen's cutlery was beginning to feel heavy in her hands.

'I'm not patronising you. I'm trying to be nice. I'm apologising.'

'Accusing me of having a sham marriage is nice, is it?'

'I'm not accusing you of anything. I'm just trying to apologise and, as usual, you suddenly jump on a small point I've made in passing and make a huge scene about it, instead of listening to what I'm trying to say.'

Helen slammed her fork on to the table, with a bang that silenced the tables around them. 'This is what you always do!' she said, her words coming out thin and high through her tight, dry throat. 'Make some awful, dire accusation, then act as if I'm being hypersensitive for even noticing that you've said it. Then you think you can come over all innocent, and accuse me of being stupid and paranoid for not accepting that we're actually having a conversation about something banal that you think you can use as a cover.'

Paul spread his arms and gripped the corners of

the table, his tendons bulging, his knuckles whitening. 'What do you mean, a cover? I'm apologising. That's what we're here for. I'm making an effort and doing my best, and taking back what I said last night and telling you that I'm sorry. What more do you want? Or do you just want to pick up on some tiny observation that is obvious to me, and obvious to Andre within ten minutes of meeting you, and probably obvious to everyone who has ever met you except Clive.'

'How can you say that? Who do you think you are? Why are you so determined to undermine me?'

'Mum, if I was wrong you wouldn't be so upset now, would you?'

Helen's eyes began to fill with tears. She stood, turned and rushed towards the door of the restaurant, then, after a few steps, turned again, scanned the room and dashed for the toilets, grabbing her handbag as she went.

Paul finished his starter, eating less out of hunger than because it was the only dignified course of action he could think of, when sitting in a restaurant being stared at by every other luncher, all of them presumably thinking he was some kind of sadist, stalker or blackmailer. He wanted to stand up and announce to the room that *she* was the sadist; she was the one tormenting him, and she'd been doing it all his life. Her tears were just another of her weapons.

He was calm in the face of her histrionics not because he was callous, but simply because he'd been in this position too many times before to find it upsetting. Larry had dealt with her wild moods in the same way. You just had to wait for them to pass

152

and hope that something better would come along soon. Helen went through more emotions in a day than Paul experienced in a month, and as a result he never took any of them too seriously. Watching her tantrums sometimes felt to Paul like observing a building site from a high balcony, the violent crashes, screeches and bangs rendered quaint and scenic by distance.

After a while, as the stares abated he began to rather enjoy his meal. By the time Helen returned, Paul was already tucking into his main course, while Helen's sat untouched across the table.

If she had stayed in the toilet long enough, would he have eaten hers, she wondered, as she watched him happily chomp away at his braised shin of veal as if nothing was wrong. Wearing a fresh coat of foundation and eye-liner, she felt in a position to make a new start, telling herself that Paul's aggression and her weakness had been wiped away and discarded along with the old smudged and smeared make-up.

She sat and took a couple of mouthfuls of her tepid pumpkin and wild mushroom tortellini, which was the only thing she'd been able to find on the menu that didn't appear to be made out of the parts of animals left behind after the supermarkets have taken the edible bits.

'OK,' she said. 'Apology accepted.'

'Great,' said Paul. 'Thank you.'

'Now how about we just leave Larry and Clive off the agenda, and try to enjoy the rest of our meal?'

'Perfect,' he said.

'My feelings, or lack of them, towards those two men is none of your business,' asserted Helen.

'Fine.'

'And you have no place speculating as to what I may or may not feel or think.'

'OK.'

'Specially when your speculations are wildly inaccurate and deeply hurtful.'

'Is this off the agenda as in we're not going to talk about them, or off the agenda as in you're going to spend the rest of the meal banging on about it?'

'Sorry. Subject closed.'

'Fine.'

'Good.'

They ate on, in a silence that grew long enough for both of them to begin to wonder if they were chewing too loudly.

'Maybe there is one more thing,' said Paul, eventually. 'I mean, now we're arguing about it, perhaps we should just get it all over with. Lance the boil.'

'I don't think we're arguing about it. I thought we'd stopped.'

'Well . . .' said Paul, dabbing at his mouth with a napkin.

'But what were you going to say?'

'It's just . . .'

'What?' said Helen.

'I mean, it's none of my business. And it's got nothing to do with me. But I know that if I don't tell you and you find out from someone else, you'll be angry with me for not telling you. I've been putting it off because I thought you might not react so well, but now we've been going through this kind of area, maybe we should just get it out of the way and move on.'

154

'What? What is it?'

'It's no big deal, really. I just felt funny not telling you. Not that it's anything to do with you.'

'WHAT?'

'It's Larry. I don't think I ever mentioned that he's had a baby. With Belinda.'

Helen swallowed her mouthful of tortellini, which went down as easily as a spanner.

'A baby? When?'

'Ooh, a few months ago. About a year.'

'A year?'

'Yeah. Ish.'

'What kind? I mean, a boy?'

'Yes. Jake.'

'Have you met it? Him.'

'Of course. Lots of times. He's my half brother.'

'It's sick! A baby that age should be your son, not your brother. It's gross. Because of that man's . . . lechery . . . because he doesn't know when to stop, our family's going to turn into some kind of freak show.'

'Let's not argue. I just thought I should tell you.'

'You thought you should tell me? Is that why you waited a year?'

'Mum, the more of a scene you make, the more it explains why I was right to not tell you.'

'Am I making a scene?'

'You're building up to it. I know the signs.'

'Well, this has been a lovely meal, and thank you very much, but I'm afraid I don't think I'm in the mood for dessert, and I really must dash. But thank you so much. Really. Don't get up. No, no. Don't.'

Helen stood and, steadying herself against the table as if she suddenly didn't trust her balance,

155

gave Paul a peck on the cheek and walked out. Something in the stiffness of her gait, and the strange, flustered slowness with which she left, gave Paul the impression that she was using all her physical and emotional strength just to get out of the restaurant.

Paul didn't go after her. It was clear that whatever it was she intended to do next, she wanted to undertake it alone.

A ROUGHER GAME THAN YOU WANTED

Helen didn't have any idea where she was going, other than out of that restaurant. All she knew was that she didn't want anyone to see her absorbing this news. Her reaction, whatever it might be, was private. Above all, she didn't want Paul to see her tears, which began to mist her vision the minute the air of the street hit her face.

She cried and walked, walked and cried, not thinking about where she was going, concentrating only on getting away from her son. The further she went, the more she found she just wanted to keep moving, keep her legs going, keep the pavement thumping past under her feet. The motion of her body and the concentration required to get through city crowds without a collision distracted her, for the moment, from the worst of her misery. She couldn't stop herself thinking or feeling, but she could do this, at least, to help numb the pain.

It was not that she wanted a baby. It was not that she felt in any way jealous. But the injustice of it wounded her like a punch in the belly. While the divorce had made her older, weaker, more tired and more vulnerable, Larry seemed with every passing year somehow to get stronger, younger and more alive.

A bad marriage is like a war. A divorce is the decisive battle of that war. Their war at the time appeared to end inconclusively, with victories and defeats on both sides. Now the real result, the judgement of history, was clear. This baby was the final, incontrovertible event that she would never be able to ignore, deny or forget. There was no longer any escaping the fact that he had won, she had lost. He had moved on to a happier, luckier, more fruitful life, while she simply plodded on, year by year, following her slow downward trajectory to the grave.

It was so unfair that men could do this: rewind thirty years and start again with a young wife. They had a second chance. A woman was stuck. For a woman, a second marriage wasn't a second chance at a first marriage; it was the tail end of a first marriage, but with a new cast.

Her tears, she realised, were tears of rage. Why did Larry always skip away from his mistakes unscathed, while every error Helen made clung to her for ever? Why did men always get to choose from a wider, more appetising menu than women? How was it possible that there was always a way for them to cheat, when for women the rules never seemed to be negotiable?

Helen found herself at Moorgate station, and without consciously deciding on a plan, she walked in and headed down into the familiar dank air of the Underground, towards the Metropolitan line that would take her back home to Pinner. She was defeated. As ever, her ex-husband and her son had devoured her, shredded her, wrung her out. This was what men did. They used you up, then moved on to someone else.

Why had she not had a daughter? Why was she not allowed a wife? Why did no one accept her love, and give some of it back? No wonder women shrivelled and shrank as they got older. They wasted their love on emotional cannibals. They allowed themselves to be eaten alive.

Only as the train pulled up to her platform did she hesitate. The doors opened, then shut. A surge of people jostled impatiently around her as the train drew away, then the platform fell quiet again. Helen looked down at the tracks. A mouse skittered along the rails, traversing with happily oblivious impunity on to the electric rail and off again, in a manner that, for a moment, reminded her of Larry.

'Hello, Larry,' she thought to herself, watching it scurry away towards the tunnel. Then she turned and looked at the Tube map on the wall behind her.

You are as weak as you allow yourself to be. If she was the victim of the family, it was because she didn't fight her corner. It should not have to come down to fighting, but if those were the rules, those were the rules. If you were outnumbered by men, you'd always end up playing a rougher game than you wanted, and it was time she accepted that and fought back.

This was her last chance, and she was not going to give up. She would head back to Hoxton.

GILLIAN AND DANIEL

SICKENING OVERTONES OF FARCE

Daniel turned the key quietly in the door and walked into his flat. He knew he'd always remember this moment. As he crossed the threshold, he felt himself passing from one phase of his life into another. Right now, at this instant, he was at long last truly becoming an adult. He was finally committing himself, for ever, to this woman, and to the family they would create together.

His body was palpitating with joy, and the sight of his home seemed to wipe out the weeks he had been away. Already, just standing there on the doormat, he could smell Erin's presence, a faint whiff of her perfume that pummelled his heart. He had never really known, until this evening, how much he loved her. He understood, finally, how blessed he was to have found her, and to be loved by her, and to have the chance to turn their love into a new person who would blend them together into one body, knit them into the ultimate in human proximity.

The lights were on in the living room, and a Nick Drake album was quietly playing. He had given her this CD a couple of years earlier for her birthday. She must have been listening to it as a reminder of him. 'I'm back!' he called.

There was no reply. He walked to the source of the music, but the room was empty. He looked in the kitchen. Erin wasn't there, either.

Daniel walked back into the hallway and called

159

up the stairs. 'Hello? Erin?'

As Daniel placed his foot on the bottom step, Erin appeared on the upstairs landing, looking confused, hastily dressed and a little cross. She was wearing a short dress that he had never seen before and no socks or shoes.

'What are you doing here?' she said.

'I live here.'

'I mean, why didn't you phone?'

'I thought we agreed not to speak. And the time's up, and I just . . . I had a revelation and I rushed over here to share it with you.'

'You should have phoned.'

Daniel could feel his legs almost giving way under him. His mouth began to fill with thin saliva.

'Are you . . . ?'

'It's not good timing, Daniel.'

'Are you alone?' he said. He could barely get the words out.

She didn't respond, or move. She didn't even shake her head. Just the way she looked at him gave the answer.

For a moment, Daniel felt as if he was going to throw up. He could feel his stomach tensing into a dry retch. His head swirled as if he had been punched. Without knowing why, he found himself striding up the stairs.

'Daniel,' said Erin, 'don't do this. Really. There's no need.'

He walked past without catching her eye and shoved his way into the bedroom. There, as if out of some plan to maximise Daniel's humiliation, to load his cuckold's role with sickening overtones of farce, was a tall blond man who was at that moment in the process of putting on his trousers.

160

Daniel didn't recognise him, except as an archetype of everything he wasn't. The man stood there, his trousers round his knees, and stared at Daniel with an air of dazed panic.

Daniel was not a puncher, but this was the closest he had ever come, less because he wanted to harm this man than because he found himself inside a cliché in which he knew instinctively what was supposed to happen next. It took a conscious effort of will to depart from the script, but even as his fingers curled into a fist, he realised that he didn't want to hit him. He didn't like fighting, he had never fought in his life, and this was no time to take up a new hobby. The man gave him what looked like an apologetic shrug.

Daniel turned, slammed the door and rushed downstairs into the living room, expecting this to be where he would find Erin. She wasn't there, but it felt beneath his dignity to chase after her, so he paced up and down, waiting for her to come and find him. For a moment he felt annoyed that she didn't come fast enough, then it occurred to him that, in the circumstances, it was crazy for this to be, even fleetingly, the focus of his anger. Then he began to wonder whether he was insane for thinking about what he ought to be thinking about instead of just being simply, straightforwardly angry. Was he incapable of feeling *anything*? Was thinking all he could ever do? Even now. Any normal person would be engulfed by a wave of overwhelming emotion, but here he was, standing there, not just thinking, but thinking about thinking. In fact, was he now thinking about thinking about thinking?

Erin appeared in the doorway of the room. She

took one step inside and leaned her back against the wall. Daniel stared at her, unable, perhaps for the first time in their entire relationship, to think of anything to say.

'I'm sorry,' she said.

'You're sorry? And is that supposed to make any difference?'

'You should have phoned. You should have rung the bell.'

'What, so you'd have time to hide him in the cupboard?'

'No, I just . . . it just feels so clumsy.'

'*Clumsy?* Is that what you're worried about? You've been fucking another guy! I can think of worse words for it than "clumsy".'

'That's not what I meant. I just . . . don't want to make it any harder for you than it must be anyway.'

'So you were going to tell me, then?'

'Of course!'

'But not yet.'

'As soon as I spoke to you!'

'But it was up to me to guess and call to find out.'

'It was up to you to call, yes. It was up to you to come back. That was the deal. That you'd go for a month, and think about it, then come back if you were ready and not if you weren't. You didn't come back. And you didn't even call. What was I supposed to think?'

'So you wait a few days and hop into bed with the next guy that walks past? Is that it?'

'I didn't think you were coming back! And if you're not even decent enough to give me a call and let me know what's happening, what do you expect? You think I'm just going to sit here waiting

162

for you for ever, with a candle in the window, in the vague hope that one day you might show up.'

Daniel heard the faint sound of the front door clicking open and shut. 'There's for ever and there's four weeks,' he said.

'You've been gone more than five weeks! Without a word!' snapped Erin, stepping out of her corner by the door, approaching Daniel with her hands slicing angrily through the air. 'It never occurred to me that you'd really walk out of the door and be so literal-minded that you don't even send me as much as a text message for a whole month. It felt like you must have been just waiting for this opportunity to walk away and forget all about me. And then when the month finished and you *still* didn't get in touch, I . . . I just couldn't believe it. It was as if you hadn't even been thinking about me and our relationship at all. I was so hoping that you'd come rushing back, and that when you'd had a chance to think about it on your own, you'd realise what we had, and what kind of a future we could make together. There was a while when I felt genuinely optimistic, and I jumped up every time the phone or the doorbell rang. Then, when there was just endless silence, for the whole month and beyond, I realised you'd just given up on the whole thing and walked away. I realised you were such a coward, you couldn't even face telling me. It made me hate you. It really did. So this evening I got sick of sitting around here brooding, and I went out with Abi and Jess, and they were trying really hard to cheer me up, and buying me all these drinks, and we were all talking about what a bastard you are, and I was trying to play along with it and act like it was helping, but I was actually

163

just feeling miserable, and that just made me drink more, then they made me go clubbing, and things got a bit wild and kind of weird and I ended up back here with a guy.'

'Why? Why would you do that?'

'I'm sorry.'

'*Why?* What went weird? What does that even mean?'

Erin began to sob, gently at first, then with her whole body, which crumpled down on to the floor. She sat on the carpet, her back leaning against the sofa, tears wrenching her body, while Daniel stood over her, watching from above, feeling strangely numb towards her misery. Some habit or instinct told him to sit beside her, to cradle her in his arms, but he fought it. This was what women did. They were simply better at being upset than men, more fluent in the language, so in a crisis they always won out in the audition for the tragic lead. But on this occasion, he couldn't let that happen. He was the wronged party here. If anyone deserved any sympathy, it was him.

'Why are you crying?' he said. 'It's not you that should be crying. This isn't about you. I'm the one who should be crying. Why the fuck should I be standing here watching you crying?'

'I'm sorry, I'm sorry, I'm sorry.'

'Why did you do it? Why did you *want* to do it?'

'I don't know.'

'You must know.'

'I don't. I didn't want to do it,' she said, her voice muffled behind her hands, which she was pressing into her face.

'He forced you?'

'No.'

'So you did want to.'

'No! I can't explain.'

'Well, you'll have to.'

Daniel knelt in front of Erin, trying to look into her eyes. She dropped her hands to her lap, but her gaze fixed unwaveringly on a patch of carpet beside her feet. 'I was angry and drunk, and I wanted to hurt you, and it made sense for a moment, in a bar, but the minute I got into bed with him, the whole thing just felt disgusting.'

'What do you mean?'

'Don't make me explain.'

'What—you think I should be sparing you embarrassment? Is that what I should be worrying about?'

'No! No! Please, there's nothing to say. I'm just sorry.' Erin stood and walked to the window. Daniel levered himself up from the floor and sat on the arm of the sofa, staring blankly at Erin's back.

'I came here to tell you I'd decided,' he said, after a long silence. 'I'd just realised that everything was clear and I knew all I wanted from life was you, and for you and me to be a family and make children together, and that would be the purpose of our lives and the best thing we'd ever do, but . . . but . . . I was wrong. You're not who I thought you were.'

'I'm sorry.'

'Sorry isn't enough. Sorry doesn't help.'

'I know.'

'Have there been others?'

'No! Of course not!' She spun on her heel and looked him straight in the eye for the first time since he had entered the flat.

He held her gaze, and spoke in a slow, flat voice. 'There's no way back from this.'

He stood, took one step towards her, then realised that in these circumstances you don't kiss, or even touch, as you part. Turning towards the door, he said, 'I'll come back and get my things another time. And I'll ring the fucking doorbell before I walk in.'

With only a quick glance backwards, Daniel left the flat, left Erin, and left the future he had only a few minutes before been certain was his.

*   *   *

Within two months, sick of his life, sick of London, sick of everything familiar and everywhere he had ever been with Erin, Daniel threw all his possessions into a van and drove to Edinburgh. Wherever he could find a phone and an internet connection, he could work. His clients never knew where he was, or cared. He'd start afresh in a new city, in what was almost a new country. He'd been there for the festival, many years before, and had liked the look of the place. It was perfect. It was far away. Nothing would remind him of anything. He'd never bump into anyone he knew or stumble across an unwelcome memory. It would be like being born again, but without the religion or the mad people, and his friends wouldn't pester him to cheer up and go out, because he'd be four hundred miles out of reach.

The move would solve all his problems, except one. But the problem of who to love, who to trust, was no longer one to which he believed there was an answer. He had lost faith in the whole idea.

YOU DON'T KNOW ANYTHING ABOUT ANYTHING

'Great news!' exclaimed Gillian. 'I've found a Jew!'

It was not yet nine in the morning. Gillian was still in her dressing-gown. Daniel had not even drunk his morning coffee.

'Er . . .' This was too much to take in. He didn't know what to say; he didn't know where to look.

'I've been making some calls, and the last piece of the jigsaw just fell into place.'

'I don't know what you're talking about, and I don't think I want to.'

'What kind of a way is that to talk to your mother?'

'It's the way I always talk to you.'

'And that makes it better?'

'Just have some breakfast, Mum. The cereal's in there.'

'I can't. I'm too excited.'

'Don't, then.'

'Don't you want to know why I'm excited?'

'No.'

'You don't want to know why?'

'No.'

'How can you not want to know why?'

'Easily.'

'That's very rude.'

'It's not rude, I'm just telling you I don't want to know. You want me to lie?'

'There's a difference between common courtesy and lying.'

'Well I must be badly brought up, then.'

'Always my fault. Everything's always my fault.'

'Toast. Why don't you have toast? There's juice in the fridge.'

'It's a mother's lot, isn't it? We're the butt of everything.'

'Just sit down, Mum. I'll do the toast.'

'Here I am, I've travelled hundreds of miles to see you—'

'Honey? Jam?'

'Marmite. Thinly spread. Margarine, not butter. Crossing the whole country from top to bottom, just to see you, not begrudging it for a moment, just pleased to be able to finally see my son who chose to run off to this God-forsaken iceberg—'

'Tea or coffee?'

'Tea. Earl Grey. Lemon, not milk. And I walk into the room—'

'I still don't have any lemons.'

'Ha!'

'What do you mean, "Ha!"?'

'I'll just have milk.'

'Why are you saying it like that?'

'Like what?'

'As if it's some huge sacrifice. I'm the one making the breakfast.'

'It is a sacrifice. I don't like it with milk. And what I'm saying is, I walk into the room, excited, not because I've done something for me, oh no, this is nothing to do with me; I'm not telling you about something I've done or bought, I'm not excited for me, I'm excited for you.'

'Yoghurt?'

'WILL YOU LET ME FINISH! It's for you. That's what I'm saying. Something I've done for you. A project which has taken no little effort, and

168

I come in here to tell you what it is and you won't even listen to me.'

'Yoghurt?'

'Are you listening?'

'Strawberry, raspberry or pear?'

'I WON'T BE IGNORED. I WILL NOT BE IGNORED. I'll have raspberry.'

'I don't want to hear. You've found a Jewish girl. You want me to date her. I'm not interested. Full stop.'

'How can you be so arrogant?'

'I'm wrong then. You're excited because you like my flat? Because you've read a good book? Because Arsenal won yesterday?'

'Will you stop this!'

'Stop what?'

'Putting words into my mouth.'

'I haven't put any words into your mouth.'

'I just want you to hear me out. For two minutes. Please. Sit down. You remember the Swimers, don't you? Joan and Ivan?'

'No.'

'On the corner. They had a shih-tzu that bit you when you were six.'

'I remember the dog.'

'Well, Joan's sister has a nephew by marriage who lives up here. I remember him from the wedding photos.'

'What wedding?'

'That's not important. Anyway, I got in touch with him, and it turns out he's moved away. Apparently the climate's just impossible—'

'No, it's not!'

'Don't interrupt. But he was very charming, and he's given me the email address of the mother of a

169

girl who used to go to playgroup with his daughter, who's just come out of a painful divorce that was apparently not her fault at all, and she's beautiful, and she's a good friend of his wife—'

'Whose wife?'

'. . . and she's beginning to think about dating again, and when I said that you were up here and in the same boat, he was very happy to pass on the email and apparently she'd love to hear from you.'

'What boat?'

'Don't be pedantic.'

'Why have you done this?'

'Done what?'

'What's wrong with you?'

'She's called Alison, and she's got a degree in politics from Manchester, and she was an NHS manager, but she's on a career break at the moment.'

'Mum—'

'That's what they call motherhood, these days. A "career break". It's outrageous, isn't it? Motherhood isn't a gap where you temporarily divert your attention from more important things. It's the most important thing of all. And it never ends, either. Motherhood never ends. You think it will, but it doesn't. Not ever. When I'm lying on my deathbed, I'll probably still be worrying about you and Rose.'

'Well, don't bother. It doesn't help.'

'I don't have the choice.'

'If you didn't have children, you'd probably spend exactly the same amount of time worrying. You'd just find a different topic. You'd get a dog, or something.'

'That's very hurtful, and I know you're just

trying to change the subject.'

'Since when have you ever not wanted to talk about worrying?'

'What we're talking about is Alison, and when you're going to get in touch with her.'

'Can I just get this straight? You think I'm going to get in touch with this woman and go on a date with her, based on the fact that she's the mother of a child who went to playgroup with the son of a man who's the nephew of the sister of the woman whose dog bit me when I was a child?'

'You can't hold the dog against her. That was more than twenty years ago.'

'I'm not talking about the dog.'

'And it wasn't a son.'

'What wasn't?'

'It was a girl who was at playgroup with Alison's daughter, who's also a girl. Phoebe. Terrible name, but that could have been the husband's fault. Apparently she's very sweet.'

'I don't care if Phoebe's sweet! I'm never going to meet her and I'm never going to meet Alison!'

'I know it might be hard for you to hear this, but at your age you have to start thinking about divorcees. The good ones were snapped up long ago. Someone's got to break the news to you, Daniel, and it looks like it's me.'

'Mum, I don't want to be rude, but you don't know anything about anything. So really, don't interfere.'

'I don't know anything about anything?' said Gillian, in an extravagantly wounded tone, as if each word was a razor blade on her tongue. 'And what would you say if you were trying to be rude?'

'Maybe that's a bit strong.'

'You can be so cutting! So brutal! No wonder you're always on your own.'

'Thanks.'

'You can't say these things!'

'Sorry. I didn't mean it like that.'

'I'm your mother. You should be nice to me.'

'It's not so easy, Mum, when you're muscling in on things that have nothing to do with you.'

'Your happiness has everything to do with me.'

'But you can't make it happen.'

'I can try. And you're not happy, are you? Are you?'

'I'm not unhappy.'

'Are you still in love with Erin?'

'WHAT?'

'You heard. I think you ran away from something. I think you ran away from her.'

'It wasn't like that.'

'Have you had a girlfriend up here? I'm not trying to intrude, I just want to know. If I don't know what you're doing or how you're feeling, it's like you're not my son any more.'

Daniel stared at the kitchen window. The pane, inside and out, was speckled with grime. He lifted a hand to his face and rubbed his eyes. The pressure began to hurt his eyeballs, but once he had started he couldn't stop. With a sigh, he dragged his hand down over his cheeks and pressed it hard against his lips.

'No, Mum,' he said.

'No what?'

'No, I haven't had a girlfriend.'

'Have you been on dates?'

Daniel examined his fingernails. They needed cutting. 'No,' he said.

172

'Has there been anything at all?'

'No.'

'Oh, Daniel. Why?'

'I can't explain.'

'What are you afraid of?'

'I'm not afraid.'

'Well, here's the email. I'm not saying marry her. I'm not saying you even have to touch her. Just spend an evening together. Get yourself out there. Stop being a hermit. It's breaking my heart.'

'Mum, please just leave me be. I can cope. I'm fine.'

'You're not fine.'

'Well, even if I'm not, it's my problem, not yours.'

'That's not true. Your problems are my problems. That's what being a mother means.'

'I'm thirty-four.'

'I don't care if you're sixty-four, I can't be happy unless you're happy.'

'You saying that just makes everything worse. You can't pressurise me into being happy in order to cheer you up.'

'I'm not pressurising you into anything. I'm just telling you that you have no right to wallow. Whatever you may think, you are not alone on this planet. You have a duty to sort yourself out. And I'm not going to argue about it any longer. It's just a fact, and you're going to have to get used to it.'

Gillian turned and left the room. Daniel heard her walk across the hallway and into the bathroom. Was she, he wondered, feeling pleased with herself? Is this what she had crossed the country to say to him? Did she think she was helping?

173

CAROL AND MATT

IT'S A TEST

Just by the sound of the key in the lock, Carol knew Matt was angry. When he entered carrying a rolled-up *Evening Standard* curled in his fist like a cudgel, her worst fears were confirmed.

'Read,' he said, slapping it on to the coffee table in front of her without so much as a 'hello'.

Carol prised open the clenched newspaper and began leafing through.

'Twelve,' barked Matt, 'page twelve,' as if only an illiterate wouldn't know exactly where to find the Mitzi Badminton column.

There was a large photo of the woman they had met in the top left-hand corner of the page, alongside her preposterous name in type large enough to be used as a road sign. The image wasn't like the blurry mug shots of journalists they used to print, but was a full-length portrait in a vaguely slutty cocktail dress. She had a grinningly quizzical expression on her face and her hands were outstretched, palm upwards, as if to say, 'Who, me?' Quite what this all meant was a mystery to Carol. Did this indicate that the article was by her, or about her? Or maybe both? And was her picture this size just because of what she wrote in the column, or was she famous for doing something else that Carol had never seen?

Every day, Carol came across one more thing that used to be comprehensible but had recently decided not to be. Things that she had never even realised took any skill or knowledge to decode, like newspapers and shop layouts, were constantly and without warning changing around her into new forms that were suddenly confusing, misleading or utterly impenetrable. She was getting old. The longer she lived, the less she understood.

'Well?' said Matt.

'Oh, I'll read it,' said Carol, trying feebly to cover for her straying attention by fumbling in her bag for a pair of glasses. She hated being hovered over while she read, but didn't feel she had the right to impose conditions. It was, after all, his flat. And the article was her fault.

She had to read the first sentence three times. She was too tense to take anything in. A long-forgotten schoolgirl deep inside her wanted to burst out in mischievous giggles, but she suppressed the urge, coughed and began to read properly.

Mitzi loves guys who aren't afraid to show they love their mommas. Can there be anything sweeter? But there are limits. Lad-about-town and *BALLS!* feature supremo, Matt Walker, has quite a reputation with the ladies, but who would have expected him to choose as his date at an exclusive London party this week his very own mother?

When I go over to congratulate him on his taste, his cool crumbles. Is that a tear I see in his eye as he goes down on his knees, literally begging poor, confused Mitzi to keep his taste in women secret? He even tries to pass off his own mother as an employee.

'Don't forget your balls!' says the

175

magazine. 'Don't forget your mummy!' says Matt Walker.

'So?' says Matt. 'Are you happy now?'

'Oh, it's not as bad as it could have been. She's quite kind about you, really.'

'You're not even going to apologise? Can't you see what you've done?'

'I've said sorry already, Matt.'

'I just want you to see what you've done. This is my professional reputation. You've dragged it through the mud. I could lose my job. Things might never be the same again.'

'Anyone who thinks you're a lesser person for being nice to your mother isn't worth knowing.'

'What if they're your employer?'

'Then they're not worth working for.'

'It's my job! It's how I live!'

'Well, I don't like annoying you, and I'm sorry if you're upset, but I've got something for you that might make up for it.'

Changing the subject had always, ever since Matt was two, been the best way of reining in his bad moods. Meeting anger with anger or strictness had never worked. Suggesting a new game— plucking a novelty from the air—was the only way of making him change tack. Even his biggest rages were usually at the mercy of his short attention span.

'What?' said Matt.

'This.'

Carol handed over a small square of paper with a central London phone number written on it.

'What's this?'

'Phone number. For Julia.'

176

'Who?'

'Julia. The girl we met at the party.'

'I didn't meet a Julia.'

'Well, I met her, and introduced her to you, then she left. Pretty girl. Very pleasant and interesting.'

'Why would I want her number?'

'To call her. Ask her out.'

'What? What are you talking about? Did you tell her I wanted to go out with her? Is that how you got her number?'

'No. She works for the PR firm who organised the party. I picked up a leaflet on the way out, and it had the name of the firm on it. Then I used the phone book.'

'Mum, I don't need your help getting dates, and I'm really not going to have my girlfriends picked by you. Sorry. Forget about it.'

'It's a test.'

'What?'

'It's a test.'

'Of what?'

'Of you.'

'Of me? What about me?'

'To see if you're lying or not.'

'About what?'

'I want to find out if you're only interested in seventeen-year-old girls, or if you were telling the truth the other night.'

'Of course it's the truth.'

Matt swept his hands angrily through his hair and made a guttural sound of frustration and annoyance in his throat—precisely what his father did when he was angry, usually immediately before storming out of the room. But in this flat there was no room you could leave, so Matt walked as far as the furthest window and stared out, in an obvious attempt to terminate the conversation.

This was as far as arguments ever went in Carol's family. Theirs was not a home where arguments were thrashed out, plates were thrown or weepers were hugged.

This week, however, Carol had junked the family rule book. Her visit to Matt was an assault on the whole way the family worked, on the central idea that you did not interfere too much in other people's business. For this week, and this week only, she was simply not going to back down obediently whenever it was asked of her. Her very purpose, for now, was to interfere, and now she had begun, there was little point in being half-hearted.

She walked to the kitchen for a glass of water, which she drank down in one gulp. She then rinsed and dried the glass, her hands clumsy and unruly with nerves.

Slowly, trying to conceal her hesitancy, Carol walked towards Matt. She spoke gently and calmly, as if offering up a casual suggestion. 'So phone her. She's your age. She's pretty. She's intelligent.'

Matt turned and stared angrily at Carol. For a moment, he appeared lost for words. 'And if I don't phone her, that means I'm only interested in teenagers?' he spat.

'No, it just means you've failed the test.'

'But . . . what is this? What are you trying to do to me?'

'Help you.'

'Men my age don't let their mothers choose their girlfriends.'

'Men your age shouldn't have girlfriends. They

178

should have wives and children.'

'Aaargh! You're insane!'

Matt was making the throat noise again, but Carol had him trapped in a corner of the flat and she was standing her ground. She could see his eyes flicking past her, looking for an escape route.

'I'm only staying till Monday. It's not much longer. I just want to find out who you are before I go. If you phone her, I'll know that you're trying: that you want something better than your horrible magazine, and that you're looking for a woman who's more than just a one night stand. If you don't, I'll know this is how you like things. I'll know this is who you want to be. It's not a test to make things hard for you, or to put you in your place. It's just a test so I can find out what I need to know.'

'What if I'm not interested? What if she just isn't my type? This is ridiculous.'

'I'm not saying anything else, Matt. All I'm asking is that you make up your own mind, and that you let me know what you did. Cup of tea?'

Matt stared at the phone number, which he was still carrying crumpled up in his hand, speechless.

'I'll take that as a yes,' said Carol, as she clip-clopped back to the kitchen with all the feigned calmness she could muster. In fact, her knees felt weak, surges of blood were booming in her head and her lungs seemed to have shrunk. She felt like she had just faced down a bear, and got away with it.

Matt's first thought, as he caught sight of Julia walking into the restaurant, was a straightforward 'too ugly'. The idea popped into his head with the kind of sound effect you hear on TV quiz shows when the contestant gives the wrong answer. Whatever might happen over the meal, this was not going to lead anywhere. She wasn't actively unattractive. There was nothing physically wrong with her: her body bulged in all the right places and her face had an open, affable quality to it. She was probably quite pretty, if pretty was your thing. But Matt had got used to more. He didn't shop from this aisle.

He thought, fleetingly, of ducking out before she saw him. He could easily sit out the evening in a pub, then go home to his mother, tell her the kind of story she wanted to hear and get on with his life exactly as before, without any further maternal interference or pressure. This was, in fact, the natural thing to do. To stay and go through with this pointless blind date simply for the sake of appeasing Carol, when he could just as easily do what he wanted and bullshit his way out of the conflict, was a little crazy.

Except that he wanted to pass the test. He had no idea why, but he did. It was not that he craved his mother's approval—he was far too old for that—but this week, for some reason, his mother's disapproval made him feel uncomfortable. And he had begun to sense, like a child again, that his mother had a telepathic ability to see through his lies.

He was usually proud of his abilities as a liar. It was a skill he felt he had perfected. But now, in the presence of his mother, he was like a scratch golfer with the yips. He had lost confidence in his ability to do the very thing he usually found easiest. Besides, to pass an honesty test by lying felt just that little bit too sneaky.

He raised his hand and smiled.

Julia gave him a long 'are you who I think you are?' peer before approaching his table.

'Matt?' she said.

'Julia?'

She sat. 'I have no idea why I said yes to this,' said Julia.

'Me too,' said Matt.

'What do you mean? You phoned me.'

'I just mean it's almost like a blind date. It seems a bit mad. But I'm glad you came.'

'Good. Good. I wouldn't normally say yes to a thing like this, but you caught me right in the middle of something, so I just said it without thinking, then I didn't have your number so I couldn't ring back and change my mind.'

'That's a shame,' said Matt.

'What do you mean?'

'I just mean I'm sorry. If it seems like an imposition. Let's order, shall we? I'm having the lamb. No starter for me. Had a late lunch. Don't let me stop you, though.'

He could be out of there within the hour, he thought. They'd both be glad to get it over with, by the sound of it. Why had he agreed to this? What on earth had he been trying to prove?

She, too, ordered no starter, and when the

181

waiter left them alone, menuless, a long silence threatened to smother their table.

Julia eventually said, 'So, your job's beneath you?'

'What?'

'Your mum told me your job's beneath you.'

'Oh, God. Did she? There's something twisted about this. Going on a date with someone your mother met first. I don't think I'm going to be able to relax.'

'We spent less than ten minutes together.'

'With my mum that's enough. God knows what else she said about me.'

'That was it. More or less. Can't remember the rest.'

'I'm sure that's a good thing.'

'And is it true?'

'What?'

'That your job's beneath you.'

'I reckon every mother thinks that about their son.'

'I didn't ask you if it's true that she thinks it, I asked you if it's true.'

There was a glint in her eye that made him look at her again. She may not have been beautiful, but there was something combative about the way she behaved that was just a little bit sexy. She clearly wasn't a lie-there-and-wait-for-it-to-be-over kind of girl.

'If I say yes to that question, you'll think I'm arrogant, won't you?'

'Not necessarily. And I didn't ask you what you think I'll think. I just asked you for the truth.'

'The truth? Well, you do your job as well as you can, don't you? Whatever it is. Even if you don't

182

really believe in it. I mean, there's no point in doing anything badly, is there?'

'You work at *BALLS!*?'

'Yeah.'

'That's what I forgot when I said yes to this date. That's why I wanted to phone back and change my mind. I wasn't going to turn up, then I thought I shouldn't be a coward. I mean, you go away stronger, don't you, if you prove to yourself that you can look your enemy in the eye.'

She sat back in her chair, folded her arms, and stared at him intently.

'Wow! Is that your chat-up line?'

'This wine's not bad.'

'That's why you're here? To look your enemy in the eye?'

'Yes,' she said, looking him in the eye, not blinking. A trace of a smirk was playing at the corner of hcr lips. She had a good mouth, this woman, an intelligent mouth. Not that an orifice can have an IQ, but the way she used it seemed always to give an intriguing hint that there was something extra, something privately amusing she was choosing not to say.

'And why am I your enemy?' said Matt, leaning forwards in his chair, making it clear that he wasn't intimidated by her stare and that he wasn't going to be the one to break off eye contact.

'You're the enemy of all women,' she said. 'You and your magazine.'

Matt found himself grinning. This was, without doubt, the worst date he had ever been on. He'd come across many strange romantic endearments in his time, but 'you're the enemy' wasn't one of them. This whole scenario was so far off the scale of badness that he was puzzled to find he was enjoying himself. The vast majority of first dates or blind dates were one long slog to fend off boredom or indifference. This was much better than that. And the more she insulted him, the more he found he liked her.

He took a big gulp of wine, glancing at his glass as he did so, conceding defeat in the staring contest. She was good. 'I'm not going to defend *BALLS!* to you,' said Matt. 'If you think it's shit, I'm not going to change your mind. In fact, I think it's shit. We probably agree.'

'Except that you work there.'

'That doesn't make me your enemy.'

'Doesn't it?'

'Maybe I'm a double agent, working to undermine it from the inside.'

'Are you?'

'Not yet. Perhaps I should be.'

'That would be good. Do you reckon you could get a story printed that was an apology to all women and a retraction of every article you've ever published?'

'That's a good idea. I'll put it up at the next editorial meeting.'

'I don't think you're taking me seriously.'

'Let's not talk about *BALLS!* all evening. It's not worth it. You think it's crap. I think it's crap. End of story. And you know what? I do think my job's beneath me, but I don't go around moaning about it because that's also beneath me. If I really meant it I'd go and get a different job, and maybe at some point I will, but it's not so easy, and sometimes you end up doing jobs you don't like and you just have to knuckle down and get on with it until you find a

184

way out.'

'You're going to leave?'

'I don't know. I've been doing some thinking lately, and . . . you know . . . oh, you don't want to hear all this. You don't even know me. Why would you be interested?'

'I'll tell you if I get bored,' she said. She was still staring at him, but for the time being she appeared to have given up on the not blinking.

It struck Matt that out of everyone he knew, he couldn't think of a single person with whom he could have this kind of conversation. His entire social circle either worked with him, or moved in worlds somehow connected to his work. Everyone he met either thought or pretended to think that *BALLS!* was a valid and worthwhile exercise. To discuss it in any other terms was as taboo as telling a fat person that they are fat.

'You know what?' he said. 'I'm enjoying this. You're all right.'

'You sound surprised.'

'It's just funny, isn't it? That you came here to tell me you hate me, and it's had the opposite effect.'

'The opposite effect? You think I've changed my mind?'

'I just meant it must be weird for you that I keep agreeing with you.'

'I suppose it is, a bit.'

'You probably wanted me to hate you back.'

'It would have been nice.'

'I can see that. Sorry to be a disappointment.'

'That's OK,' she said, with a half-smile. 'We can work on it.'

As Matt sloshed out two large top-ups, it

occurred to him that maybe his mother wasn't as mad as she seemed. You couldn't judge someone's sex appeal on a quick glance. It was when you saw how a woman talked and moved and used her eyes, mouth and hands that you knew. The models he had slept with were always beautiful, but never sexy. Precisely what they were missing, Julia had. It came off her like a radiator gives off heat.

In the end, the meal lasted three hours, with dessert, then coffee, then a couple of brandies each. For Matt, it felt a little like a holiday romance, when you meet someone from another world and find yourself lying on your back, looking at the stars, talking about your life in a fresh, open and dreamy way. He felt as if he could say anything to her, and was surprised to find how unfamiliar this sensation was.

The difference, he realised, was one of tone, of sincerity. He could talk about anything, more or less, with his friends—there were no boundaries of taste, vulgarity or frankness—but it simply wasn't done to be too sincere. His social group dealt with sincerity in the way he imagined Victorians might have handled flatulence: it was to be avoided at all costs, and if some slipped out by accident, everyone present was honour bound to pretend it hadn't happened, and to move the conversation on as seamlessly as possible.

At one point in the evening, Matt realised he'd been talking too much and turned the conversation round, asking Julia what she did and what her ambitions were. This was the way teenagers spoke to one another when they were up past their bedtime, and Matt was loving it.

In fact, he was so excited by the type of

conversation they were having that his side of the interrogation didn't go very far. He was having such fun asking teenager-type questions that he found himself concentrating more on what else he could ask her than on listening to the answers she gave. It was something of a novelty for Matt to be asking anyone anything, and as he struggled to keep his side of the conversation flowing, he recognised that his technique in this area was rusty.

It wasn't his fault, though. It was the world he lived in. Among his colleagues, the ability to listen was about as useful a skill as knowing how to light a fire with twigs. His peers exchanged information fluently and wittily enough, but no one really listened, asked or probed. You might be challenged and needled on an abstract argument—plenty of people would dig away at a factual or logical flaw in something you said—but no one would ever draw out another person's ideas or feelings.

As Matt got to the end of this thought, he realised that Julia had stopped talking. She had answered his previous question, which he could no longer remember, and he hadn't heard her answer. He wanted to ask her to repeat herself; he wanted to explain to her that the only reason he hadn't responded was because he'd been suddenly struck by how awful it was that he and his friends had lost the ability to listen, but he didn't feel confident he could get this idea across in a way that would show him in a flattering light. Instead, he opted for a sympathetic nod and an intense stare. If he gave the impression he was thinking deeply about what she said, he could rely on her to move the conversation forwards without too much of an embarrassing glitch.

He didn't even try and get her into bed. With a woman like Julia, you had to play the long game. You could ruin everything by making the wrong move at the wrong time. Women like this wanted you to behave like a eunuch, while at the same time demonstrating that you were capable of virility should it ever be required of you.

He pointedly ordered a cab and, as any virile eunuch would, commandingly sent her off in it with a chaste but authoritative kiss on the cheek. That he had moved from 'the enemy' to someone you'd kiss on the cheek felt like ample progress for one evening. Besides, he was exhausted. The evening had tired him out more than any session at the gym.

*   *   *

When he got home, Carol was still awake, waiting for him, killing time with her fourth news broadcast of the evening. She flicked off the TV the instant he walked in and looked up at him expectantly.

'It was good,' he said. 'I like her.'

Carol smiled. 'Oh, I'm so glad. Did you have fun? I took to her the minute I saw her. She was very kind to me at that party.'

'I'll tell you tomorrow,' said Matt, retreating to the privacy of his bedroom. There was nothing his mother liked better than an in-depth social post-mortem, and Matt really wasn't in the mood. He wanted to be alone to savour the bubble of happiness the evening had generated around him.

He smiled at her, wished her good night and closed the door.

'There's been an earthquake in Bolivia!' Carol called after him.

'Whatever,' said Matt.

HELEN AND PAUL

THAT'S NOT THE ARRANGEMENT

Andre let Helen into the house and immediately, in the tone of voice you'd use with someone who had just been in a car crash, offered her a cup of tea. Helen gathered that, in the wake of her dismal lunch with Paul, she was perhaps not looking her best, and she gratefully accepted.

While he was in the kitchen, she went to the bathroom to assess the damage. Looking in the mirror had once been one of her favourite hobbies. Lately, it had become a daily trauma. Many years ago, she had heard a woman described as having 'the remains of a beautiful face'. Her memory, cruelly, had never allowed her to forget the phrase, and had saved it up, semi-dormant in the back of her mind, for the moment when it applied to her.

The bone structure was still there, but the skin sagged and drooped on it like a blanket on a dog basket. Her hair, though more expensively done than ever, had lost its lustre and bounce through excessive colouring, as she endlessly strove for that pure, radiant black which had once been the beacon around which she constructed her wardrobe. She was not yet an old crone, but her

189

sex appeal had long since dried up and blown away. She was an ex-beauty. She had entered the invisible years.

As an exhausted athlete near the end of a training session might reach for a bottle of water, Helen fumbled through the pouches of her sponge bag for her cleanser. She wearily washed her face and put on fresh make-up, for the third time that day.

She didn't want to speak to Andre, she didn't want to speak to anyone, but she was simply too tired to be out of the house any longer, and was still, for now, successfully fighting the urge to retreat home.

Helen returned to the living room just as Andre walked in with two steaming mugs and a packet of chocolate digestives. He sat down and smiled, tentatively. This time she would have been happier to see only one mug, and for Andre to withdraw, but she could see his intentions were kind, so she thanked him and smiled back.

They sat for a while, blowing on their drinks, until Helen, uncomfortable with the silence, asked Andre if he had any sisters.

'Two,' he replied.

'Do they get on well with your mum?'

'More or less.'

'Better than you?'

'That's very personal.'

'Sorry. It's just, things with Paul . . . as you know . . . can be tricky, and you forget what's normal. You want to be reminded.'

'You're very keen on that word.'

'What word?'

'Normal.'

190

'Am I?'

'You were talking about it last night as well. What was it Calvin said? "Who gives a shit what's normal?"'

'Is that what you think?'

Though Paul never mentioned Helen to Andre without some kind of moan or grievance, and though Andre had been up until one in the morning listening to Paul complain about her 'emotional incontinence', he still didn't quite understand. It was forbidden, of course, to take her side—Andre's role in all this was simply as a maker of tea and a sounding board—but he could see why she had come round unannounced, given the efforts Paul made to keep her at bay.

Andre could see what Helen was trying to do. She just wanted Paul to like her. It wasn't too much to ask, in the circumstances, and as far as Andre could tell, she appeared reasonably likeable. But with other people's families, you never knew anything. More often than not, the more you saw, the less you understood.

While trying to stay on the tightrope of what was acceptable for a man to say to his boyfriend's mother, he decided to help her. 'Pretty much,' he said. 'It's what I try to think. It's what we should all try to think.'

'Maybe. But we all need reassurance, don't we?'

'Of what? That we're normal?'

'Something like that. Not in every way. Just reassurance that our problems aren't because we're crazy or weak or stupid—that other people have the same difficulties.'

This was one of Helen's most private, shameful thoughts. It was an idea that floated around

191

anxiously in her head all the time, but she had never even mentioned it to her husband or her closest friends. Now—she had no idea why—she had revealed it to a man who was little more than a stranger.

'I'm sure you're not crazy or weak or stupid, and even if you were, I don't think that would make you any less normal. Plenty of extremely normal people are all three.'

'You think?'

'Of course!'

There was a silence while they sipped their drinks, with Helen trying to figure out if this idea was of any comfort. At first, it appeared to be. But she had never seriously doubted whether or not she was normal. Apart from her lost beauty, Helen had always felt that her utter, profound normality was never in doubt, and was in fact one of her flaws.

When she thought about what Andre was saying, his theory seemed to suggest that her averageness in fact made her more likely to be crazy, weak and stupid, not less. That was definitely the implication. She was sure he meant well, but this was not, however you looked at it, reassuring.

'Maybe,' said Andre, 'if you ditched the "normal" thing, you might find it easier to get on with Paul.' It had taken Andre ten years to get this idea into the head of his own mother, a woman who was at heart more interested in coasters than self-awareness. Helen was getting the five-minute crash course.

'What do you mean?' she said, baffled by his conversational logic.

'Just try not to think like that. Forget "normal". Pretend it doesn't exist. I have to go and do some work.'

He stood and walked to the stairs.

'What do you do?' said Helen.

'I'm a student.'

Before she could ask what he was studying, or if he was paying rent in cash or by sleeping with the landlord, or if he just slept with Paul, or if he slept with everyone, or if everyone slept with everyone, he had disappeared.

Helen kicked her shoes off and closed her eyes. She wouldn't sleep. Not in the middle of the day. Only cats, babies, geriatrics and vagrants slept in the afternoon. She'd just allow herself a little quiet time to mull things over.

The next thing she heard was Paul's voice, telling her that dinner was ready, as he squeezed her shoulder and peered at her face from alarmingly close range.

It is not easy to make a dignified performance of waking up when you aren't even aware of having fallen asleep, when you can't remember where you are and have drooled copiously down your chin. In the wake of her resolve to take a stronger, more assertive stance with Paul, this wasn't a great start: less warrior stateswoman than Alzheimer's patient.

'I was asleep,' she said, as much to herself as to Paul.

'I know. You've been asleep most of the afternoon.'

'I'll just freshen up,' she said, conscious as the words came out of her mouth that this euphemism had gone out of fashion several decades ago.

'Take your time,' he said. 'It's just me and you

193

for dinner. I've heated up a pizza.'

'Oh. Lovely.'

Even after splashing her face and wrists with cold water and reapplying yet another full mask of make-up, Helen still felt groggy and confused. She was about to go back to Paul when the news he had given her at lunch stabbed its way back into her mind. She gripped the sink, breathed deeply and gave herself a silent little team-talk. *You are doing well. You are being brave. You haven't gone home, which means you are not weak or stupid (though you may be crazy). Now you will face your son, and be yourself, proudly.*

Her body felt old, wobbly and wayward, but she sniffed, practised a smile in the mirror, and walked out of the bathroom.

A slice of pizza was already cooling on her plate by the time she took her place. Paul had an untouched slice on his plate, and clean cutlery, but the shape of the remaining pizza in front of them gave the definite impression that he had snaffled a piece with his fingers while waiting for her to arrive.

Paul ceremoniously poured out two glasses of wine, making a slight point, Helen felt, of having held back on the wine until her belated appearance.

'To family,' said Paul, raising his glass.

Helen had no idea what this meant, nor any way of discerning whether there was a darker purpose to this choice of toast. Was it a roundabout way of forcing her to raise a glass to Larry's new child, as part of her family? She decided not to ask.

'To family,' she said, taking a small sip that almost against her wishes became a lengthy swig.

'And thank you for coming to visit me,' said Paul.

Again, Helen was floored and perplexed by what Paul was saying. It didn't seem ironic, but she couldn't understand how it might be sincere, given how much they had argued. But with his constant accusations towards her of being paranoid and oversensitive, she knew she had no choice, if she didn't want to slip into one of their old arguments, of doing anything other than appearing to take what he said at face value, which she feared made her come across as an idiot.

She had barely opened her mouth, and already Paul had somehow cornered her into a choice between paranoia and idiocy. She opted for idiocy.

'Well thank *you*,' she said, 'for having me and for making me feel so welcome here.'

Perhaps this was the point. In the politest possible way, was he somehow turning this into a farewell dinner? Was he kicking her out?

'You *are* welcome here,' he said. 'It's been nice to see you.'

Nice? Was that the most enthusiastic word he could come up with?

'And I'm really glad I met Andre at long last,' said Helen, beginning to wonder if the two of them were capable of being pleasant to one another without conversing in stiff platitudes.

'We've only been together a few months.'

'You know what I mean,' said Helen. 'And thank you for lunch. It was very generous of you. I'm sorry I left in such a rush.' They still appeared to be stuck in a tutorial conversation from an English language textbook.

'I hope I didn't upset you,' said Paul.

195

'Nonononono. I'm glad you told me.'

'I'm glad you're glad.'

'And if I was upset it wasn't because of you. I'm sorry I made a scene. It's just . . . you know . . . a big thing when you divorce, and your life goes one way and theirs goes another. You never quite get used to it. It's like a bit of yourself has broken free and is getting on with things on its own. Like having a child, I suppose.'

'Maybe that's the problem, Mum. You have to stop thinking of him as a bit of you, because he isn't.'

'No, I don't mean it like that. I just mean that . . . that every day we make a thousand choices, and all we get to do is live on one branch of this infinitely branching tree, on this tiny thread of choices that we've made, but when I see you, and you talk about Larry, it's like I can suddenly see across to this other thread out there that's got my name on it. Or had my name on it. Do you see what I mean? I'll always know I could have stayed with him and that thread would have been my life.'

'But what he's doing now isn't what he'd be doing if he was with you. So it's got nothing to do with any kind of life that might have been yours if you'd stayed together.'

'I know, but it just makes you think these thoughts that it's easier to live without. Life's so much simpler when the alternatives fall away. If they stay around and live on, in the same city, day in day out, they can haunt you.'

'They're not your alternatives that live on, though. They're his.'

'But they feel like mine. Sometimes. I know they shouldn't, but they do.'

'Well, at least we've managed to talk about him without it turning into an argument,' said Paul.

'Yes,' said Helen. 'Exactly. It's important that we can have a normal . . . I mean average . . . I mean just kind of a civilised conversation about him. It's not like we have to talk about him every time we see each other, but it's good to know that if we do, it won't automatically become a row.'

'Exactly.'

They ate in silence for a while.

'Nice pizza,' said Helen, as she finished her slice.

'Mmm,' grunted Paul, through a full mouth, dumping a second piece on Helen's plate with his fingers and grabbing a third one for himself. After another lengthy pause, it was Helen, again, who broke the silence. 'And it is amazing that he's had a baby, isn't it? At his age.'

'I suppose so.'

'That poor child. He's going to have an eighty-year-old for a father when he's still a teenager.'

'Not quite.'

'It's very selfish, don't you think?'

'I'm sure if you ask Jake, when he's sixteen, whether he'd rather have an old dad or not exist, he'd choose the old dad.'

'It's just typical of Larry. Of the way he thinks of himself. That just when he should be becoming a grandfather, he flips out and decides to have another baby, even though he doesn't like babies, just to try and make himself feel young.'

'Mum, you haven't spoken to him for years. I don't think you're in a position to guess his motives.'

'I'm not guessing. I'm telling you the truth. I

197

know how he thinks.'

'What if how he thinks has changed?'

'I'm not talking about his *opinions*. I'm talking about who he is.'

'I don't know why we're even talking about this. I thought we agreed not to.'

'I mean, it's not as if he was ever going to become a grandfather, because of . . . well, how you are . . . so you'd think he might have been able to put off the crisis a bit longer.'

'How I am?'

'Yes.'

'And how am I?'

'You know. Gay.'

At that moment, the fridge shuddered off, sending the room, which had already appeared silent, into what now sounded like an extra layer of deeper silence, as if a snowfall had instantaneously blanketed the kitchen.

'And gay people can't have children? Is that what you're saying? We're all sterile, are we?'

For some reason Helen couldn't fathom, Paul appeared riled. Helen took a nervous sip of her wine.

'Er . . . not sterile, but . . . I mean . . . two men can't have a baby. Are you telling me I shouldn't say that?'

'They can adopt. They can have children by another means.'

'Another means? What other means?'

'The nuclear family isn't the only unit that exists, Mum. There are hundreds of thousands of people who live in different ways by different rules. You can't just assume that everyone lives or wants to live how you live.'

'But biology is biology.'

'Gay men have sperm, lesbians have wombs, and we can live whatever kind of lives we want. We don't need straight people to tell us what to do.'

'Why are you telling me this?'

'Because you ought to know it. Everyone ought to know it. Ignorance is prejudice.'

'But why are you using that tone?'

'What tone?'

'Angry.'

'I'm not angry.'

'You are, Paul. You're angry.'

'Like I said. Ignorance is prejudice.'

'It's more than that.'

'More than what?'

'This isn't something you'd do, is it?'

Paul didn't respond.

'You wouldn't, would you? Do you think it's acceptable? To put a child through that?'

'Through what?'

'Through . . . having to live like that . . . in some weird set-up where they don't know who's who or what's what or how many mothers and fathers they've got.'

'The world is full of horrible families who screw up their children. You're infinitely better off with two gay parents who love you than with two straight ones who don't.'

'So you think it's normal. You think it's acceptable.'

'It's not normal, but it is acceptable, yes.'

'You wouldn't do it, though? Not you.'

Paul looked at his hands, his face immobile and unreadable.

'Would you?'

He still didn't look up, or speak. Helen's pulse began to accelerate.

'Paul, what are you saying? Have you got something to tell me?'

'No.'

'Are you sure?'

'Yes.'

'Have you done this?'

'No.'

'Tell me the truth, Paul. Look at me and tell me the truth. Have you done this?'

Paul raised his head and held Helen's stare. The room around them seemed to dissolve as their eyes locked together. Only by the feel of her heart hammering in her chest did Helen have any sense that time was still passing.

'Yes,' said Paul.

'YES?!'

'Yes.'

'You have?'

'I have.'

'With a lesbian?'

'Yes. A lesbian couple. They're friends of mine. They asked me as a favour, so I said yes.'

'You said yes?'

'I said yes.'

'When? I mean, how? I mean, did it work? Is there a baby?'

'Yes.'

'Yes?! When? How old?'

'Two months. A girl.'

'A girl!'

'A girl. Ella.'

'Ella.'

'But I'm not the father.'

'What? You're not?'

'Genetically I am, but not in reality.'

'Not in reality?'

'No. The birth mother is the mother and the other mother is the father. That's the deal.'

'What deal?'

'That's the arrangement. That's what they wanted.'

'But if you're the father, you're the father. You either are or you aren't.'

'Well, then I'm not. She's the father. The mother's partner.'

'But she's not the father. She's a woman. You're the father.'

'That's not the arrangement.'

'I don't understand the word arrangement.'

'You want a dictionary?'

'In this context.'

'That's the deal. They didn't want a father. They already had the father. All they needed was some sperm. And they're good friends of mine and I like them and trust them, so I had a fresh AIDS test and gave them some sperm. It's no big deal. It was a favour I did for some friends.'

'NO BIG DEAL?'

'No. We should never have got into this. I can tell you're not going to understand.'

'NO BIG DEAL?'

'Let's just drop it.'

'Drop it? You've just told me I'm a grandmother and you're telling me to drop it?'

'You're not a grandmother.'

'I am. You just told me that you've had a baby.'

'I haven't had a baby. I've just given my friends some sperm. The baby already has four

201

grandparents. It doesn't need six.'

'So the mother's girlfriend's mother is the paternal grandmother? Not me. Is that what you're saying?'

'Yeah. Apparently she's quite keen.'

'Oh. Right. And that's why I'm just going to drop it, is it? Because I'm surplus to requirements?'

'It sounds bad if you put it like that, but if I'm not being the father, you can't be the grandmother. It doesn't work like that.'

'It works how it works. I'm her grandmother.' The feel of that phrase on her tongue felt exquisite, each word a delicious new flavour. She had never thought she would ever get to say it. For years, she had been certain that the grandmother club was closed to her; now, in the space of one brief conversation, she was in.

'Sorry, Mum. I should never have told you.'

'I'm her grandmother.'

'Mum, drop it.'

'I am her grandmother.'

'Mum, don't come over all psychotic on me.'

'I'm her grandmother.'

'Right,' said Paul. 'OK. I think this conversation's over.' He stood and walked towards the door.

'COME BACK HERE RIGHT NOW!'

Paul stopped and turned, for the first time in almost twenty years genuinely afraid of his mother. Her face bore a purity of rage that he hadn't seen since the time, aged seventeen, when he borrowed the family car without asking and crashed it into the neighbour's garden wall.

'SIT! NOW!'

He sat.

'Have you met this child?' she said.

'Of course. They're close friends of mine.'

'Take me to her.'

'What?'

'Take me to my grandchild.'

'But—'

'Take me to her. Tomorrow.'

'I . . . I . . .'

'This is what's going to happen. Tomorrow morning, you are going to call in sick to work. You can say there's been a family crisis. Then you will phone the mother of your child. You will tell her that you are visiting with Ella's grandmother. You will ask her what time is convenient for her and for the baby, so we don't disturb them. You will be as flexible and as understanding as possible. But you will tell them that we are visiting tomorrow.'

'I. I don't think you—'

'This is not up for debate. You have made me a grandmother, so I intend to be one. Now I have a lot of thinking to do, and I have to phone Clive. Good night.'

IT ALL SOUNDS VERY MODERN

Clive always answered the phone after precisely three rings, even if he was sitting right next to it. This was one of his many annoying quirks. The fact that none of his quirks were interesting was another one.

The phone rang three times.

'Clive speaking,' said Clive.

203

'Hi, it's me,' said Helen.

'Hi, love. I was just thinking about you.'

'Oh? What were you thinking?'

'Just about you. Nothing specific.'

'Oh.'

'What's up? How are you doing?' he said.

'Fine. Fine. You?'

'Yes. Good. Just watching some telly.'

'Anything good?'

'No. It's all rubbish.'

'Oh.'

'How are things at your end? Paul OK?'

'Yes. He's well.'

'How's his new home?'

'Oh, it's not new, really. He's been here months.'

'Is it nice?'

'Yes. It's a lovely house. It's a gay commune.'

'Oh. And it's nice, is it?'

'Yes. It's nice.'

'Good. Good.'

'Clive? Did you hear me?'

'I'm not sure.'

'What did you think I said?'

'I'm not sure I should repeat it.'

'Why?'

'No reason. I just think I might have misheard you.'

'So you thought you'd pretend I didn't say anything?'

'No. It just sounded for a moment like you said . . . I mean, it's ridiculous, isn't it . . . but I thought you said it was a gay commune. HA! HA! Hahahah!'

'That is what I said.'

'Oh.' There was a considerable pause while

204

Clive digested this information. After a long think, he said, 'Well, as long as it's nice.'

'I'm sorry?'

'I mean, as long as he's happy there.'

'Well, he seems to be.'

'Good, good.'

'And it turns out he's had a baby with some lesbians, but he doesn't want to acknowledge himself as the father. He says the mother's girlfriend is the father, even though she's a woman.'

There was another long pause.

'Well!' said Clive.

'Well?'

'I mean. I don't know. Gosh!'

'Gosh?'

'I . . . I don't know what to say. It all sounds very modern.'

'I'm not talking about a building, Clive. This is a person I'm talking about. A baby.'

'I just meant the arrangement. Very modern. What people do these days!'

'This isn't "people"! This is my son and grandchild.'

'Well, you always wanted to be a granny. Every cloud and all that.'

'Er . . . thanks for your insights, Clive, and I'm glad we had this chat, but I have to go to bed now. It's been quite a day.'

'OK, dear. And you mustn't worry. Everything will be OK.'

'If you say so.'

'I do,' said Clive, Helen's sarcasm sailing far over his head. 'You have to remember that boys will be boys.'

'Um . . . I don't think I understand what you're talking about.'

'Just, he's a big boy now, and things change very fast, and the world we're used to disappeared into the big computer in the sky long, long ago. And we can't expect to understand what people like Paul want to do with themselves. We just have to be grateful for what we've got.'

These few days on her own had been enough for Helen to forget quite how much her husband irked her. He was a man with many personal qualities, but putting thoughts into words was not one of them. He wasn't stupid—he could repair cars and install kitchens and do crosswords, and he remembered the names of every sportsman and politician ever mentioned in a national newspaper—but he wasn't capable of responding to new ideas on the hoof. In a day or two, he'd be able to discuss Helen's new discoveries about Paul. For now, there was simply no point in prolonging the conversation.

'Well, good night,' said Helen.

'Night night. Don't let the bedbugs bite,' said Clive.

Clive possessed just about enough intuition to tell when he had annoyed or disappointed Helen. He inevitably responded by becoming jovial. This, needless to say, did not have the desired effect. Helen hung up.

GILLIAN AND DANIEL

HER SALT ON HIS TONGUE

At first sight, it was the hair. They were at one of those university functions that happen during freshers' week where, for some reason you don't understand, you go and listen to someone whose identity you never quite catch explain lots of rules you immediately forget. After that, you stand around like delegates at a sales conference, sipping nasty wine and making uncomfortable conversation with students you'll never meet again. And across the room, through a thicket of tedious-looking people with tedious-looking hair, Daniel saw Erin. She was wearing knee-high boots, green stripy tights, and denim hot-pants skimpier than an average pair of knickers.

The first time he glanced at her, she was already looking at him, and their eyes locked. They both smiled. He knew what she was thinking; she knew what he was thinking. Three thoughts:

1) I'm bored and you're bored.
2) If we were speaking to each other, we wouldn't be bored.
3) You've got big hair.

Daniel hadn't cut his for three years, but it was still defying gravity. Thick, black, dense and wiry, it just grew up and out. His mother regularly told him it was a disgrace. He was more proud of it than any other achievement in his life. Erin's was longer, curlier and wilder, but lacked the ability to resist the laws of physics. You couldn't call it a mess— this was carefully looked-after, well-loved hair— but you could call it a disgrace, and Erin's mother regularly did.

*   *   *

Imagine needing a new coat. It's autumn, the wind is turning icy, and you simply don't have anything to keep you warm. So you head out and stand, shivering, at the bus stop, waiting for a ride to the shops. Imagine waiting eighteen years.

This was how Erin felt about university. University was that bus, and now, at last, it was here. She'd hated the small town where she grew up: she argued constantly with her parents, she shared not one square millimetre of common ground with her two football-obsessed brothers, and every day she spent at school felt like a month of tedium doled out minute by minute.

She was bored of the place, and she was bored of her friends, and her friends, she sensed, were bored of her. There were two escapes: pub or university. Among her peers, she was the only one interested in the latter option, a choice which carried with it all the social cachet of leprosy. Her friends drank and worked their way through the local boys, who were sampled in precisely the same way as the limited selection at the town's video rental shop (from which, in the long run, everyone watched everything), while Erin just stayed in, night after night, doing her homework and revising for exams.

She would probably have been bullied for it,

were it not for something in her nature that rendered her unbullyable. She was not aloof so much as simply different, apart, uninterested or perhaps even unaware of what it might mean to fit in. She was a giraffe in a pony enclosure. Most people were civil to her, the rest chose to pretend she wasn't there, while she waited, year after year, for passage out.

The instant she saw Daniel, she recognised something in the face of this big-haired, badly dressed boy who looked not quite English but not exactly foreign, either. She saw in him, in the intelligent, mischievous curl of his mouth, in the murky glint of his dark eyes, a fellow giraffe.

*   *   *

They argued, years later, about who approached who. Daniel always insisted that she came to him; she clearly remembered him sidling towards her, then being too shy to say anything. They both agreed, however, word for word, on how the conversation had started.

'Big hair,' said Erin.

'Thanks,' said Daniel. 'Yours is pretty big, too.'

'Thanks.'

Erin smiled at Daniel; he smiled back. She wanted to keep talking to this boy, but momentarily felt at a loss for anything to say, so she reached up and gave his hair a pat and a gentle rub, like a tailor assessing a swatch of cloth. 'Interesting,' she said. 'Unusual.'

'Oh, yes.'

'It doesn't go down, does it?'

'Exactly.'

'It just goes up. And up.'

'You know what they call it? The look?'

'What?'

'A Jewfro,' he said, proudly.

'A Jewfro?' It took her a minute to mentally divide up the word, and piece together its meaning. So that's what he was. She wasn't sure she had ever met one before.

'Yup. They're very rare. Very prized. Can I have a go on yours?'

'OK,' said Erin, worried that she might be beginning to blush. She hadn't intended the conversation to become this flirtatious, and wasn't sure if the development was her fault. Was he going to think she was slutty, or too keen?

Daniel reached up to Erin's hair and mimicked her pat and rub precisely. 'I'm going to need two hands for this. Will you hold my glass?'

She took his glass and he felt again, this time pushing his fingers through to her skull and allowing them to linger briefly on the groove at the back of her neck. She looked into his eyes as he did so, and he stared right back, not blinking. It didn't take any great expertise in male psychology to guess what he was thinking. He wanted to strip her naked and fuck her. As soon as possible.

The thought of it made her smirk with happy anticipation. She even toyed with the idea of cutting to the chase and dragging him by the hand, then and there, back to her room. But that wasn't how people behaved. She was in a new place, and she probably ought to leave it for a few days to see how things worked. She had her reputation to consider.

'Not bad,' he said, letting go of her hair and

210

taking back his glass. He held his ground, remaining within touching distance.

'Thanks.'

'Big, but not clumpy.'

'Exactly.'

'And soft. But I bet it can't do this.'

'Do what?'

'It's the only interesting thing I can do, though,' said Daniel. 'If I do this for you now, any further time we ever spend together will just seem pale by comparison.'

'I'll take that risk.'

'You sure? I can save it for later, if you prefer.'

'Now's good.'

'OK. Are you ready?'

'Yeah.'

'Sure?'

'Just get on with it.'

'OK. Here goes. Take my glass again. And try not to blink. This isn't a trick. Everything you are about to see is real.'

'You've got two seconds to get started, or I'm off.'

Daniel closed his eyes and took two slow, deep, pseudo-yogic breaths. He raised his hands to shoulder height and wiggled his fingers. He then did a few more clenches and stretches with his hands, shook them out, touched his toes, and rolled his head in a long, circular neck stretch. After two more breaths, this time taken through his mouth, he reached up and tucked his fingers into his hair. Like a circus mind-reader, he proceeded to prod, poke and rub. Then, slowly and with intense care, he drew out his right hand. Held between his fingertips was a biro.

'Da daaaaaaaaaa!' he said.

'Is that it?'

'There's more.'

Daniel reached back into his hair. Sensing that his circus act was wearing a little thin, he went faster this time, but it soon became apparent that he couldn't find what he was looking for.

'Have you lost it?' said Erin.

'It's in here somewhere.'

'Do you need some help?' said Erin, laughing now.

'Maybe I do.'

'When did you see it last?'

'I can't remember.'

'Let's have a go.'

Daniel bent at the waist, and Erin began to finger through his hair. 'What am I looking for?' she said. 'A mouse?'

'No, but that's a good idea. I'll remember that.'

'People are staring at us,' she said.

'Tell them it's an emergency.'

'They probably think you've got nits.'

'Hang on! Here it is! Thank God!' Daniel pulled out a small, crumpled bit of paper and flattened it out on his sleeve. 'Da daaaaa!'

'That's it? A piece of paper.'

'Yeah. Paper and a pen. See? Now, what's your phone number?'

'Oh, right. It's that. It's a sleazy for-the-girls thing.'

'Sleazy?'

'A showing-off thing.'

'It's a party piece. Everyone needs a party piece. I had a friend who could push a condom up his nose, pull it out of his mouth, and floss his sinuses.'

'Wow.'

'So, what's your number?'

'There are already three numbers on there.'

'Are there? They're old. I don't even know who they are.'

'Yeah, right. I'll see you around.'

'Where are you going?'

'Am I supposed to be flattered to be the fourth number on your list?'

'I told you, this is ancient. There's a new one in there somewhere. I must have lost it.'

'How often do you wash your hair?'

'Often! Not that often. Just . . . you know . . .'

'Well, nice to meet you. I'll see you around.'

'What's your name?'

'Erin. Bye.'

'Don't you even want to know my name?'

'Not really,' she lied.

'It's Danicl.'

'OK, Daniel. Bye, Daniel.'

She walked out of the party and, for three weeks, out of his life.

She was easy enough to spot. He was sure he'd bump into her somewhere around town, or on campus, but by the time it happened, he already had a girlfriend: a girl who had only remained his girlfriend for a fortnight (she turned out to be anorexic, borderline agoraphobic and psychotically obsessed with attendance at lectures), but by the time it was over, Erin had a boyfriend (a Russian doing a PhD in marine biology) who she stuck with until the end of the year.

Much later, Erin told Daniel that she did actually see him during those three weeks, but he never saw her. Via a mutual friend, she had heard

213

he was going to be at a particular party, and she had deliberately put on her slinkiest outfit and her very finest underwear (right down to stockings and suspenders, with knickers over the suspender belt for quick removal) in order to seduce him. But when she saw him at the party, he'd been zeroing in on the anorexic agoraphobic, leaning in, hanging on her every word, and, yes, she'd even seen him pull a pen out of his hair.

'Leaning in!' she had always stressed. 'Leaning in!'

She seemed to enjoy taunting him with her descriptions of this evening, of how she had planned exactly what she was going to do to him, and where, but how it had never happened because he'd been too interested in this other girl, whose name he had long since forgotten. As a result, it had taken them years to get together. Daniel was now, more than ever, tortured by those lost years, wasted on people they never loved, not to mention the hundreds of missed fucks.

In their second term, they found themselves on the same course and a friendship developed, though nothing more, since by this time they were both in relationships: Erin with her Russian; Daniel with a viola-, piano-, tabla- and fretless bass-playing music student, Christine, who, through Daniel, became close friends with Erin. Over the years, various girlfriends and boyfriends came into and left their lives (Christine ditched Daniel when she realised it was her record collection he really lusted after), while Daniel and Erin's friendship became ever closer and stronger.

After university, they both moved to London and, throughout their early twenties, as they

214

passed through a series of decreasingly inappropriate jobs and gradually reined in their big hair, they saw each other more or less every week. They went to films, gigs and restaurants, lent each other books, argued about the books, took one another to repertory screenings of favourite films, and explored obscure corners of the city in long, slow Sundays that always seemed to be held together by one magical, endlessly engaging, inexhaustible conversation. Again and again, they talked one another through break-ups and get-togethers, until they were closer than either of them ever managed to be with their respective lovers. And yet, since those first three weeks, back when they were students, they were never both single at the same time. One or other of them always had someone.

The only clue either of them gave to any non-platonic feelings was a hint of excessive interest in the other's sex life. Both Erin and Daniel were strangely overeager to help in the other one's search for love, always doing whatever they could to hook one another up with suitable acquaintances. When these matches failed, they were both insistently, perhaps unhealthily, curious as to precisely why.

Beyond this vicarious desire to get one another bedded by friends, there was no flirtation, no intrigue, and no hint that this was anything more than a friendship. They never once talked about a repressed, troubling, nagging idea which privately tormented them both: that they might be in love with one another.

The subject was the only taboo between them. Over the years, they had discussed everything, it

215

seemed, except this.

Then, eight years after they first became friends, Daniel met up with Erin at a bar in Soho and told her that Lucy had moved out of his flat. Erin reached out, in sympathy, and put a hand over his fingers, which were knotted around a salt cellar. Other than to kiss hello and goodbye, they never touched. A thought flashed into his brain, like a warning message over a motorway: YOU ARE BOTH SINGLE. No sooner had she touched him than her hand suddenly veered away, as if she'd been simultaneously struck by the same thought.

It was a whole summer before their hands touched again, the strangest summer of Daniel's life.

They began to see each other three or four times a week. On the days they didn't see one another, they usually spoke on the phone. They parted now with a hug as well as a kiss, and over the course of the summer the hugs became longer. Daniel now knew exactly the contours of her ribs and the texture of the soft skin on her cheeks. He could conjure up the precise feel and smell of one of Erin's embraces whenever he wanted, relishing the memory of their brief moments of physical closeness and the delicious pain of his thwarted desire. But he could not bring himself to confess what he felt for her.

He could not imagine living without her friendship. He could not risk a physical lunge or an embarrassing speech that might find itself unreciprocated, nor could he think of an indirect or tentative way to raise the subject. There was no question of trying things out with her for a while, then going back if it didn't work out. He was

216

utterly in love with her, with her mind and her spirit and her body, but he had no idea if she felt anything sexual for him whatsoever.

Again and again, throughout the summer, he found himself on the brink of confessing his feelings, but he could never bring himself to speak. He knew there were two possible reactions. She'd either be horrified, perhaps slap him, and their friendship would be ruined, or she'd fall into his arms and they'd love one another for the rest of their lives. He wanted this more than he had ever wanted anything, but he simply couldn't risk being rebuffed. Perhaps it was too greedy to want more of her. He effectively had her already. Everything except her body was his. If he needed sex, he could get a girlfriend. It wouldn't even have to be someone great. There was a status quo here that worked. He was happy. It would be mad to destroy it all out of simple greed, out of lust.

Then Christine arrived in London, visiting for a week from Japan, where she'd been living for three years, first working with a chamber orchestra, then with a 'punk jazz outfit'. She had shaved her head and acquired a diamond-studded nose ring.

Christine suggested the three of them go away together to catch up, and Erin managed to get hold of a country cottage that her boss had said she could use if ever she wanted to. 'No mod cons' was the billing, which sounded perfect.

As they drove up, Christine talked at length about how 'no one can play tabla for shit in Japan', and how much they loved fretless bass, but how, for some reason, Japanese men had found her physically repulsive. 'For two years, I've been a big-nosed, sweaty, huge-footed monster. I've been the

217

ugliest girl in the playground. It's quite an interesting experience, but now I'm randy as fuck.'

The place, just over the Welsh border, had two bedrooms, both with double beds, both freezing cold. The first night, they drank and talked until three in the morning, staggered upstairs together, had a lingering three-way hug in the hall, then Erin and Christine flopped into one bed, Daniel into the other.

For a moment, it had seemed as if they might all tumble into one bed, as if a whole new realm of adventure was about to open up for Daniel, but at the key moment Erin had slipped away and the atmosphere evaporated. A perky, indefatigable erection taunted him long into the night, keeping him awake with its malicious biological jeer.

The other thing that bothered him was the darkness, which was thicker and deeper than any darkness he had previously experienced. They were miles from the nearest streetlight, and the moon was the merest sliver in the sky, only fleetingly visible through the dense Welsh cloud. While trying and failing to get to sleep, he experimented by putting his hand in front of his face, and was disquieted to realise that only when his hand was almost touching his nose did it become visible. He didn't like this. He didn't like it at all.

The following day, not long after breakfast, which started so late and went on so long it also turned out to be lunch, Erin went out to buy supplies for dinner. As the sound of the car receded, Christine gave Daniel the look he'd been waiting for. She ripped off her jumper and T-shirt, tossed them at his feet and ran upstairs. Daniel

218

followed and found her naked in bed. It had been two years since he'd last seen her, eight years since they'd last slept together, but he slipped into her as you would into an old pair of jeans. The mattress squeaked, the bed frame groaned, the floorboards creaked and the headboard whacked out an insistent beat on the wall, but the only living things for miles around were sheep. There was no reason to be quiet. The noisier it became, the louder they made it. By the end, it sounded more like rodeo than love-making.

Sweaty and spent, it was a while before either of them spoke.

'Still feel like the ugliest girl in the playground?' Daniel said, eventually.

'Maybe not quite so badly.'

That afternoon, the three of them went for a long walk. Erin was in a strange mood, alternately hyperactive and strangely quiet. It was clear she sensed what had happened while she was out. In the cold air and high winds, the fug of desire hanging over the three of them seemed to dissipate, and a strange, uncharacteristic cordiality settled over the rest of the day. Everyone was friendly, the conversation never flagged or became dull, but the spark of excitement between the three of them had suddenly gone.

He told them about his dislike of the intense darkness, and about his hand experiment in the middle of the night, thinking they would find this hilarious, but they both gave a muted response. 'You can't tell if your eyes are open or shut!' he complained. They laughed, but didn't launch into the tirade of affectionate mockery he had been expecting, or wrestle him to the ground as they might have done the previous day. Erin didn't even appear to be listening.

The same atmosphere prevailed through dinner: an improvised hodge-podge of boiled artichokes, mashed potato, roast asparagus and a baked fish. By midnight, they were all in bed, relatively sober, Daniel plagued again by the same biological taunt, though this time it didn't keep him awake. Rather, he soon found himself in an intense erotic dream, in which Erin was in that very bed with him, below the covers, sucking him.

He had dreamt about sleeping with Erin before, many times, but never once of this act, and never with such vivid intensity. As the dream became more arousing, his eyes opened. Or at least he thought they opened, but for a moment it was hard to tell, because no light entered his eyes, and because the physical sensation of his dream continued. This meant he had to be still asleep, but he could feel his eyelids blinking, leading him, with a few seconds' befuddled calculation, to the conclusion that he could only be awake. And yet he still felt a remarkably realistic sensation of fellatio.

The information his body was receiving from his various senses, at this instant, simply didn't add up. He seemed to be awake, but he was also still dreaming. He touched his face, which gave him the sensation of fingers on his face. Real fingers, awake fingers, on an awake face.

He recalculated. There was only one configuration of events that now made sense: he was awake, and someone was sucking his penis. He reached out and confirmed the presence of another body in his bed. This new information gave him an instant, disbelieving thrill, twinned with the pang of smug relief you get on solving a crossword clue.

He reached down under the covers, and felt the stubble of Christine's head. Disappointment is not a sensation compatible with skilled fellatio, but for a fraction of an instant, Daniel felt the tiniest pang of it at the difference between reality and his dream.

Feeling the touch of his hand on her head, Christine rose up from under the covers and slid Daniel into her. She kissed him swiftly on the lips, a waft of penisy breath filling his nostrils, and still he couldn't see her face.

'You had a hard-on when I came in, you dirty man,' she whispered into his ear.

'What time is it?' he said.

'Two,' said Christine. 'But a woman has needs.'

'How do I know it's you?' he muttered.

'Maybe it isn't,' she said, raising herself up, beginning to push against him in an exquisite, slow rhythm.

On his histrionically squeaky bed, they could barely move without a cacophony of howling joinery filling the room, an impediment which added a titillating edge of masochistic self-denial as they ever so slowly pushed one another on and held one another back, inching towards two clench-mouthed, vein-busting orgasms.

The following morning, they woke to find Erin gone.

For a week, Erin wouldn't return Daniel's phone calls, nor did she answer her door, until one evening when he rang her doorbell for half an hour and she eventually opened, greeting him with a face screwed tight in rage and hatred.

221

'I just want to say two things,' said Daniel, 'then you can slam the door in my face. One: I apologise, for being a lecherous, insensitive idiot. And two: I love you. I've loved you for years, and I've always been too scared to say it, because I couldn't face the idea that it might destroy our friendship, which is the deepest and closest friendship I've ever had. But now it seems like you hate me anyway, so there's nothing to lose, and I can finally say it. I love you.'

Erin didn't react. The only sign that she had heard him came when her arm rose to touch the wall, as if she needed extra support to stop herself falling over. Silently, a tear squeezed itself out of her left eye and rolled down her cheek.

Daniel reached out and wiped it away with the back of his index finger. Without thinking about it, or knowing why, he lifted the finger to his mouth and licked it, savouring the sharp tang of her salt on his tongue. After all these years, this tear was his first taste of her.

The instant they touched, it seemed miraculous, preposterous, that they had avoided it until now. It was a long night. They talked and fucked, fucked and talked, until everything ached. They agreed that this was it, for ever.

Their night together didn't feel like the start of a relationship. There were no doubts, hesitations, obstacles, niggles or qualms. They already knew each other like a married couple. They had both waited years for this love to be consummated, and the act felt more like a conclusion than a beginning. Only now could they acknowledge to themselves, and to one another, how long they had been holding back, how they had both yearned for

222

this simultaneously yet secretly, for year after year, the same desire hanging unexpressed but unignorable in the air between them.

Suddenly, their years of chaste, platonic friendship seemed like one long tease, like a ludicrously prolonged act of foreplay. They couldn't decide now whether to relish or regret this delay, whether to laugh or cry or just fuck and fuck again.

The future, their life together, suddenly shone with clarity and hope. They talked, half-jokingly, about whether they should have two, three or four children, and where they would spend their retirement. Erin, at four in the morning, declared that she couldn't possibly make such a big commitment without giving Daniel a thorough medical, which turned out to be more sex, after which she told him she had memorised the positions of every mole and scar on his body. If he died in a plane crash, she'd be able to identify his body from one limb. She told him that the only thing she hadn't already loved about him, through the years of their friendship, was his body, because she hadn't really seen it. Now she loved that, too. Daniel told Erin that her body was the first thing he'd noticed about her, after her hair. Everything else had come later.

You could not ask for more from life than this, and they, at last, had found it, in one another.

'Every other woman I've ever been with was Milton Keynes,' said Daniel. 'You're my Venice.'

'I'm glad.'

'Maybe I've had one or two Birminghams.'

'What about Christine?'

'She's Beirut.'

223

Erin laughed, then rolled on to her side and fixed Daniel with an intent stare. 'She told me it wasn't your fault. She said she didn't really give you a choice.'

'It's true.'

'I told her that was the stupidest thing I'd ever heard.'

'Really. What did she say?'

'She said I don't know shit about men.'

'I wouldn't say that,' said Daniel, kissing her on the lips.

'The day after you, she had the bloke who came to fix her mum and dad's boiler.'

'Really?'

'In the garage. Her parents hadn't even gone out.'

'She's quite something.'

'She is,' said Erin. 'Why did you do it? If you really do love me, how could you do that with her?'

'Because I thought I couldn't have you.'

Erin stared at Daniel, her eyes wide and unblinking. 'Wow,' she said, with a shake of the head.

'What?'

'That's the worst reason for having sex with someone I've ever heard.'

'Mmm.'

'It's just an amazing piece of logic.'

'Maybe it only makes sense if you're a man.'

'Maybe it only makes sense if you're you.'

'Possibly.'

Erin stroked Daniel's cheek with the back of her index finger. 'If you ever cheat on me, I'll cut your balls off,' she whispered.

'I love you, too,' said Daniel, with a kiss.

'This one first,' she said, giving his left testicle a gentle squeeze, 'then this one.'

'That's good to know,' he said, wondering if it was too early in their relationship to let her know that having his balls touched made him feel nauseous. He rose up on his elbows and rolled on top of her, releasing himself from her grip. 'I haven't given you your medical yet,' he whispered.

'I'm too tired. I have to be at work in three hours.'

'It seems a shame to stop, though.'

Spent and sore, they did, eventually, fall asleep. Despite stumbling through their day's work on two hours' rest, they barely managed any more sleep the following night. It was a month before they spent the night apart. For a year, they never argued. But after three years, when Erin decided it was time to start a family, and Daniel resisted, the long prologue of friendship began to seem, for the first time, like a hindrance. They couldn't lie to one another. And Erin knew she couldn't just wait for Daniel to change his mind, because in all the years she'd known him, he never seemed to change his mind about anything.

Erin always remembered that he had promised her children on the first night they spent together. She told him she'd meant it when she asked, and she had taken him at his word when he answered. He repeatedly swore that he did want children, but not yet.

Erin couldn't trust Daniel's 'not yet'. She knew he put off difficult decisions until they went away. She sensed that in his heart he didn't want to be a father and, if this was true, he had betrayed her. They should have simply remained friends. Their

225

years together had been a waste. She had thrown away the most important time of her life on a man who would never give her what she most wanted. Having children, she felt, was the ultimate purpose behind everything. If she never became a mother, her existence on earth would amount to nothing. Her later life would be lonely, empty and pointless.

By the time she sent him away to make up his mind, she had lost patience with him. She loved him, but she was so angry with him for his prevarication and (as she saw it) his huge lie at the start of their relationship that she wanted to hurt him. She wanted to pick up the love they seemed to have for one another and hurl it on the floor to see if it smashed. If she succeeded in breaking it, she would be free to start again with another man, a potential father.

CAROL AND MATT

I CAN READ YOU LIKE A MAGAZINE

It was the biggest meeting of the week. All the big *BALLS!* players were there. Matt, as ever, was at the top of the table, sitting at the editor's right hand.

They were discussing the June issue. The favoured idea for a cover story had been put forward by an ambitious young pup on work experience, who had bypassed Matt and emailed his suggestion straight to Daren, the editor. This breach of etiquette might have got Pup into trouble had Daren (who had taken one 'r' out of his name by deed poll) not loved every word of it. The idea was written at the top of the conference room whiteboard, in huge capitals: THE SUN CREAM CHALLENGE—SHOULD TITS BE SHINY?

Pup, who would normally have considered himself lucky just to be bringing cups of tea to a meeting of this importance, had been given a special seat at the bottom of the table, in which he squirmed with pride and glee. The look he had given the other work-experience kid, at the moment when sub-Pup had been forced to ask promoted Pup if he wanted tea or coffee, had been priceless. Never before in the history of human communication had the words 'tea, extra milky, three sugars' been pronounced with such overtones of commanding superiority and self-satisfaction.

The topic under debate was whether the shininess idea of the original proposal was the one they should pursue, perhaps with a reporter dressed as a cricket umpire measuring the reflectivity of various differently smeared breasts using a light meter, or whether they should rethink it as a TV advert spoof taste-test, with someone sent to taste the array of breasts, and write it up Gonzo/*Loaded* style.

Pup was hanging on every word of the debate, too overwhelmed to speak, visibly quaking with the agony of watching his precious idea being roughly tossed around with scant regard for its integrity or genius. Whenever the taste-test angle appeared to be winning out over shininess, Pup's face turned faintly green with the sheer physical pain of seeing his loved one fighting for survival.

Uncharacteristically, Matt found himself unable to care either way. It was his job to have a strong opinion on matters like this, and usually he would have been leading the discussion, stamping his authority on the meeting and on the magazine. In this particular debate, it was more important than ever that he spoke up, in order to eradicate the lingering slight of having been bypassed on the key email. It was obvious that he ought to have been pushing for the taste-test angle, ideally taking it in a new direction in order to send Pup back down to where he belonged and to assert some personal ownership of the idea, from which everyone round the table knew he had been initially excluded. But, as yet, he had not spoken a single word on the subject. As the debate stalled, the table divided more or less equally between the two options, Daren turned to him.

'You're very quiet today,' said Daren.

'Mmm.'

'What do you think?'

'About what?'

'Shininess or taste-test, Matt. Come on, get with it.'

'Mmm. Not sure.'

'Not sure?'

'I mean, I'm not sure I go for the whole idea.'

'What, the Sun Cream Challenge?'

Pup, at the bottom of the table, went white. For a moment, it looked as if he might faint.

'It doesn't do it for me.'

'Matt, the Sun Cream Challenge is a winner. That's not even up for discussion.'

'OK.'

'OK? Don't you even care?'

'I've said what I think. I don't like it. But if you all love it—'

'Why? Are you just down on it because Scott didn't go to you first? Because I've told him about that, and he's going to send you an apology. It was a simple mistake, and I've told him how things work, and he knows exactly what to do from now on. He knows you're the man. Don't you, Scotty?'

'Oh, absolutely,' said Pup. 'One hundred per cent. And I'm really sorry. I mean, I didn't know. No one told me. It was a mistake. No one told me.'

'Calm down, Scott,' said Daren. Pup was hyperventilating, on the brink of tears. 'Go and get a drink of water.'

'OK.'

Pup stood up, with some difficulty, and staggered out of the room.

'He's a kid,' said Daren. 'You're bigger than this.'

'It's not the email,' said Matt. 'It's the idea. I just don't like it. But if you're committed to it—'

'WHY? How can you not like it? It's a winner.'

'I just . . .'

'What?'

'. . . think maybe it's a bit . . .'

'What?'

'Nothing.'

'What? You think it's a bit what?'

'Well . . . degrading.'

A long silence settled over the conference table.

'To who?' said Daren, eventually.

'You know.'

'No, I don't know,' said Daren, who clearly did. He was making Matt say it, forcing him to bask in his shame.

'Women.'

'*Degrading to women?*' said Daren.

'Just a bit.'

It was as if the oxygen had been sucked out of the room. The lights gave the impression of dimming slightly.

Pup walked back in, his trousers faintly speckled with urinal splash-back. Sensing the atmosphere, fearing that he was the cause of it, he turned and fled, slamming the door behind him.

'OK, take five, everyone,' said Daren. 'Matt, my office. Now.'

Daren strode out. Matt followed, not catching anyone's eye as he left the room.

When Matt entered Daren's office, Daren was standing at the window, looking out, in the manner of angry bosses on US cop shows. Matt took a seat. Daren didn't move. Matt coughed. Daren still didn't move.

'What's up?' said Matt, eventually.

Slowly and carefully, as if he had just slipped a disc, Daren turned to Matt.

'Precisely,' he said.

'Precisely what?'

'I couldn't have put it any better myself,' said Daren, with a cryptic leer.

'Put what any better?'

'What's up? You said it. And that's what I want to know.'

'With me?' said Matt.

'Yes, with you. Not with the fucking . . .' Daren's eyes scanned the room, searching for a prompt to complete his witticism, '. . . computer-repair IT person.'

'Nothing's up.'

'Don't lie to me, Matt.'

'I'm not lying.'

'I know you, Matt. I can read you like a magazine. And I know when you're lying. Is it drugs? What did you take last night?'

'Nothing.'

'*Nothing?*'

'Well, a bit of coke,' Matt lied, in order to sound normal. 'But nothing unusual. Nothing I can't handle.'

'Is it something else? Is there some kind of family crisis? Yvonne tells me you've been taking calls from your mother.'

'Er . . . there is a little bit of a family situation, but it's not affecting my work. I promise.'

'It better not be. Now listen to me. There's plenty of people could do your job. I want you to get back into that meeting and show those guys that this magazine is in safe hands. Do you understand me? I want you to go in and get behind one of these two ideas before I begin to think you're losing your judgement. Got me?' At moments of stress, Daren's mockney accent slipped a little, revealing the faintest trace of Surrey, the merest whiff of tennis lessons and cucumber sandwiches and rugger.

'Sure. Sorry,' said Matt.

'And I don't want any fucking apologies.'

'OK.'

*   *   *

Matt opted for the taste-test. Pup never looked him in the eye again. Pup-made tea never tasted quite right, either, and after a while Matt stopped

231

drinking it.

HOW TO COME ACROSS AS VAGUELY SOCIALLY ACCEPTABLE

Just the way Julia said hello made his stomach lurch and his fingers clench tighter around his phone, which was so expensively tiny that it threatened to shoot out of his hand like an orange pip. The date, he could instantly tell, hadn't done for her what it had for him.

'So,' said Matt, his mouth suddenly dry and claggy, 'what have you been up to?'

'The usual,' said Julia.

Matt never had trouble talking to anyone. He was never tongue-tied. Except now. All she had said was 'hello' and 'the usual', and already he felt as if their conversation had run aground. He tried to mask his fear with false confidence.

'So when are we going to have dinner again?'

'Matt . . . it was a fun evening. And it certainly didn't go how I thought it would go. I mean, you're not nearly such a bad guy as I was expecting, but . . . we're really not well suited. Nothing's going to happen, and we're not exactly cut out to be friends, either, so why don't we just forget about it and move on?'

'Why?' he said, not even pausing to think before the word came out of his mouth.

As anyone over the age of thirteen knows, this was the most humiliating thing he could possibly have said. How it had popped out of his mouth he couldn't imagine, but it had, and now it was out

232

there he decided to let it hang. With that one word, he had instantly sunk too far to claw back any pride, so he decided he might as well wallow. Besides, he wanted to know the answer.

'Why?' she said, shocked to discover this arrogant man to be a wallower. 'Are you asking why?'

'I'm sorry. I know I shouldn't. It's terrible, isn't it? I feel like even more of a prick for asking why than I do for being turned down.'

'So I don't have to answer?'

'No. Sorry. I was just surprised, that's all.'

'To be turned down? It's that unusual, is it?'

'Er . . . well, it is, actually. But I just meant by you. I mean, I thought we got on.'

'We did.'

'So why aren't you interested?'

'Why do you keep asking why?'

'I don't know. Sorry. I just want you to tell me.' Matt was beginning to feel like someone standing with one foot on land and the other on an unmoored rowing boat. He was clearly going in the water, regardless of whether he turned back or lunged for the boat, and since all dignity was already lost, he decided he might as well lose it in an advance as a retreat. 'It's stupid, but I can't help wondering,' he said.

'You really want me to say?'

'If you wouldn't mind.'

'Are you sure?'

'Just so I can understand.'

Like water vapour forming into a cloud, Julia could feel a short, angry speech beginning to take shape in her brain. She knew precisely what was wrong with Matt. It was more or less the same thing that had been wrong with every other guy over the years who had bored her, betrayed her, let her down, or all three. And not once had she ever had such a good opportunity to speak her mind— to deliver her verdict. Now she was getting the chance.

It was unfortunate that Matt would be the one to hear it, since at heart he seemed less bad than most of the others, even if his job was a pinnacle of obnoxiousness, but he was asking for it, so why shouldn't she give it to him? It would be cathartic. And he could take it. In the long run, if he listened, which was unlikely, it might even do him some good.

'Well, OK,' she said, trying to rein in the hint of glee in her voice. 'If that's what you want. But there's no point unless I'm honest.'

'Exactly.'

'As in brutally honest. But you're pretty impervious, aren't you?'

'Impervious?'

'Yeah.'

'I'm not impervious,' said Matt, offended without quite knowing why.

'I just feel like whatever I say, it won't hurt your feelings.'

'Of course it won't.'

'Exactly. You're impervious.'

'No, I'm not.'

'You just admitted it. Before I've even said anything, you've already got this amazing confidence that nothing I could ever say might possibly upset or undermine you. That's what impervious means.'

'It's not bad breath, is it?'

'Er . . . this is a bit more fundamental, Matt.'

'Worse than bad breath?' Matt was horrified. His palms had become sweaty, and his tongue felt as if it had doubled in size.

'I don't know why we're even having this conversation, because I'm really not going out with you again, and that's not negotiable, and I don't feel I owe you anything.'

'But as a special favour, if I beg, you might be willing to explain why you think I'm a prick.'

'You don't have to beg.'

'Good. Go on, then.'

'Are you sure? I wouldn't usually do this.'

'Sure.'

'OK.' Julia took a deep breath. The question was not so much what to say as where to start. 'You're just one of those guys, Matt. One of those men who seem interesting and intelligent and witty while they're talking about themselves and their world, then the minute they stop being the centre of attention, their personality kind of disappears. Someone at some point has taught you that you're supposed to ask the odd question—that it's bad manners to talk about yourself all evening—so you kind of go through the motions of showing an interest in other people, but it's just something you do off a checklist of how to come across as vaguely socially acceptable. You don't mean it. You don't listen. You don't give a shit about anything or anyone other than yourself. Nothing really exists for you outside your own ego. You're a toddler in a man's body, which, let's face it, is in the end just boring.'

Julia paused and listened to the silence on the other end of the line. She was perhaps imagining it, but the sound of his breathing seemed to have acquired a chastened, wounded air. The effect wasn't due to Matt being an unusually communicative breather, but was because this was the first time she had said anything to him that had failed to engender an instant comeback. Or rather, it was the first time she had said anything to Matt on the topic of Matt that had caused this response. Every time she'd said anything about herself, there had been similar pauses before he'd been able to respond, but these silences always had a quality of daydreaming, not of reflection.

As the silence grew, she sensed herself beginning to feel sorry for him, though to an extent she'd felt sorry for him from the first moment they met. Perhaps she'd been too harsh. At heart, he wasn't so bad. At least, he wasn't any worse than other men. But she'd said her piece. She'd done a good job of shaking him off. If she tempered or qualified her judgement of him now, there was a risk he might latch on to her consolation and use selective deafness to launch a fresh attempt.

'Sorry,' she said. 'Don't feel bad. I mean, it's very common. And you're quite good-looking. Anyway, have a nice life. Bye.'

Click.

Never had a dialling tone sounded so hollow or mournful. Matt hung up, slowly. What was the word for this? For this emotion. Not since he was a desperate teenager failing to get a dance partner for 'Careless Whisper' had he felt anything even vaguely similar.

Crushed. Yes, that was it. He was a grape; Julia was a foot. This was the balance of power, and she had chosen to step on him.

The last time his heart had beaten this fast was during a World Cup penalty shoot-out. In fact, the mix of emotion was curiously similar to a lost penalty shoot-out: a strange soup of rapture and despair.

His misery at her rejection and her damning verdict of his character was comprehensible enough, but the masochistic pleasure that went with it was more mysterious. Perhaps it came from the excitement of rediscovering lost emotions, or of finding a new depth of feeling. That he could feel this upset, that he could be brought so low by a phone call with a woman he had only knowingly met once, was somehow a confirmation that he was fully alive, and that a part of him he thought might have died was in fact in full working order.

There was a novelty and a perverse gratification to rediscovering this lost chamber of pain in his heart. Poets and artists lived in there; until now, he'd lost the key and forgotten where the room even was. It wasn't a place he'd want to hang out for long, but just knowing where it was, and that the lock hadn't rusted over, was on some level a relief.

But there was also another thrill. The words 'not negotiable' always excited Matt. To his ears, they meant the opposite. Negotiating the non-negotiable was his favourite sport. Julia hadn't really turned him down. She had set him a challenge. Something about the way she had told him he was good-looking made him wonder if the whole thing was a joke. Or not exactly a joke, but a provocation. She was, perhaps, simply trying to take her revenge on his magazine, on what she thought he stood for. Maybe she didn't really mean any of it, but was setting out to treat him the way she thought he treated women. Her behaviour was quite possibly just a bad impersonation of a sexist man. All along, this could well have been her plan: not just to look her enemy in the eye, but to feed him a dose of his own medicine. Which was admirably feisty, and even quite amusing, now he understood what she was up to, but to let her get away with it would be to acknowledge that she was right about him, and he wasn't going to let that happen.

He couldn't force her to like him, but he could refuse to be beaten so easily. It was a matter of pride to let her know that he understood her game, and to explain (again) that she was wrong about him.

He picked up the phone and called her back.

'Hi, Julia. It's Matt.'

'Matt?'

'Yeah. How are you doing?'

'I'm fine. Did I imagine the conversation we just had? Did it not really happen?'

'We always have fun, don't we?'

'Do we? What are you talking about?'

'You're honest with me; I'm honest with you. You said yourself that you're never usually this honest with anyone, and the funny thing is, that's exactly how I feel about you. It would be crazy to just throw that away, wouldn't it?'

'I was honest enough to tell you I don't like you, it's true, and that is a bit unusual, but it's not really a good basis for a love affair.'

'Or is it? I think we should meet up again and talk about it.'

'What is there to say?'

'We should get to know each other better. I feel as if we're on to something.'

'That's nice for you, but I'm afraid I don't.'

'Julia, I find you really exciting. I haven't felt this way about anyone for ages. I don't know anyone like you. We're from different worlds, and there's lots about us that clashes, but I think we're striking sparks. I think this is good. If you gave me some time, I think you'd find you don't know anyone like me, either.'

As he had dialled her number, Matt's intention was to mimic Julia's aloof, game-playing tone, but again, without knowing why he was doing it, he found himself gushing at her with a catch in his throat, straining to hold back the whining, begging tone that threatened to take over his voice every time he thought about the idea that he might never see her again.

'But I know lots of people like you,' said Julia. 'I'm temping at a PR firm. I'm surrounded by people like you every day, and I don't like any of them.'

'Except I'm not like them. That's the whole point. That's what I'm trying to say.'

'Because your job's beneath you?'

'Yes. No. That sounds terrible. I just mean I have broader interests.'

'Do you? Like what?'

'I . . . I'm not going to give you a list of hobbies on the phone. This isn't a job interview.'

'You have hobbies?'

'No! Yes! Look—this is a ridiculous conversation.'

'So you're not really talking about interests? You're saying the other people in the office are

239

beneath you in some other way?'

'Not beneath me. I'd never say that about anyone.'

'So what are you saying?'

'THAT I LIKE YOU! Is that such a terrible thing to think?'

Realising that he had shouted, Matt looked up from his desk and noticed that he had forgotten to shut his office door. Daren was at that moment handing a message to Yvonne, his head turned towards the sound of Matt's raised voice. Daren stared at him, frowning, his expression a mixture of concern and admonition. Matt looked away and stretched out his leg to push the door shut.

'Right. OK,' said Julia. 'Thank you. I knew that, anyway.'

Another silence opened up between them. It was Matt who eventually broke it.

'So why are you tormenting me?'

'I don't know,' said Julia. 'It just seems like fun.'

'Oh.'

'And why are you pursuing me when I've already told you I don't like you?'

'Because everything you said about me is right. The me you don't like is the me I don't like, either. But there's another me you haven't really met, and that's the me you'll like. I think maybe I've got stuck being someone I don't want to be, and you're the only person I know who wants me to be the real me.'

'I don't want you to be anything. It's none of my business. And what do I get out of this, anyway?'

'You get to torment me. What could be better? Everyone wins. Let's meet tonight, and you can torment me over dinner.'

240

'I'm working tonight.'

'So skive off early.'

'I am skiving off early. To go home and work. Write an essay.'

'Tomorrow, then.'

'I can't write it in one evening.'

'Saturday. No one should stay in working on a Saturday night.'

'Maybe. Call me on the day.'

'I'll need your home phone number.'

'You can have my mobile. 07929 378223,' said Julia, astonished to hear the numbers rattling off her tongue.

'What?'

'Did you miss it?'

'I got the first half. Say it again.'

'You were too slow. Bad luck.'

'WHY ARE YOU DOING THIS?'

'I told you,' she said. 'It's fun. And it's kind of interesting.' She meant it, too. For all his flaws, she did enjoy talking to him. It brought out an acerbic side to her character that only rarely got taken for a spin, like a racing car kept under dust-sheets in the garage. Talking to Matt, she felt funnier and sharper than she did when she was talking to people she actually liked, which, strangely, made her like him. He was a sport she had discovered she was good at. She wasn't stupid enough to let herself become his girlfriend, but seeing him again wouldn't necessarily be an unpleasant experience.

'Why?' bleated Matt.

'Well, the more I do it, the more you seem to like it. It's just very weird that you haven't told me to piss off.'

'It is weird, I know. I'm having trouble figuring

241

that out myself.'

'You must enjoy it. Do you have a domineering mother?'

'I don't think it's anything to do with—'

'Oh yes, you *do* have a domineering mother. I've met her. Oh, God. Perhaps this whole thing is unhealthy. Maybe we should forget it.'

'STOP DOING THIS. PLEASE!'

'378223.'

Then she hung up. This time he had a pen ready.

HELEN AND PAUL

A NICE BIG STONE

Helen's eyes snapped open at seven o'clock. She felt alert and excited. She couldn't remember the last time she had woken up feeling this way, like a child, immediately ready to leap out of bed and start the day.

The house was still and quiet. She showered and grabbed a quick breakfast. As she began to hear the first footsteps upstairs, she slipped into her coat and dashed out of the house. This was no day to lounge around chatting. She had things to do. She wanted to be in Oxford Street, outside John Lewis, ready for them as soon as the doors opened.

The Tube was filled with sour, dead-faced commuters, stumbling through their trip to work like automatons. Helen stared at them, amazed that they could look so grim when life was so full of wonder and joy. She wanted to tell them all that no matter how bad they were feeling now, some amazing and thrilling piece of news might be waiting for them when they got home that night.

She had the urge to go round the carriage, telling every last one of them that only yesterday she had felt alone, unloved and irrelevant, and today she was suddenly a grandmother. There was a tiny, adorable little baby curled up somewhere in this city who was hers: her grandchild.

Helen hadn't consciously changed her mind about Ella. She hadn't even really had a chance to think about it. She had simply gone to bed confused and overwhelmed by the news, and had woken up happy. It was as simple as that. In an ideal world, the circumstances would be different, but nothing could be done about that now, and her dream of anything remotely resembling an ideal world with regard to what Paul might do with his life had been shattered long ago. He was her only child and he was gay, therefore she would never be a grandmother. She had been reconciled to this for a long time (if you can call it reconciled when the idea in fact made her sad every single time she saw a baby or heard one or thought about one), but now, out of the blue, almost magically, her dearest wish had been granted. All her grievances and complaints about the manner in which it had been done, and about the confusing life into which the baby had been born, when put up against the fact of this living, breathing baby, felt like mere quibbles.

She existed, she was alive, and Helen was her grandmother. This was more than Helen had ever dared hope for. Now she had Ella, she wouldn't demand anything more of anyone. Helen's life had been miraculously blessed and she would not, she vowed to herself, forget it.

With this sudden, novel surge of happiness pumping through her veins, a gate opened in her mind, and she allowed herself to acknowledge how alien this sensation was. Up to this day, for many, many years, she had been unhappy. Only now it was over could she admit it. She had never got over Larry; the years on her own had been one long tangle of anxiety; the marriage to Clive was nothing more than a shell to hide in. She had held back these thoughts, year in, year out, afraid of what they might do to her if she let them in, but now she was ready to end the denial. She was strong enough. She had a future to live for.

Only a few minutes earlier, she had wanted to walk round the compartment telling the commuters that life was better than they thought. Now, she realised, people were staring at her because she was crying.

She fumbled in her handbag for a tissue and wiped her face. Whether these were tears of misery, prompted by the sudden admission to herself of her own unhappiness, or tears of joy at her new role as a grandmother, or simply tears of relief that her suffering was over, she didn't know. All she knew was that it felt good. She cried, wiped, blew her nose, then cried some more. She didn't care what the other passengers thought. If she wanted to cry, she'd cry. She'd earned the right.

Stepping into the John Lewis baby department had a strange effect on Helen's physiognomy. She instantly felt lighter and younger. Around her were pregnant women and harassed-looking couples peering wearily at unfamiliar bits of lurid kit, while Helen felt she was almost floating. As if guided by divine inspiration, Helen quickly found herself in front of a rack of minuscule Babygros, each one barely the length of her forearm.

She hurriedly reached for more tissues. The tears were coming again. She took four pink Babygros, two newborn, two 3–6 months, and walked away before she made a scene. Suddenly, she was face to face with a rack of socks. The teeniest, tiniest socks she could ever remember seeing. Had Paul's feet ever really been that small?

She gave up on self-control and allowed herself to sob. People here would be used to public emotion. It was probably a rarity for anyone to look at these socks and not cry. She bought a pink fistful, wondering if it would be weird to keep a pair for herself. Then she saw a tiny pink jumper with a picture of a bunny rabbit on it, which she simply couldn't walk past without buying, as well as a woolly hat to go with it and a pair of booties that made a colour match so perfect it would have been madness not to get them.

She then went to the ground floor to get some knitting needles and some balls of pink wool. There was no time to knit anything before the visit today, but she could at least get started. Then she thought it would be good to give something personal, so she also bought a needle and a box of brightly coloured thread, and took the lift back up to the baby section to get some plain white bibs. She couldn't remember how long embroidery took (she had no memory of doing it since school), but she thought she might at least be able to stitch an 'E' or maybe a little picture of a cat on to one, so that Ella would get something that had Helen's love sewn into it. A first little thing to bond them together. A token of the years of devotion to come.

Then she went to the toy department.

Helen was carrying two large bags and had spent over a hundred pounds by the time she left the shop. The money, however, meant nothing to her. This was beyond money. This was beyond everything. This was a new, fresh, unblemished, uncynical, perfect human being to love: the closest real life ever got to the miraculous.

She arrived back at the Hoxton house still on a dizzy high and rang the bell. There was no answer. She waited and waited, but no one came.

Helen took her mobile out of her handbag and switched it on. She dialled Paul's office.

'Isn't Andre there?' he said, when she told him she was locked out.

'No.'

'He must be at college. Sorry. I forgot.'

'But I thought you were taking the day off. What about the visit?'

'That's what I was about to tell you.'

'What?'

'I was all set to take the day off. I was. I can see how important it is to you.'

'But?'

'But they said no.'

'What?'

'They said no.'

'What do you mean they said no?'

'I don't know how else to put it.'

'How can they do that?'

'I thought they would. I tried to warn you. It's not Andrea.'

246

'Which one's Andrea?'

'The mother. I don't think she would have minded. But it was Rebecca who answered the phone. She's the other one, and she's always been a bit funny about me keeping my distance, and she's the one who wanted to get all exact about rules for everything and everyone's rights, and my name not being on the birth certificate. She's just very intense and serious about it, which is understandable, I suppose. And she got me to make lots of promises about what I would and wouldn't do, and what claims I might make on the baby, and when I said you wanted to visit, she said no.'

'But she can't.'

'She did.'

'But she's my granddaughter. I have rights.'

'Let's not have that conversation again. I just want you to know I did my best.'

'No you didn't.'

'I did!'

'One phone call is your best, is it? You're ridiculous and lazy, and frankly at the moment I think you're being extremely stupid. What's their address?'

'Er . . .'

'Come on.'

'I don't think—'

'I'm standing on the doorstep of your house, locked out, carrying two bags of presents for my granddaughter, and I'm not going to stand here for the rest of the day. What's the damn address?'

'You can't just—'

'I can and I will.'

'They said no, Mum.'

247

'They said no to you, not to me. If they're going to say no to me, they can say it to my face. Now tell me.'

'I don't think I should.'

'I'm going to give you one more chance. This isn't about you and the lesbians. It's about me and Ella. Now I've had enough of this conversation. If you don't tell me in the next ten seconds, I'm . . . I'm going to start smashing the windows of your house. One. Two. Three.'

'Mum, don't be ridiculous. They'll turn you away.'

'Fine. They can do it to my face, then, so I'll need the address.'

'Mum—'

'Four. Five. I've found a nice big stone. Six.'

'Mum!'

'Seven. Eight. Nine. Don't test me, Paul.'

'This is crazy.'

'Nine and a half.'

Helen kicked Paul's recycling box, which produced a gratifyingly glassy clatter.

'WHAT ARE YOU DOING!' shrieked Paul.

'What do you think I'm doing?'

He gave her the address. Helen thanked him, told him his windows were untouched and walked straight back to the Tube station, buying an *A–Z* on the way.

BEYOND LOVE

The address was in Stoke Newington, where Helen had never been before. Not knowing her way around this part of the city, she got a train to Finsbury Park and stumbled around the bus terminus for a few minutes, trying in vain to find someone who wasn't too scary to ask for help, then, assisted by nothing more than a faded and filthy map, climbed on to a bus with only the vaguest confidence that it would take her in the right direction.

Helen sat bolt upright in her seat, anxiously following on her *A–Z* as the bus inched past Turkish, Ethiopian and Moroccan restaurants, alongside innumerable small supermarkets selling unfamiliar fruit and misshapen vegetables to people who, for all she knew, were genuine Turks, Ethiopians and Moroccans.

After a while, the density of shops thinned out and the bus drove past a park, to an area that reminded Helen slightly of Hoxton, having the same mix of ominous high-rise council estates and the kind of health-food shops where you can buy kumquats and organic polenta. This was Stoke Newington.

The address turned out to be a flat above a second-hand bookshop. The door was windowless and unadorned, at first sight looking more like a fire exit than an entrance to a home. There were two buzzers, one with a smudged, semi-legible, consonant-heavy surname, the other saying 'Andrea + Rebecca'. Helen was in the right place. But she couldn't ring. Now she was finally here, her confidence faltered, for the first time all day.

It occurred to her that she had perhaps already invested too much in the idea of this child, from whose life she could quite easily be banished. She had let herself imagine that she was transformed into a grandmother, when in fact her condition was still hanging in the balance. The next conversation would decide it.

What she chose to say, whether or not she managed to make these women like her, might have some bearing on the outcome, but essentially the matter was out of her hands. If they categorically did not want her to have a relationship with her grandchild, nothing she could do would make any difference. She could ask, she could beg, but she could not demand or insist upon anything.

A few doors down, Helen spotted a pub with a picnic-style bench on the pavement. She decided to sit there for a while, have a cup of tea and watch the door—not in a sinister way, just to see if there were any comings or goings, just to settle her nerves and allow herself to feel comfortable in this unfamiliar environment.

If she could catch a glimpse of one of these women first, she'd know what she was up against. When someone came out, she might even be able to see where they were going, and find a way to get into conversation with them. In fact, that was probably her only chance. She couldn't make her first approach from behind that blank door, speaking through a crackly entryphone. She couldn't allow such a critical conversation to take place so impersonally.

Two cups of tea and one very modest sherry later, the door opened. The first thing to emerge was a pram. Helen's pulse surged. Her granddaughter! Helen had been so intent on the way she was going to approach the mother(s), she'd almost forgotten that her waiting tactic would possibly also yield a first glimpse of Ella. From this distance, Helen could see nothing of the baby inside the pram, but she already felt herself palpitating with love.

After a brief struggle with the threshold and the heavy door, a woman, who had to be either Andrea or Rebecca, came into view. If this was what a lesbian looked like, thought Helen, she had no way of knowing how many others she had met before.

She had known the odd lesbian on the Soho party scene in the sixties, but in those days there was a uniform. Or not a uniform, exactly, but a look. She hadn't even known what it meant when she met her first lesbian, but once you clapped eyes on one, it didn't take much explaining. Larry had always been particularly keen on them, and tried several times to get one back to the marital bed for a threesome, but without any success. A girl with short blonde hair and ruby lips had once told Helen that she'd gladly come, but only on condition that Larry would be locked outside in the garden. If the plan hadn't been quite so impracticable, Helen might even have said yes.

Andrea (or was it Rebecca?) walked straight towards Helen. As she got closer, Helen could see she was attractive, with a thin, intelligent face and stunning, deep-brown eyes. The pram, unfortunately, was high, and Helen's bench was low. As her grandchild was wheeled past her, Helen still couldn't see in without standing or craning her neck. Though it took all her self-control to refrain, she didn't want to draw any attention to herself yet, so she forced herself to stay seated, and to look away as they passed.

She could even smell them as they went by, in a

subtly glorious cloud of fecund, milky mother-babyness. She had not smelt that aroma for years, not consciously, and had certainly not been part of it as she was now. As she took this first secret sniff of these two strangers, she thought to herself, 'You are my family, and you don't even know it.'

She stood and followed, keeping her distance, watching closely as this woman and her grandchild went into various food shops, buying small bags of this and that, before suddenly turning round and walking straight towards her again.

Helen momentarily panicked, and almost dived behind a van to conceal herself, but realised just in time that the best way to stay unobtrusive was simply to keep walking. She had noticed while following them down the street that it was quite normal for women of her age to gaze with undisguised curiosity into passing prams, so this time, as they walked by, she allowed herself her first look at Ella.

She was asleep on her back, with her arms up, as if surrendering, though her limbs were so small that her tiny fists didn't reach any higher than her head. She was so deeply asleep that her features had crumpled together, with a pout and a frown of total concentration. Helen's glimpse was only fleeting, but if she were never to see the child again for the rest of her life, it was a face she would never forget. She had never known such a brief instant to burn itself so irrevocably into her mind. She had never seen anything more beautiful.

First there was Larry, then there was Paul, now there was Ella. For the first time in thirty-four years, Helen felt in her heart the exquisite, horrifying plummet of falling suddenly, irreversibly in love.

She had simply forgotten how to deal with emotion of this magnitude. She felt like an Eskimo dumped in the middle of New York, struggling to make sense of the view, straining to compute a new sense of scale. It was all too much, and yet not enough. She wanted to stop time and have a chance to comprehend what she was feeling, and at the same time yearned to race forwards into the future to experience more of it.

What she wanted most of all was to know the feeling of Ella in her arms. She wanted to hold her close and smell her neck. If she could have that, just for one minute, her life's share of happiness would have been fully dealt out to her. It would be enough. There would be more, with luck, but she wouldn't expect it or demand it. Anything further would be an additional, fortuitous blessing. For now, all she needed was that cuddle, a single dose of grandmotherhood that would lift her to the summit of elation.

A gap had now opened up between them. Helen turned and followed Ella and her mother back home, though to her surprise, Andrea/Rebecca walked past her front door and on to the park, where she made a small circuit round a duck pond, then sat at a secluded bench and pulled out a book from under the pram.

Helen hovered. She had three choices. She could hide and watch from a distance, she could go and sit next to her, or she could walk on past for one last look, then head home to plan a more careful approach for a later date. The one thing she couldn't do was stand there in the middle of the path, staring and dithering.

This had been a bizarre week. Helen had never known her self-confidence to soar and plummet like this on a daily basis. Her predictable, boring life had been shattered. There was suddenly no knowing what would happen tomorrow. If her legs were capable of carrying her to that bench and sitting down next to the woman who had borne her grandchild, she had to do it. She might never have the opportunity or the willpower again.

Still carrying a hefty John Lewis bag in either hand, trying not to worry if Andrea/Rebecca would notice that this was their third encounter, Helen approached the bench. Her legs felt frail, her lungs suddenly incapable of pulling in air to a regular rhythm. Doing her best to conceal the psychological mayhem rampaging through her brain, Helen took a seat on the vacant half of the bench and let out the type of sigh she thought a woman of her age might make when taking a rest from carrying heavy shopping bags.

Andrea/Rebecca didn't look up from her book. Helen didn't try to catch her eye. For a long time, Helen simply sat there, staring into space. Was this suspicious behaviour, she wondered? How long could a person legitimately sit on a bench staring into space without seeming like a tramp?

A mewling sound emanated from the pram, a tiny, muffled whine like a squeaky door. Andrea/Rebecca put down her book, stood, stretched, and as the mewl built to a howl, lifted Ella out.

Ella's face was now purple with rage. Her feet and fists flailed and pounded, protesting at the affront of the brief delay between sleep and food. Andrea—it was finally apparent which of the two

254

women this was—deftly released several buttons and clasps concealed in her clothing, and tenderly latched Ella on to her breast. Andrea gazed at her daughter as she fed, occasionally giving her cheek tiny, adoring strokes with the back of one finger.

Although they were sitting next to Helen on a bench, Andrea and Ella seemed to be on a faraway planet of mutual adoration. The only sign they gave of any awareness of the world around them was when Andrea laid a muslin square over her breast and the baby's head to stop people staring. Or rather, not so much to stop people staring, as specifically to stop her, Helen, staring. Only now did Helen realise she had been shamelessly gawping at this entire procedure since it began.

She forced herself to look away, and tried to think of what she could say to open a conversation. She decided to wait until the feed was over. She had to pick her moment carefully.

It wasn't long before Ella was propped up on Andrea's knee, Andrea gently winding her with strokes and pats on her minuscule back. In this position, Ella was looking straight at Helen, who took this as her moment.

'Hello!' she said to Ella, for some reason an octave higher than her usual speaking voice. 'Hello! You're a beauty, aren't you? Aren't you? Eh?'

Ella burped, loudly and with gusto.

'Oop!' said Andrea. 'There we go.'

'She's beautiful,' said Helen.

'Thank you.'

'How old is she?'

'Three months.'

'Three? I thought it was two.'

'Sorry?'

'I mean . . . I just mean I thought she looked a bit younger than that. But I don't know anything about it. I just thought she looks so tiny and adorable, she must be a bit younger than three months.'

'She's quite big, actually. For her age.'

'It doesn't show. I mean, she's lovely.'

'Thanks.'

Andrea looked away, as if trying to end the conversation there.

'What's her name?'

'Ella.'

'Ella! How lovely! After Ella Fitzgerald?'

'No. We just liked the name.'

'Right. Well, that's the best reason, isn't it? The only reason, in fact.'

'Mmm. Well, must be off.'

Andrea stood and put Ella back in the pram. Helen had to think fast. Her big opportunity was slipping away.

'Actually, I don't know why I asked her name, because I already knew.'

'Oh,' said Andrea, utterly without interest. She was now picking up her book from the bench and placing it under the pram. She kicked the brake off and began to walk away.

'I'm Paul's mother,' Helen blurted.

Andrea stopped walking. 'Sorry?'

'I'm Paul's mother. Ella's grandmother. I came to meet her.'

'What do you mean? How did you find us?'

'I went to your flat.'

'But how did you find me here? Were you following me?'

256

'No. Not really. I just went to your door, and I lost confidence and couldn't ring the bell because I was too worried that you'd turn me away, then while I was thinking about what to do you came out of the flat. So I just watched where you went, and when you came here I thought it might be an opportunity to say something. To meet you.'

'But you've been sitting there for ages.'

'I didn't know how to start.'

'Just watching us.'

'I didn't know what to say. I'm sorry. I don't want to seem like a stalker, it's just a funny situation. There's no easy way of doing it.'

'I suppose not.'

'Do you mind if I have a look at her?'

Andrea stared at Helen, deep in thought. 'OK,' she said, eventually, putting the brake on and taking one small step back.

Helen leaned in. 'Hiya!' she said. 'Hiya! Aren't you gorgeous? Eh? Aren't you? Aren't you a little chicken? Eh? A wee chicky-chicken. Chicky-chicky-chicken. Eh? Aren't you? I've got something for you. Wait there.'

Helen delved into her John Lewis bags, and after a long rummage emerged with a rattle. She roughly yanked off the price tag and leaned over the pram. 'What's this? Eh? What is it? Can you hear it? Can you? It's a rattle. Yes. Rittle rattle rittle rattle. Isn't that good? Look. This is white. That's yellow. White. Yellow. Rittle rattle rittle rattle.'

Helen had no idea how much time had passed when she turned her attention back to Andrea, who was eyeballing her with what looked like a mixture of suspicion and contempt.

257

'I'm really sorry to spring this on you,' said Helen. 'But I didn't know what else to do.'

'You phoned this morning, didn't you?'

'Paul did, yes. But he was a bit vague about the response. I had to come and find out for myself.'

'He spoke to Rebecca.'

'Yes, I think so. And he said her response wasn't very positive, but I wasn't going to give up. I couldn't just give up. This is my granddaughter. I'm her grandmother. And I can't pretend I'm not because someone I've never met at the other end of a phone line tells my son I'm not needed.'

'What is it you want?'

'I don't want anything. I'm not asking you for anything. I'm just saying what I am, which is her grandmother. And I'd like to be a good grandmother instead of a bad one, if you'll let me.'

'That's very nice of you, but she's got grandmothers.'

'I know she has. And I'm one of them.'

'That's not the arrangement.'

'This isn't about arrangements. This is biology. It's a fact.'

Andrea sat back down on the bench, with a sigh. 'I thought you'd come,' she said, eventually. 'We talked about it before the birth and everyone thought we could set things up exactly how we wanted them, to a plan we could make up from scratch, but now I've had Ella, now I know what it feels like, I . . . well, I know that when she has a baby, if she has a baby, nothing will keep me away. Nothing. War, flood, earthquake. I'll be there.'

Helen was suddenly at a loss for what to say. Relief that she had been understood washed through her body, eradicating all other thoughts and feelings. The beginnings of a sob started to tingle at the end of her nose. She turned and rummaged frantically through her handbag for a tissue. Andrea, it seemed, did not intend to crush her hopes. This baby, in some way or other, would be part of her life. She was, after all, a grandmother.

'I brought you some presents,' she said, when her mind finally cleared. One by one, with trembling hands, she picked out the clothes and toys from her John Lewis bag, realising as she did so that half the clothes were in newborn size, and were already too small. 'I'll take those back,' she said. 'And those. And those. Sorry. Wasn't thinking straight. She was such a new idea to me—I mean, I only discovered she existed yesterday—that in my head she was newborn. I knew she wasn't, but I just got overwhelmed when I saw all the baby clothes, and I think I went kind of doolally. I might have been a bit emotional. I'm sorry. I'll change them for something else.'

'It's OK. You don't have to.'

'I will. I will. I'd like to. It was stupid.'

Helen twigged, from Andrea's lukewarm response to the presents, that something else about them was wrong, too. Then she realised that Ella's clothes, hat, pram and blanket were in a range of colours, all without the slightest hint of pink.

'I'll get different colours next time,' she said. 'Something more masculine. I mean, less girly. Just not pink. I . . . I didn't know what you'd like. But now I've seen her, I think maybe I can guess a little better.'

'Don't worry about it.'

'Can I hold her?'

259

Andrea didn't answer. She simply continued examining the clothes and toys as if she hadn't heard.

'Please.'

Andrea looked Helen up and down, as if inspecting her for flaws.

'Rebecca would kill me,' she said.

'She doesn't have to know. We can worry about that another time.'

'I can't really say no, can I?'

'I hope not.'

'I'll lift her out and pass her to you. You have to support her head.'

'I know.'

'In the crook of your elbow, like this.'

'I know.'

'And I have to get back soon. I'm sorry, but I said I'd be home by now.'

'That's fine. Just a quick cuddle.'

Then, suddenly, there Ella was, a miracle of life, writhing and nuzzling in her arms, as Paul once had, and for the first time they looked into one another's eyes.

Helen had once read that a woman's heart becomes physically bigger during pregnancy, to pump round the extra blood needed for the foetus. She felt, at this moment, as if the same thing was happening to her now. This soft, dense, utterly *there* little person in her arms was made of her blood. They were the same. Apart from Paul, every other human being on the planet was just another person. But Paul was also part of her, and now so was Ella. From this moment on, there were two living creatures who would not exist without her, two lives made from her life, two people she would die to save.

This was beyond love. This compared to mere love in the way amputation compared to cutting your fingernails. This was as far as you could go, as much as you could feel, as irreversible as birth.

GILLIAN AND DANIEL

YOU CANNOT KNOW THE EGG IN ONE STEP

Quite why he got in touch with Alison, the mother of the child who went to playgroup with the son of the nephew of the sister of the woman whose dog bit Daniel when he was a child, he didn't know. It may have been to appease his mother; it may have been because he found himself agreeing with some of the criticisms she'd made of him. She was right that he had become a hermit, and he knew he wouldn't be happy staying like that indefinitely, even if at any given moment the hermit option seemed preferable to a sociable alternative. He had to think more about the future, less about the past. He had to force himself out.

So out he went, to Sardi's, a restaurant low-key enough for the evening to feel informal, but with good enough food for there to be some pleasure to fall back on should the conversation fail.

The conversation, in the end, didn't so much fail as blow up. At first, Alison seemed pleasant enough. He was surprised to find, when she first walked into the restaurant, that she was actually attractive, so much so that he assumed it couldn't

261

be her. The idea that his mother might be capable of putting him in touch with a woman he'd find alluring was simply not plausible. She was wearing a sweeping, asymmetric coat, and a glossy heap of thick black hair sat high and slightly chaotically on top of her head, clipped into place in a manner that could have taken ten seconds or an hour. The coat came off to reveal a swoopingly low-cut dress and a genuine somewhere-to-hide-a-letter cleavage.

Daniel was not, historically, a tit man, but this was quite a sight. He couldn't look at breasts like these without thinking about sex, and he couldn't sit opposite this woman without looking at her breasts. He instantly regretted his choice of restaurant. Perhaps he should have chosen somewhere more classy, more datey, more cleavagey. Perhaps the meal would not constitute their whole evening together, after all, but might be a prelude to further adventures.

The first five seconds of the date were superb. From there on, it went downhill. The descent began in earnest when Daniel asked about Alison's divorce.

'You don't want to know,' she said, with, as Daniel would discover too late, some accuracy. He made the mistake of inviting her to explain, if she felt like it, what she had been through.

She explained. Thoroughly.

'You cannot imagine,' she said, 'you simply cannot imagine what it is like to be married to a man who denies you. Who negates you. Do you know what I mean?'

This was the only chance he was given to bail out, but he failed to take it. He didn't react fast

262

enough. He didn't say anything.

'We married too young. That was the problem. It was an accidental pregnancy. It should have been our cue to split up, but I couldn't go through with another abortion, I just couldn't. You don't want to know this. I'm sorry. I'll skip the gory details. But I just couldn't. And maybe I could have had it on my own and things might have been OK, but we were young and stupid, and I was afraid of being alone, and I hated my job, so I thought maybe it was good timing and it would be a chance to spend some time at home and think about what to do next, and he said that he couldn't let me down or his unborn child, so he would stand by me and marry me and be a proper father to the baby, which sounds nice enough if you put it like that, but I now know that's how he works. That's him all over. He's an alpha male. He sees himself as dominant, and his mission was to crush me. The child was just an excuse. I mean, when you quote exactly what he said, it never sounds like he's saying anything bad, but that's what makes him so evil. It's like everything on the surface is kind and decent and understanding, but what he's doing all along is undermining you and taking away your choices and ruining your ability to think for yourself and live your own life. Do you understand? Because now there I was, alone at home all day with a baby, which, I don't know if you know this . . . do you? Maybe you don't. It's wonderful but it's awful and no one's ever allowed to say it, but it's also the most boring thing ever, and then he'd come back from work, having had his exciting day, and be all full of how great it was to be a father, and he never knew what it was really

263

like, and he'd just smother us completely. Do you understand? It was just, "Do you want this? Do you want that?" I can't explain it. Do you know what I'm saying? Everything he did just undermined me. He had a way of being mean that was just so insidious, because he'd be mean by being kind, and the more I resented it, the more I could never explain it, and the worse it got, the more my status as an intelligent, independent woman just got completely eroded by his need to provide and nurture and smother and he never understood that his behaviour was killing me. But the thing was, I didn't even understand it myself at the time, because I was internalising all my negative feelings for him into self-hatred, which is apparently very common. I was falling out of love with him, but all I thought was happening was that I was falling out of love with myself. And the most evil thing you can ever do to anyone is kill their self-love. It's taken me a lot of therapy to realise this. Do you get what I mean?'

'I'm not sure I do.'

'Look—think of yourself as an egg.'

'An egg?'

'Yes.'

'How do I do that?'

'Just think of yourself as an egg.'

'I'm finding that a bit hard. I don't really—'

'WILL YOU LET ME FINISH?'

'Sorry.'

'Think of yourself as an egg.'

'I'm trying.'

'This egg is you. It's your self-love. It's your self-worth.'

'Is it?'

'Yes. Can you picture it?'

'I'm not sure. I can see an egg, if I try.'

'Will you stop interrupting? Now Good Love presses on the ends of the egg. And what happens when you press on the ends of an egg?'

'Nothing.'

'Exactly. Good Love challenges the egg, it puts pressure on the egg, but it allows the egg to stay whole. To remain itself. Under the forces of Good Love, the egg retains its essential eggness. And what does it take for Good Love to turn into Bad Love?'

'Er . . . I'm not sure.'

'The egg twists. That's it. The pressure is on the sides, and what happens?'

'Omelette.'

'Exactly. And the key question is, who twisted the egg? That's all you need to know.'

'And?'

'And what?'

'Who did twist the egg?'

'HIM! Weren't you listening?'

'I was, I just—'

'And what happens when an egg is broken?' she continued.

'I . . . I don't know.'

'Can you put it back together?'

'Er . . . I wouldn't think so, no.'

'That's the wrong question.'

'What is? I didn't ask a question.'

'No, I did. Can you put it back together? No. That's what people try to do. Put it back together. But they're wasting their time, aren't they?'

'I suppose so.'

'So what's the alternative?'

'What alternative? To what?'

'This is what it all comes down to. This is what I'm trying to tell you.' She leaned over the table, revealing an extra inch or so of cleavage, which Daniel was rapidly deciding was an overrated crevice, bearing as it did far too close a resemblance to bum. She began to whisper, enunciating with precise, actorly care. *'You don't fix the egg. You let it go. And when you have truly, in your heart, bid it farewell, you will find that it is not gone. You will find a new egg.'*

Alison gave Daniel a one-day-you'll-understand smile and leant back in her chair.

Daniel didn't know what to say. He also had no idea what to do with his face, the muscles of which suddenly seemed determined to behave as if he had a lemon on his tongue. He decided to resort to silent eating, which Alison would be allowed to interpret however she chose, either as rudeness or as plain gastronomic intensity.

It did not occur to him that she would see this as philosophical reflection. She, too, ate in silence for a while, before saying, 'You know what I'm seeing?'

Her obscure choice of tense threw him. 'I'm not sure.'

'In you.'

'In me?' he said. 'You're seeing something in me?'

'A broken egg.'

Daniel laugh-coughed. 'Oh. OK.'

'I'm right. Aren't I?'

'I'm having a bit of trouble with your metaphor, to be honest.'

'That's quite normal.'

266

'There's an egg, and it breaks, then it comes back again, and, I . . . I'm a bit lost. The egg thing isn't working for me.'

'That's very honest of you to say so. I respect you for that.'

'Thanks.'

'Before you can know that the egg is broken, you have to know the egg. And you cannot know the egg in one step. It takes time, and a lot of thought, and a lot of emotional spadework.'

'Can we move on from the egg? I thought the weather was nice today. Windy, though. Edinburgh's often windy, isn't it?'

'I see a lot of pain,' said Alison.

'You use interesting tenses. It makes a nice change to talk to someone who speaks in so many tenses.'

'I see a lot of defences and a lot of pain.'

'I eat pizza. I drink wine.'

'Defensiveness is normal. Aggression is to men what love is to women.'

'Did you talk to your husband like this? I'm just wondering.'

'If only. I only discovered the vocabulary of my self-worth after he left me.'

'So he left you? It sounded like you were building up to saying you left him.'

'We left each other.'

'And how's his egg? Did you break it?'

'Are you being facetious?'

'Er . . .'

'Can you hear *me* trampling on *your* beliefs?' said Alison.

'Kind of. Logic, for example.'

'Where did you get this *hostility*? You are a very

267

broken man. You are so damaged.'

'Let's skip dessert, shall we?' said Daniel. 'I'll ask for the bill.'

'Why do you hate women?'

'I hate hundreds of men, but very few women, though one does spring to mind at the moment.'

'Your ex.'

'That's not who I meant.'

'Not who you think you meant, but we all say far more than we mean.'

'I thought it was windier in the afternoon than the morning. Didn't you?'

'You hate her and you love her. For men, the two aren't mutually exclusive. That's why marriage is a doomed institution. It contains two lovers and one hater.'

'You don't hate your husband, then?'

'I do now. Of course. But not then. That was the whole problem. I wasn't yet empowered enough. Men know how to hate. Women have to learn.'

'Well, good luck with that. I get the feeling I may even have helped. I'm going to go and settle this bill at the bar. And it was very nice to meet you.'

'Don't lie to me. Why are men addicted to lying?'

'Er . . . OK, it wasn't that nice to meet you. Is that better?'

'At least it's honest. It's a glimpse of the real you.'

'Bye, then.'

'That's right, run away. Run away from your issues.'

'OK. Will do.'

Rarely had fresh air felt so fresh, nor had the sensation of walking away from another human given him such simple joy. As Daniel strode home, crossing the Meadows with a fast stride, almost running, for the pleasure of feeling blood pulse through his body, an awful thought struck him. Despite the intensity of his dislike for Alison, despite the scorn he felt for her sanctimonious, accusatory self-pity, it dawned on him that perhaps, in her, he saw a glimmer of himself. He was dealing with it in a different way, but, just like her, he was allowing his life to be dominated by resentment towards an ex-lover.

He glanced up at Salisbury Crags, the wide, high escarpment that loomed over the city, and it seemed to grin down at him like a vast set of decayed teeth. He shivered and hastened his step, almost bumping into a gaggle of students heading the other way, dressed either for clubbing or prostitution or a medical study of hypothermia. He avoided a collision at the last moment by standing still, and the group parted fractionally and re-formed on the other side of him, as if he was an inconveniently located tree. He stood there for a moment, listening to their receding chatter, breathing in the squall of perfume they had left in their wake. Only when their sound and scent had tailed away to nothing did he continue on his way, out of the city, away from the students and nightclubs and restaurants, away from Alison, towards home, where his mother would be waiting for him, expectantly.

As if the evening hadn't been bad enough already. Now he'd have to go through it all with his mother. Gillian was not a woman you could brush off with a sketchy summary. She'd want to know it all: who said what, and when, and in which tone of voice. Given half an opportunity, she'd probably want to discuss Alison's table manners.

How would he describe Alison? Was it worth saying how much he had loathed her? As he tried to think of a way to encapsulate the essence of the evening into an informational nugget that would get him off the hook with his mother, and quickly into bed, he began to worry again that the intensity of his dislike for Alison had been caused not by the differences between them, but by their similarity. He hated to admit it, but he couldn't deny that he had seen in her a reflection of his own bitterness.

Could he really be as obsessed with Erin as Alison was with her ex-husband? Was he, perhaps, just as consumed with anger, just as wracked by betrayal and disappointment? Were they both, above all, prisoners of their wounded self-esteem?

Alison's egg metaphor was preposterous and meaningless, but as Daniel crossed the cobbles of Warrender Park Road and turned into his own street, he found himself picturing an egg plummeting through the night sky and smashing at his feet, a perfect miniature of violent metamorphosis.

Yes, he thought, Erin *had* smashed his egg. He couldn't put his finger on precisely what this egg was supposed to signify, but the act of smashing it was exactly what she had done. The bitch had taken his egg and chucked it on the ground, and it was the only egg he liked. He didn't want another damn egg. That was the only egg for him and now it was shattered and useless, and it was all her fault.

Maybe the only real difference between Alison and Daniel was that Alison had tried, with the dubious assistance of whatever self-help manuals she had stumbled across, to think her way free of her problems, while Daniel simply chose to cohabit with them. Alison, in her own way, was at least moving on from her divorce, while Daniel let himself stagnate and fester in a marinade of old rage.

She was, by a clear margin, the most annoying woman he had ever dated. But was she, perhaps, braver and smarter than him?

BUT I REMEMBER LESS OFTEN

It wasn't late when Daniel got home. He found his mother gazing listlessly at the TV, watching a garden makeover show on which a man in a yellow sweatshirt was having a tantrum about decking. She switched it off as he walked in.

'Well?' she said.

'Well what?'

'How was it?'

'Hard to describe.'

'Good?'

'Not really. There was a fundamental problem.'

'What?'

Daniel slumped heavily into a chair opposite his mother. 'I detested her,' he said.

'Oh, Daniel,' sighed Gillian, her disappointment mitigated only by the fact that she had known this would happen. When he was young, he had been such a warm, loving and sociable boy. Aged three, when Helen and Carol's boys had still been clingy and shy, Daniel had been in the habit of grabbing

271

visitors by the hand, regardless of whether he had even met them before, and dragging them off to private corners of the house to read him stories or play with his toys. He had, initially at least, instinctively and unreservedly loved people. He'd always just assumed that people liked him, and would enjoy his company, and as a result they usually did. Then, at the point in his adolescence where you'd expect it to happen, he changed his mind.

The hating-people phase, which Gillian had thought would last a few years at most, had somehow never quite ended. Daniel was no longer angry or sulky, but one last shred of teenage anti-sociability had remained stubbornly in place. His social life appeared normal, but Gillian could sense that he didn't depend on it. Friends, for him, were optional. As for strangers, his default responses seemed to range from suspicion and hostility to (if he was feeling generous) recalcitrance and indifference.

From the first moment of Daniel's life, Gillian had always enjoyed his company. Even before he could talk, he'd known how to make her laugh. He was fun and he was funny, he was clever and warm, but he chose to hide these qualities from the world as if he were ashamed of them, and she'd never been able to understand why. For almost twenty years, she had worried silently about this aspect of Daniel's nature.

In many ways, she felt she shared her son's flaws, and she understood his tendency towards pessimism and misanthropy. The fundamental difference between them was that he laid out on public display the very character traits she tried

272

hardest to repress, conquer or hide. This was what never ceased puzzling her about her son. They were so alike, yet so unalike—cut from the same pattern, yet somehow inside-out versions of one another—in a way that sometimes made her feel as if their oppositeness was an expression of their similarity.

'Why are you oh, Danieling me?' he said.

'You know why.'

'Why?'

'I know what you're like. When you're in this mood.'

'What mood?'

'You choose to hate people. To hate everyone.'

'I don't hate everyone. There are lots of people I like.'

'New people. You get in moods where you're just not going to be open to new people, and I saw it on your face as you walked out, and it's just . . . such a waste.'

'A waste of what?'

'You're too old for it, Daniel. It's childish.'

'Listen, I didn't hate her because I'd decided to hate her in advance. I actually quite fancied her until she opened her mouth.'

'You can be so critical.'

'How is that bad?'

'How is it good?' snapped Gillian.

'You think it's better not to care? To just be indifferent to everyone without thinking about who you like and who you don't?'

'You just ought to give people more of a chance.'

'Why?'

'Because it would help you. It would make your

life easier.'

'Rubbish. My life's a lot easier having decided I hate this woman straight away, instead of dating her for a month, then figuring it out.'

'No it isn't.'

'Of course it is.'

'It isn't, because in that month you could have found out new things about her that you might have liked and that might have made the relationship worth pursuing. You can't just write people off.' As the words slipped out of her mouth, she suddenly heard the sound of this very phrase coming from her mother's lips. She could picture the moment. She could see her mother in a lilac twin-set, her stiff back set at an irate angle, telling her off in the same words for the same offence, in the front room of the poky East End house where Gillian had battled unsuccessfully to introduce her parents to the then-novel notion of the teenager.

'Some people I like, some people I don't,' said Daniel. 'The quicker I know which camp they're in, the easier things are for everyone.'

'And when did you last meet a new person you liked?'

'It's not that simple.'

'You just said it is that simple. When? It's not recently, is it?'

'What does it matter?'

'When? I want to know.'

Daniel rubbed a hand against his forehead, running an index finger along the groove above his eyebrows.

'I can't think. Not recently,' he mumbled.

'Exactly,' said Gillian, her voice resonating with a hint of triumph, a hint of doom. She felt they

274

were now, at last, zeroing in on the conversation she had travelled four hundred miles to have.

Daniel looked at her, scrutinising her face, as if demanding an elaboration but unwilling to ask for one. Gillian could see in him a reluctance to pursue the subject mingled with a curiosity about where her hints were leading. She forced herself to wait for his response, not wanting to dive in with another accusation that might cause him to lose patience with her and walk away.

'Exactly what?' he said, eventually, fiddling with the cuff of his shirt, refusing to catch her eye.

'You're depressed,' she said. 'You're hiding from the world, most of all from the people who love you, and you don't seem to go anywhere or do anything or enjoy anything, and you're just disappearing into yourself, into your own unhappiness, and it's breaking my heart. You're depressed.'

'I'm not depressed,' he barked.

'And the longer you deny it, and pretend it isn't happening, the worse it's going to get.'

'This whole conversation's stupid.'

'Why did you come here, Daniel? Why did you come all this way, where there's no one who knows you or cares for you or loves you?'

Daniel picked up the remote and switched on the TV. The man in the yellow sweatshirt was now standing up to his waist in a garden pond, gesticulating enthusiastically with a fistful of algae. Gillian leapt from the sofa, stamped over to the set and flicked it off at the plug. 'I asked you a question,' she said.

'I've had a terrible evening,' said Daniel. 'This really isn't the time.'

'It's exactly the time. I'm asking because I care about you and I want to understand what's going on.'

'Please leave me alone.'

'No,' said Gillian. 'You're my child, and I will not just leave you alone.'

Daniel looked down at the remote control in his hands. With his little finger, he began clearing away the dust that had collected between the buttons. He could quite easily stand up and leave the room. He was under no obligation to pursue this discussion. He was an adult, and he was free to do as he wished, but he sensed a uniqueness to this moment.

He felt it had taken several days to reach this point between him and his mother. If he didn't respond to the lifeline she had just this once managed to throw to a point within his reach, then he might simply be swept away, alone, for good.

It was a long time before Daniel spoke. When he did, he told her from start to finish, in a way he had never told anyone, the whole story of his friendship and love affair with Erin, right up to his discovery of her infidelity. As he spoke, he realised that his life, from the moment he met Erin, had been dominated by one simple idea. Since that encounter, now fifteen years in the past, no one else had ever matched up. It had taken them years to become lovers but immediately and irreversibly, in some way, she had become his yardstick.

Throughout the last decade and a half, Daniel's entire adult life, all other women had been measured in Erins. Or rather, in fractions of an Erin. And as this occurred to him, he realised he was definitively stuck, utterly lost, for ever.

276

Because even if he did meet the perfect woman—more beautiful than Erin, funnier, kinder, cleverer—he'd still be measuring her in Erins. She had become his calibration, and that would never change. She was engraved into him.

As things stood now, the only meaningful relationship in his life was with Erin's absence, and he could not imagine that ever changing. But he could never go back to her. She had humiliated and betrayed him. She had smashed his egg.

Daniel confessed to his mother that he had, as she thought, simply run away from his life. But he didn't regret it; he didn't see an alternative. Physical distance was the only thing that helped him forget.

'But it hasn't helped you forget,' she said.

'No,' he replied, 'but I remember less often.'

CAROL AND MATT

A LITTLE PRIDE

On Saturday morning, Carol suggested that she and Matt take a walk in Hyde Park. Matt didn't like walking, and he wasn't keen on parks, either, but he felt it would be churlish to refuse.

It was one of those London days when you're too hot if you wrap up and too cold if you don't; when it's not exactly raining, but it isn't what you could call dry; when there's simply nothing to be gained by being outside. It was the kind of day when all you want to see of the weather is what you can make out from your local pub's football coverage.

The park was swarming with children, dogs, pigeons, kite-flyers and roller-bladers: every variety of life that Matt most despised, a significant proportion of them at any given time engaged in the act of public defecation. Carol, however, seemed thrilled by the place.

'I should come here more often,' she kept saying. 'It's not as if I'm so far away, is it?'

Matt didn't want to encourage this line of thinking, and protested to her that central London was a dirty and dangerous place that a woman of her age ought to avoid.

Carol told Matt the latest news from home and from his father, but he didn't appear interested and failed to ask any further questions. After raising a couple more topics that also fell flat, Carol decided to let Matt take over the conversational running.

She was disappointed, if unsurprised, to discover that this resulted in silence. As the *longueur* between them grew, she found herself welling up with anger at his selfishness. She didn't want her annoyance to show, so she didn't let herself stare at him, but a few glances in his direction showed him seemingly unperturbed by the ever-deepening chasm in their attempt at a chat, unaware that his mother was taking an experimental measurement of his self-absorption and rudeness. Then, suddenly, he put a hand on her shoulder. 'Thank you for coming,' he said.

Carol's irritation, at a stroke, was transformed into thrilled gratitude. 'Well . . . it's been a pleasure,' she said, colour rising to her cheeks as she almost went on to suggest that they do the

278

same again soon. But she stopped herself. She'd ruin the moment if she pushed her luck. And, on reflection, she wasn't sure she even wanted to. Her week had been interesting, but she'd need a good long while to recover from it.

'I've . . . er . . . I'm still in touch with that girl. Julia,' said Matt.

'Oh. That's good.'

'I'm seeing her tonight, I think.'

'You think?'

'I have to call her.'

'Oh, I'm so glad you hit it off.'

'I ought to ring her this afternoon. I don't want to seem too keen, but it's just driving me mad, waiting. I might have to do it now.'

'OK. Don't mind me.'

'It's not that. I just ought to play it a bit cool.'

'Oh, women hate that. There's nothing better than a bit of keenness.'

'You think?'

'I'm positive.'

The mobile phone in his pocket had been pulling him all morning like a cigarette packet taunting a smoker. Matt looked at his watch. It was barely eleven o'clock, but he couldn't wait any longer. There was no sense in letting the tension ruin any more of his day.

Matt excused himself from his mother and walked away, behind the nearest tree. Julia's number was already programmed into his mobile. After a couple of rings, she answered.

'You still haven't given up?' she said.

'No. I'm not going to, either.'

'Men think women want to hear that, but they don't. The whole stalker thing really isn't a turn-on.'

'Is that what I said? Did I say I was going to stalk you?'

'I'm not sure. Are you?'

'No. Where shall we meet?'

'I still don't know why I even gave you my number.'

'Maybe you couldn't help yourself.'

'Er . . . yes, you're irresistible, Matt. You're every woman's fantasy.'

'Maybe I know what you're doing,' he said, with an intonation that was intended to convey penetrating intelligence. He wasn't sure how well he pulled it off.

'What I'm doing? What *am* I doing?'

'We both know what's going on here, Julia. I'm not stupid. And I respect you for it,' he said, attempting to hint at her sexism-reversal game before immediately losing confidence in his theory the second the words began to come out of his mouth.

'Respect me for what?' said Julia. 'For trying to get rid of you?'

Matt could feel the conversation slipping away from him. Talking to Julia reminded him vaguely of school sports days, of the way it felt to do something you are bad at, in public, knowing before you've even started that you are going to lose.

He knew he just ought to give up, for the sake of his dignity, but he couldn't. He wanted her too much, and part of him felt he deserved the humiliation she inflicted on him, as if it was another test set in some obscure way by his mother. If he could survive it, and win Julia over,

280

he sensed that he would have proved something to himself and to Carol. It would be a way to demonstrate that he had a grasp of his flaws and intended to tackle them. Or, at the very least, that he would try.

The longer he talked to her, the more opportunity Julia had to turn him down, which she was liable to do at any moment, just for fun. The best tactic for staving off rejection, he decided, was simply to keep it short.

'I'll see you at the Coach and Horses in Soho,' he said. 'Greek Street. Eight o'clock.'

He hung up without waiting for her answer, his trembling thumb at first missing the tiny red button on his phone. He'd done well. He'd shown her that he wasn't going to let her have it all her own way. He'd salvaged a little pride.

She'd come. A little late, maybe, but she'd show up. She had, after all, given him her number. Julia could see, like his mother, that he was a better man than he appeared.

CHARACTER ASSASSINATION CALLED FLIRTATION

Matt waited in the Coach and Horses for three hours, but Julia never came. He hadn't previously waited longer than fifteen minutes for a woman in his whole life. This time, he only stopped at three hours because the pub closed.

He could have phoned Julia as soon as it was clear she was a little late, to ask if she was on her way, but he hadn't wanted to come across as too keen. Then, by the time he'd left it half an hour, he realised that if he phoned her now, whatever he said, he wouldn't be asking 'are you coming?' but 'why aren't you coming?' And they'd been through that conversation once already.

He may have been feeling crushed (again), depressed, shocked and hurt, but he was still in possession of the shred of dignity that stopped him picking up his phone. She didn't want him. She didn't like him. He just had to accept it like a man.

So he did. He drank.

Of all the places to be stood up, a pub is not a good one. The consolation at hand isn't of a useful kind, and is almost impossible to resist. By closing time, Matt was so drunk that five cabs drove past him before he managed to pass himself off as sober enough to be worth picking up.

Back at his flat, which was dark, silent and apparently empty, Matt forgot about his guest. 'FUCK!' he shouted, kicking the sofa. 'FUCKFUCKFUCK! BITCH! FUCKING BITCH!'

'Are you OK?' said Carol, standing behind him in her nightie and dressing-gown.

'Mum!' said Matt. 'Oh, Mum.'

His inhibitions were down. His defences were in tatters. His self-control was long gone. He was four again. He stretched out his arms and lunged at her. 'She didn't turn up!' he stuttered, wrapping his arms around her neck.

'Who?'

'Julia! She said she would, but she didn't. I sat there for hours.'

'Oh, I'm sorry.'

'I LIKE HER! SHE'S REALLY NICE!'

'I know she is, dear.'

'WHY DOESN'T SHE LIKE ME?'

'I don't know. Well, as long as you tried. That's the main thing.'

'I DID TRY! I LIKE HER! SHE'S REALLY NICE!'

'You just said that, dear. Would you like a coffee?'

'I don't know.'

'I'll make you a coffee.'

Carol pulled herself free of his grip and coaxed him towards the sofa. She knew a precious window of opportunity was about to open up, after he calmed down and before he sobered up, when she'd be able to ask him anything and he'd be likely to give an unguarded answer. She made the coffee strong, but not too strong.

'Why don't you tell me what happened,' she said, sitting herself opposite him, in the narcolepsy chair. 'From the beginning.'

'I told you already. We went out. We got on. We spoke on the phone. We made a date. She didn't show up. The end.'

'Maybe something happened. Maybe she was held up somewhere.'

'No, it's not like that. She kind of said she wasn't coming, but I thought it was a joke, and I only realised it wasn't when she didn't arrive.'

'What sort of a joke is it to say you're not coming?'

'The whole thing is a joke. Kind of a game, where I tell her I like her and she says she doesn't like me. It's a flirting thing.'

'Flirting?'

'Yes.'

'So does she like you or not?'

'Well, I thought she did. But obviously she doesn't. Maybe I just thought it was flirting, but she actually meant it.'

'I don't really understand.'

'She even told me why.'

'Why what?'

'Why she doesn't like me.'

'This was part of the flirtation? Telling you why she doesn't like you.'

'Yeah.'

'And what was the reason?'

'Oh, God. It was some big speech. I can't remember the whole thing.'

'What was the gist?'

'Something about how I seem like a nice guy when I'm talking, but when I start listening I turn out to be a tosser because I'm only pretending to listen instead of really doing it. Which is bollocks. I mean, just because you can't remember what someone's told you, that doesn't mean you weren't listening when they said it.'

This girl was smarter than Carol had thought. After only one evening, she already knew the essence of Matt better than he knew himself, like someone snapping a stick of rock in half to read the text inside. Quite how this accurate and pointed character assassination could be called flirtation was beyond her. But the window was open. Matt was having a moment of what, for him, could be classed as introspection. The template of family reticence told her to walk away and leave him to it, but again she forced herself to ignore the rules and press on. This was what she had come for. The door she had been knocking on all week was beginning to creak open. She decided to give it

284

a yank.

'You really believe that?' said Carol. 'You think you listen carefully to what people say—to what women say—and show them respect and courtesy?'

As she watched him do it, Carol realised she had never before seen her son think. Whatever you asked him, he threw back an answer straight away. On the rare occasions he reconsidered one of his opinions or changed his mind about something, the thought process was always conducted in private, after which he'd come back with a convoluted retraction or an elaborate explanation of why events had caused him to modify his view. What she never saw was this: live action thinking. She had put him a question, and he was mulling it over from scratch, right in front of her. He was drunk, of course, but you had to take what you could get.

'Maybe I could do a bit better. With the listening stuff,' he said. 'But it's not my fault. It's the world I move in. I've just fallen out of practice.'

'And how is it not your fault?'

More thinking, this time with a maudlin sag slowly creeping across his features.

'OK, maybe it is my fault. But I don't want to be like that. I don't.'

'So don't be.'

'It's not that easy.'

Matt could feel the caffeine beginning to percolate into his brain, and with it came a horrible realisation. The self-hatred drawer was now wide open, its contents scattered shamefully all over the floor. He hated his job. He didn't like his friends. His life had led him somewhere he never wanted to be. He lived in a hermetic bubble of ambition, surrounded by loathsome people who believed that

285

producing *BALLS!* was an appropriate pursuit for an intelligent adult, rather than a daily assault on the soul. He was weak and stupid, no better in any way than the colleagues he despised.

He had wanted to do good things with his life. Like anyone else, when he was young he'd hoped to win the admiration of the people he admired. He'd never had it in him to be a doctor or an aid worker—he'd never aspired to great altruism—but he'd felt confident he would end up doing something vaguely worthwhile, or at least a job that wasn't actively malicious or immoral. Now, only thirty-four, he had already betrayed every last shred of his adolescent idealism.

Julia had been the first person he'd come across for years who'd stirred in him any memory of his lost ideals. In her company, he'd felt the first inkling of a long-dormant desire to improve himself. She would have been his salvation. With her help, he could have begun to turn himself into the person he wanted to be. Without her, there was no incentive, no assistance, no hope.

'And is that it with Julia?' said Carol, as if she had been reading his thoughts from across the room. 'Is it all over?'

'You can't really say it's over when it never even started. She just doesn't like me.'

'Because you don't listen?'

'Seems like it.'

'So why don't you show her that you do listen?'

'How?'

'By listening.'

'To what? It's over. I can't call her now and offer to listen. It's too late.'

'Well, show her that you did listen before. Act

286

on something you remember her saying when she thinks you weren't listening.'

'Well, the main thing she said is that she doesn't like me.'

'Can't you think of something else? What did she talk about on your date? There must have been something you didn't listen to that made her take against you for not listening.'

'Um . . . can't remember.'

'Well, what do you remember? What did she tell you about herself?'

'Not sure. She talked about her studies a bit. Her MSc.'

'What did she say about it?'

'That it was about development.'

'What kind of development?'

'Don't know. Not sure if I asked.'

'You didn't ask? So it could be property development or child development or Third World development, and you didn't think to ask which? You weren't bothered?'

'I might have asked. I'm not sure. But I can't remember the answer. I was distracted. It was a confusing evening.'

'Well, luckily for you, I did.'

'You did what?'

'Ask. About her MSc. It's Third World development. She's writing something on child nutrition in Kenya. I think she said it was the Masai.'

'Maybe I could find it on the internet! I could Google her name and Kenya and something might come up. I could read up on it.'

'If you think it would help.'

'Of course it would help! I can prove to her that

I listen and that I'm interested in what she does.'

'Are you?'

'Am I what?'

'Interested in what she does.'

'Yes! Yes! Absolutely.'

'You're not just trying to get her into bed?'

'No! I have to go back to her with some proof that I'm not who she thinks I am. This might do it.'

'It's only proof if it's also true. If you're just tricking her with something I've told you and something else you've found out on the internet, then it'll catch up with you. She'll find you out. You have to mean it.'

'I do mean it, and it's not a trick. You've just given me a toe-hold. I really do want to know more about her. I'm interested.'

'Well, I hope it works. And I hope she doesn't hurt you.'

'She won't. What about me hurting her?'

'That's not going to happen.'

Carol drained her coffee, kissed her son on the forehead and went back to bed. She didn't know whether to be more or less worried about Matt than she had been before her visit. She had come in the hope of rediscovering who he was, and had found him in such a state of flux and confusion that there didn't seem to be anything solid or permanent to know. The minute she thought she understood something about him, he'd tell her he was on the brink of changing it.

You'd expect this with a sixteen-year-old, not someone in their mid-thirties. His intentions sounded positive, so she supposed she ought to be grateful for him at least professing the desire to change for the better, but if he hadn't managed it yet, was there any real chance of him starting now, at his age?

Frankly, she'd believe it when she saw it. She loved him, and wanted intensely to believe him, but he'd always had a streak in his character that bent too easily with the current. He was never a leader. As a child, he had often borrowed personalities from other, more charismatic kids. Now, perhaps, he was agreeing with Carol for only so long as she was in his flat. She had no real confidence that when she left, his life wouldn't revert to exactly as it had been before she came.

There was always a slim possibility that he meant what he said, and would follow it through. It was conceivable that he had decided now, this week, to grow up. But she doubted it. Matt always had grand plans for himself, but he never acted on them. He was a dreamer more than a doer. He zoned out more than he zoned in. Julia, by the sound of it, had seen through him in one evening. Smart women would. He didn't stand a chance with her. But the attempt was the important thing. He was at least heading in the right direction, and having his heart broken might even do him some good.

She should never have drunk that coffee. It would be hours before she'd get to sleep.

Carol got out of bed and began to pack. She'd leave the next morning. She was missing home, and she'd found out what she wanted to know. Whether Matt changed or not was, in the end, none of her business. He was an adult. He had the right to live how he wanted to live, and Carol had to accept whatever he chose. She had to love him regardless of whether she liked him or not. That was a mother's job.

Without even thinking it through, Carol found herself taking off her nightie and getting dressed. Somewhere in her purse, for emergencies, was the card of a twenty-four-hour minicab firm. She'd leave right now, go home, and slip into her own bed without waking her husband.

She phoned from her bedroom and tiptoed out as quietly as she could, though if she'd been wearing clogs it would have made no difference. Matt was out for the count, slumped on the sofa, still fully dressed down to his shoes. Carol knelt on the floor and undid his laces. This felt like a fitting end, somehow. This was how things were supposed to be. She was being a mother; he was being a son.

Of course, it shouldn't still be like this. At Matt's age it should have been him on his knees, taking off Carol's shoes. The roles should have reversed by now. But perhaps Carol had been hoping for too much, and maybe she had been seeking the wrong thing. There was something to be said for this. Matt remaining a child prevented Carol from becoming a geriatric. She couldn't let herself age until he did. Only one of them could be the taker-off of shoes and, for now, she would rather it was her.

Watching him sleep took her back thirty years, to a time when you'd pop in last thing at night, ostensibly to check that your child was all right, but in reality just for another dose of them, for one last glance at their beauty, for a sniff of their sweet, perfect, faraway slumber. It was astonishing that this snoring, unshaven man, stinking of booze and fags, was the same human being. This large creature, this uncontrollable force, capable of exerting huge good or evil on the world, had once lived inside her, had been fed at her breast. She had made him.

She rearranged Matt's body into a less twisted shape and looked around the flat for a blanket. There was none to be found. She looked through all the high cupboards in the flat, but could only find unidentifiable electronic devices, discarded sports equipment and three cookery-book stands, all of which she vaguely remembered having given him for different birthdays. A duvet would do, placed over his legs so he didn't get too hot.

She wanted to leave a note, explaining that there was nothing sinister in her sudden departure and thanking him for his hospitality (if that was a word you could use for what was on offer from someone like Matt). Another search around the house ensued, but she could find no pen or paper. Perhaps she'd have to send him a text message. Then she remembered her own handbag. Tearing a page from the back of her diary, she wrote:

Thank you for having me. Couldn't sleep, and decided to leave a bit early. Missing Dad terribly. So nice to spend time with you again. I only want you to be happy.
love
Mum
xxxx

It looked so kitsch and empty, that final sentiment, but she couldn't think of what else to say. The truth was, she wanted much more than that. She wanted him to be good and honest and decent, and loving to someone worthwhile who'd love him

291

back. But 'I only want you to be good and honest and decent, and loving to someone worthwhile who'll love you back' would not have struck the right note, and wouldn't have fitted on to a page of her diary.

At least, perhaps, in the course of the week she had communicated this to him without having to say it. Not that she could possibly make a difference. She had to remind herself that she hadn't come to change him. She had just come to satisfy her curiosity, which she had achieved. It had been a successful week.

She switched the light off and slipped down the stairs. He would do his own thing in his own time. She had done her best with him. At heart, he was not a bad man. She was not a bad mother.

GILLIAN AND DANIEL

PRAGMANTIC

Gillian stared at Daniel across his living room, which felt embraced by the dense quiet of the sleeping city around them. It was now after one in the morning and Edinburgh, in a way that never happened in London, had gone silent. Gillian couldn't remember when she had last been up this late, but she didn't feel tired. Honesty had the same effect on her as caffeine.

Daniel's history of his love for Erin had not surprised her. She wasn't sure how, but she somehow already knew almost everything he'd told her. She felt she'd understood the depth of

Daniel's love for Erin even before he had, even while they were only friends. And yet, to hear Daniel unburdening himself came as an exquisite relief to Gillian.

She knew that by talking about his unhappiness he was not automatically curing himself of anything, but, equally, she felt certain that his previous denial of it had doomed him to indefinite misery. A corner, she sensed, had been turned. There was no guarantee that the next thing would be better, or easier, or happier, but at least there would be a next thing, and by beginning to acknowledge his problem and accept it, Daniel was allowing his life to acquire a forwards momentum.

Gillian left the room without a word, returning a while later with two cups of tea. He smiled sadly at her as she sat down, and they drank for a while in easy silence.

As the mug began to cool between her palms, Gillian told Daniel that she, too, had something important to say. She'd never thought she would tell Daniel this particular story, but now the events of one distant summer's day suddenly felt relevant, even pressing.

Gillian's story was almost twenty-five years old. She began by asking Daniel if he remembered a camping holiday they had taken in Gloucestershire when he was eight. A group of Pinner families had all gone together, and taken over a campsite that had turned out, when they got there, to be a very sketchily set up sideline for a farmer who had done nothing more than rig up a crude shower in an outhouse.

His advertising campaign had been as half-hearted as every other aspect of the enterprise, and even though it was high summer, the group had ended up sharing their field with no one other than a few sheep. On the first day there had been a few moans to Ian, Daniel's father, who had made the booking, but once they settled in, the place proved to be perfect. The children could shout as much as they liked, roll around naked in the mud whenever they felt like it, and generally run wild without anyone worrying that there was anybody around who might be annoyed, disturbed or offended.

Daniel's strongest memory was of a pair of peacocks who acted like they owned the place and were always strutting around near the farmhouse. For a whole week, the peacocks were the only creatures who seemed to attempt to tell the children off for anything, shrieking with outrage when they got too close.

As Gillian started talking about this farm, a powerful memory of a fallen tree also came back to him. It was a huge oak, long dead, that lay like a felled giant in the middle of the field. This tree had been the centrepiece of their week, alternately a pirate ship, a jungle canopy, a castle, a transport network and a battleground. It was too high to be safe, but too irresistible to go unclimbed, and the parents soon gave up their attempts to keep the children off it. The only injury had been when Paul fell into a bed of nettles that infested one end. Daniel remembered clearly that Matt had pushed Paul off, but Gillian recalled it as an accident. Perhaps only Daniel saw the incident—and had never told anyone the truth.

'Why did we never go back?' Daniel asked. It had, after all, been a near-perfect week. 'In fact, why was there never another group holiday?' After that one magical week, it had never happened again.

'Because it was far from perfect,' Gillian replied. 'That's why I'm bringing it up.'

There had been one disastrous day, which had begun with Larry getting a mild electric shock in the shower. He had gone to speak to the farmer about it, but the farmhouse was empty. No one had seen him or his wife since the day they had arrived. Larry had another look at the shower, and decided all that was required to make it safe was some insulating tape. Since this was the only place everyone could wash, he decided to do it himself. Ian knew the area, and had a vague memory of having seen a hardware store somewhere in one of the local towns. He couldn't describe it, but he thought if he went he'd be able to find it. This, at least, was the story Larry and Ian had spun to the rest of the group.

The two men went off in Larry's car, with an arrangement that they would meet up with everyone else at the cheese-rolling contest they were all due to visit that afternoon.

'The cheese-rolling! I remember the cheese-rolling!' said Daniel, sitting up sharply.

'We never saw any cheese-rolling.'

'Are you sure?'

'I couldn't be more positive.'

'I remember the idea of it.'

'It must be that.'

The morning had been hot and muggy, dedicated to a seemingly endless game of French cricket, and to a picnic lunch made by Carol involving an avocado salad that Matt, for some reason, had smeared into Paul's hair.

It began to rain just as they were finishing lunch, and the other families decided to hunker down at the campsite. Only Gillian and Helen opted to persevere with the cheese-rolling outing, in order to make the rendezvous with their husbands. By the time they got near, they were caught up in a downpour of folklore-obliterating proportions. Even if they had reached their destination, they wouldn't have wanted to get out of the car, besides which, the cheese-rollers, whoever they were, and whatever it was they were hoping to do, would almost certainly have gone home and taken their cheese with them. Larry and Ian would understand what had happened, and they'd all find each other later at the campsite.

Despite protests from the children, they decided to head for a local museum, which was the only dry activity the two women could think of. The promise of a complete skeleton and some antique surgical tools, as described in a guidebook, with the added bribe of a cream tea, put a stop to the whining from the back of the car.

It was as they were pulling into the museum car park that Gillian saw Larry's car approach. What she saw next imprinted itself on her brain not as a moving image but as a single still glimpse that even now was as clear to her as the moment it happened.

It was, of itself, an ordinary sight. Just a car containing two men and two women. Larry was in the front, with a woman who looked around ten years younger than him in the passenger seat. Ian was in the back, alongside a woman of the same age. All four were laughing, too absorbed in their

296

joke and in each other to look out of the window at the gawping figures of Gillian and Helen on the pavement.

The children, already dashing ahead into the museum, saw nothing; the men in the car saw nothing; but in that moment, all their lives changed. There was no possible innocent explanation for what they had seen. Had the two women been in the back, there was a possibility they could have been hitch-hikers, but the arrangement of the bodies in the car spoke of coupling-up, of intimacy, of sex.

Straight away, the story of the unsafe shower seemed strange, and the joint mission to a hardware store sounded like a pretext. The men had not just lied, they had planned their lies. They had arranged a day off from domesticity, from childcare and from marriage. The more Gillian thought about it, the more this plotting, this utter lack of spontaneity in their arrangements, struck her as the greatest evil of all. Whatever her husband had done with this woman, whether he had slept with her or not, the fact of having schemed the day out in advance, with rehearsed deception, was unforgivable. After all, for every rehearsed lie there are a thousand casual ones while you wait for your moment, feigning devotion, planning your escape.

The men didn't arrive back at the campsite until late. They smelt of beer, of pubs, and ever so faintly of the kind of air freshener used in cheap hotels. There was too much bounce in their walk. They radiated ill-suppressed glee. Between them, there was a palpable secret hanging in the air.

They jauntily related a long story involving a

297

breakdown and a garage who had sworn to repair the car while they waited but then took much longer than promised, but as it dawned on them that their wives' anger was not just because they had stayed away too long, and as their story began to be tested for precise geographical details and timings, the alibi unravelled. When they were told that they had been spotted, they lied their way in opposing directions, tangling themselves in knots of mutual contradiction.

The two men were put in charge of getting the children into bed, while Gillian and Helen sat and thought. Neither had anything to say to the other. When Larry and Ian emerged from the tents, the women demanded the truth. Strangely, though Gillian remembered so many details from that day, what exactly her husband had done, or claimed to have done, was now slightly hazy in her memory. The essence of it was that Larry had a mistress, or an ex-girlfriend, who had recently moved to the area. She had come down for the day to see Larry. Larry had told Ian that she was coming, and asked Ian if he thought it would be fun if she brought a friend. Ian had agreed. Part of the afternoon had been spent at a hotel. Ian had tried to protest that only a few precise things had happened in the hotel room, while other key things hadn't happened or even been desired, but these details Gillian did not want to know. He had told her enough.

A few days after returning from the camping holiday, Gillian told Daniel that she was going to her mother's for a week. Daniel remembered this, though not that the timing had been so close to the camping holiday. He had never doubted this was where she had gone, and the only thing that struck him at the time as weird was that she took the car. It was strange enough to be looked after by his father, but to be carless at the same time felt like a double deprivation. He remembered his father being tense and tetchy, an unnerving mix of over-keen and neglectful in his attention to Daniel and Rose's needs. The week had been odd, but his mother not being there was explanation enough for any unusual atmosphere or behaviour. It had never occurred to him to wonder why she had gone; less still, where.

The truth was, she had simply got in the car and driven. She did not want warmth or comfort; she didn't want anything that might seem like a holiday and distract her from the thinking she had to do, so she drove north. Without making any kind of plan, without even having in mind any particular destination or purpose, she headed for the M1 and drove. She stopped to pee, she stopped to eat, but she kept these pauses to a minimum, the harsh lighting and screamy acoustic of motorway service stations jarring on her mental state. The radio stayed off, and her eyes barely strayed from the road. One part of her brain drove, the other part thought. Neither, it felt to her, were using language or logic. Her thoughts were not coherent or purposeful; she was not yet even trying to work out what she would do, she was simply setting a mental peristalsis to work on the events of the previous week. Until she had broken down her husband's betrayal and digested it, no decisions could be taken.

Though she was driving, in a way that seemed to her perfectly safe—overtaking when she had to, checking her mirror, indicating, changing lanes—

her mind felt more asleep than awake. She was not really inhabiting her body or her thoughts. She simply did not feel as if she was there, in the car. She was not anywhere.

As darkness fell, Gillian's sense of unreality deepened. The motorway now seemed less like a road containing other cars driven by other people, more like an abstract corridor of lights down which she was effortlessly passing. Occasionally she would jolt to her senses and remember what she was doing, but most of the time she felt neither time nor distance impinge on her. She almost forgot that she was going anywhere. She passed Manchester, passed Glasgow, went beyond the end of the last motorway, and still she kept driving.

She didn't look at her watch until she felt her eyes drooping. It was almost midnight. A sign told her she was approaching Ullapool. At the next B+B hoarding she turned off the road and rang the bell. Gillian knew you were not supposed to arrive at places like this unannounced, late at night, and she tried to think of a plausible story, but her brain was not capable of it.

A landlady wearing a dressing-gown answered the door, angrily at first, but she saw something in Gillian's face, something Gillian didn't even know was there, that changed her manner. Kindly, solicitously even, she showed Gillian to a room and told her that she could have breakfast as late as she liked. Gillian didn't even ask her the price. She just thanked her, stripped off, and within seconds was fast asleep.

The following day, Gillian walked to the centre of town, which was empty and appealingly desolate. She found a pub with a view of the harbour and lingered over a bowl of soup and a coffee, staring out at the bobbing, rusting ships. It was mid-afternoon, and no one had bothered her, when a huge ferry hooted its arrival. For ten minutes the town was suddenly abuzz with lorries, motorbikes, cars, caravans and pedestrians, then it went quiet again, as if the momentary bustle of activity had been a fleeting hallucination.

She paid at the bar and asked about the ferry. It would be leaving that evening, heading out to Stornoway, on the Western Isles: what they used to call the Outer Hebrides. Gillian wanted to keep going, further out, further away, but did not yet want to get back in the car. This was perfect. When the ferry left, she was on it.

Gillian was on deck to see the sunset: stripes of orange and pink bashfully hovering between the sea and the sky, as if embarrassed to be so beautiful and so richly coloured. The islands rose out of the sea ahead, a mass of pure, calm bulk. Gillian closed her eyes and let the cold, salty tang fill her lungs. It was hard to be angry here. If ever there was a place to put aside the now, this was it. She could leave Ian; she could kick him out. She could let her life as she knew it be destroyed. Or she could stay with him, weakened and humiliated, waiting for the next infidelity.

There was a map somewhere in the back of the car, but Gillian still didn't look at it. She drove off the ferry and kept going, putting more distance between herself and home. If she went far enough, she felt she would find her answer. Another anonymous B+B housed her for the night, but this time she was up and back in the car even before breakfast, leaving cash for the room under a pink ashtray on her bedside table.

Only weeks later did she look at a map and find out where she had been. Her journey further out through the islands had, though she didn't realise it at the time, been leading her closer to home. As she drove further from Stornoway, hopping from island to island on causeways and two small ferries, the archipelago was in fact taking her back southwards, from Lewis to Harris, North Uist to Benbecula to South Uist, and finally over a short strip of water to Barra, then Vatersay. Here the road ended. She could go no further.

She stopped the car and got out, a blast of cold wind slapping her across the face. The road ended on a high ridge. Ahead of her stretched a featureless slope of rocky grass, dotted with sheep. Down below, on either side of the road, were two beaches of pure white sand. One beach, on the right, was pummelled by vicious breakers. The other, down a short slope to her left, was a calm bay filled with the kind of clear turquoise water you would expect to find on a tropical island. In the water, looking at her with quizzical poise, was a seal.

She had passed no cars for the last hour. She had not seen a single person on the entire island. Gillian allowed the wind to buffet her a little longer, then quickly stripped off all her clothes and ran down to the calmer of the two beaches.

The water clamped itself down on her ankles like a threat, a punishment, but she didn't falter. As soon as the water was up to her knees, she threw herself in, over her head. The shock of the cold made her want to scream, but when she resurfaced and opened her mouth no sound came

302

out. Her lungs were in a vice, incapacitated, unable to push out enough air to make any noise. She felt as if her body might solidify, give up on her, literally petrify in the water, but she was in now. She kicked as hard as she could, and set off with the fastest front crawl she could manage. When her breath began to shorten, she switched to breast-stroke. Soon she was at the spot where she had seen the seal. The cold was no longer so painful. In fact, her skin was now giving off a shrill buzz that felt a little like warmth.

She stopped and turned, treading water and looking back at the shore. She had left the car doors open. She looked down, into the water, which was such a limpid, crystalline blue that she could see her toenails as clearly as if she was standing in air. Lifting her head again, something small and brown floated past in the water. It was a neat, dry sheep turd. She laughed. She had almost forgotten what if felt like to hear this sound coming out of her throat.

Gillian swam back to the shore, ran out of the water, dried herself on a T-shirt, dressed as fast as she could, and got back in the car. Then she drove home, her skin tingling, warming her like sunburn. Something had led her here. She had not known where she was going until she found it. Here, at the end of the last road, at the limit of the furthest island, the answer she was looking for had come to her. This place—these two beaches, one exposed, one sheltered—had told her what to do. She had made her choice.

After driving through the night, she arrived home shortly before dawn. Slipping into bed, she accidentally woke Ian, who asked where she had

303

been, what she had done, and what she had decided.

'I've come home,' she said. 'Now I have to sleep.' She would not tell him any more.

Ian soon gave up asking. She had come back. That was enough. Anything that had to be said, she would say in her own time.

She never did talk to Ian about where she had driven. She wasn't warm or loving to him on her return, nor did she go out of her way to be overtly hostile. They simply got on with their lives, and eventually, when enough time had elapsed, things returned to normal. Something crucial at the centre of the relationship seemed to have died, but slowly, over the ensuing months, like a bulb pushing up through the soil, their love was miraculously reborn.

Though Gillian explained this marital resurrection to Daniel as a miracle, the truth was in fact perfectly logical and comprehensible, if a little hard to explain, particularly to one's son. Gillian's anger may not have been discussed, but it wasn't ignored, nor did it just disappear with the passage of time. The issue was simply tackled physically rather than verbally.

For several months, Gillian didn't touch Ian. She had not intended to do this, nor had she known in advance that it would happen, but she didn't want to, and he didn't force himself on her. He tried to seduce her once or twice, but he soon realised that she was making him wait. Only as he understood it did Gillian grasp what she was doing. It was rather neat. A year would be good, she thought.

Without a word being spoken, it somehow

became clear that this withholding of sex was his punishment. He understood, and he waited. He allowed her to be absolutely in charge of the bed. His physical reticence in response to hers became a form of repentance.

Verbally, they pretended his violation of their marriage had never happened. It was physically that they negotiated it, that he paid his penance, and that she allowed him to know when he was forgiven.

Occasionally, after she had fallen asleep, she found herself woken by the odd strange shudder in the bed frame, but she always pretended she hadn't noticed. She began even to feel a little sorry for him.

Slowly, long before the intended year was up, she began to touch him. At first, she just lay a little closer to him. Then she began to curl herself round him. The rules, however, remained the same. Everything was to advance at her pace. Gently, half-jokingly, she refused to let him touch her, even as she began to touch him more affectionately and more intimately. She gave herself to him bit by bit. It became a test, a punishment and a joke, all at once.

This was the most erotic phase of their marriage. The slightest touch made him hard, and his hardness aroused her, too, but still she made him wait, bringing him to the brink, then stopping, telling him he was still being punished. By then, the truth had ebbed out of the joke and it had become simply an erotic game. When she finally ended his torment, they had a night more passionate than any other in their life.

To this day, they had more sex and (from what

she could glean) far better sex than her friends. She knew it was due to this interruption of their sexual routine twelve years into the marriage. It had made them think about sex again, just when it was becoming easy to treat it as another household chore. Their sexual fast and feast had reminded them how much the other one needed it and enjoyed it. This reminder had stoked up their mutual desire, and kept it burning for longer than they ever could have hoped.

Though Gillian wanted to tell Daniel this part of the story, she couldn't say it. Now she had got to the end, she began to feel this was perhaps the most important part, was the essence of what she was trying to tell him. But no one wants to hear this kind of thing about their parents. Instead, she told him, with as much authority and conviction as she could summon into her voice, that trust is not made of glass. It is not an object that irreparably shatters. It is a muscle. It can be wounded. It can stop functioning for a while, but it can heal, if you take things slowly enough. If you keep tearing at the same wound, stretching it before it is ready, the muscle will never recover. But if you are careful, if you allow it to, it will heal.

Returning to Ian, Gillian told Daniel, was the bravest thing she ever did, and she felt she had been rewarded for it ever since. As she was driving back towards London, trying to justify to herself the decision she had made, Gillian had found one word echoing round her head. It wasn't even a real word. Pragmantic. It was a word the language needed; it was a word for what every marriage depended upon. A man and a woman cannot last a lifetime together just by being pragmatic, nor by

306

only being romantic. Anger, moral outrage and revenge were all very tempting, but they would not help. They would not make her any happier, or her marriage any stronger, or contribute to the welfare of her children. The only way to be, the only path to follow, was the pragmantic one.

Helen reacted differently. She didn't stop to think. She raged and spat, she threw Larry out, she took him back, she forgave too easily while at the same time not really forgiving at all, and it was only a matter of time before the marriage ended. Maybe that was the right thing for her. Larry probably never had it in him to be a good and loyal husband. Perhaps, however Helen had behaved, he would never have been capable of repentance or fidelity. But the difference between the two marriages, between the two men, had not stopped Helen judging Gillian for her choice, and resenting it. Helen always acted as if Gillian had betrayed her, let down the sisterhood, by allowing her marriage to be saved. Their friendship had never quite recovered.

'I've always understood you, Daniel, without you having to say anything,' Gillian said. 'When you were a child, I knew when you were going to get angry before it happened. I could always tell when you said you were tired but were actually hungry, and when you said you were hungry but were actually tired. I always understood what made you tick in a way I never have with Rose. Dad used to laugh at both of us when you had tantrums. He always said the only person he'd ever come across as stubborn as his wife was his son. And when you came up here, just blindly heading north, I knew what had happened. I understood it, and I

307

understood your reaction. But if you want to be happy, and if this is the only woman you love, and all the time you've been away from her doesn't help you fall out of love, then you have to go back to her. If you really thought you could never trust her again, I don't think you would have carried on loving her for so long.'

Gillian stood, walked across the room, and kissed Daniel on the top of his head.

'Life isn't going to reward you for nursing your wounded pride,' she said. 'It's humiliating to forgive someone who has hurt you, and that's why it's hard, and that's why it's brave, but I think you're strong enough.'

'I thought you didn't like her,' said Daniel.

'If she made you happy, I'd learn to like her. I'd learn to love her.'

'What if she's found someone else?'

'There's only one way to find out.'

'She probably has.'

'Even if she has, maybe she still loves you.'

'Maybe she doesn't.'

'There's only one way to find out.'

'Stop saying that.'

'Come with me, Daniel. I'll drive you home.'

'This is home.'

'I don't think it is. I really don't think it is.'

Daniel looked around his starkly furnished, bare-walled, curtainless lounge. He noticed for the first time that, with his white wallpaper and black furniture, the only colour in the room came from the spines on his bookshelves. She had a point. This was somewhere to live, but it wasn't home.

HELEN AND PAUL

NOT A WOMAN HE KNEW

Paul left work early and travelled home with dread
in his heart. This had been an appalling week, and
every day his mother stayed on it somehow got
worse. There was something to be said for the way
the air had been cleared between them, and it was
a relief to have unburdened himself of the various
secrets he'd been keeping from her, but he'd only
be able to appreciate this once she had left. While
she was still there, he couldn't relax for fear that
some new horror, trauma or tantrum might leap
out at him when he least expected it.

Now, the most painful chore of the week
awaited him. His mother would be waiting at his
house, having been turned away by Rebecca. They
would have said to Helen exactly what they'd said
to him. She was bound to have argued and cajoled
and wept, but nothing in Helen's emotional arsenal
would have made any difference. Rebecca and
Andrea knew what they wanted, and it certainly
wasn't Helen. She didn't figure in their plans, and
she was powerless to divert them from their chosen
path. Helen would be forced to relinquish her
claim, and Paul would have to deal with the
wreckage.

Having a mother like Helen, he sometimes felt,
was like having faulty plumbing. You could never
quite relax. You never knew when and where you
would next be mopping up.

Paul was not a pub person. He found them

oppressive and unfriendly. They didn't feel like his territory, even when they were apparently empty and calm, since at any moment he knew they might suddenly fill with hordes of beer-swilling men in lurid polyester tops roaring at giant TV screens. But today, as he walked the familiar route from Old Street station to his home, he found himself wanting to go into every one, to hide for a while, gather his strength for the confrontation to come, and fortify his nerves against the inevitable onslaught.

At the last pub before home, he succumbed. A double whisky didn't last him long, but it did the job. It took the edge off his anxiety, and reminded him that it wouldn't be long before Helen left and he got his life back again. It also gave him a little pat on the back for being a good son. He had been under no obligation to invite her into his home and allow her to stay as long as she wanted, but he had done the decent thing and given his ageing mother what she asked for. He felt proud of himself. However things turned out with Helen over the baby issue, he had done well. He had been a good, hospitable and generous son to his demanding, awkward and hysterical mother. In fact, he deserved a reward. He deserved another whisky.

He nursed this one, instead of gulping it down with quick medicinal swigs, and by the time it was finished, he realised that his well-intentioned decision to leave work early for the sake of his mother had now been rather undermined by his choice to spend all the time he'd saved sitting in the pub. It had done strange things to him, having his mother in the house. He was beginning to behave like a heterosexual, perhaps even like his father.

After the second whisky, he knew he could delay no longer. He dragged himself outside and walked slowly home.

He found Helen in the kitchen, busily and at first glance contentedly slicing aubergines. 'Hello, dear,' she said, and kissed him on the cheek.

'Hi.'

'Good day?' she said.

'OK. You?'

'Yes. Fine.'

'Fine?'

'Yes. Well, actually a lot more than fine. Wonderful, really. Miraculous, in fact. I met Ella, and she's the most delightful, beautiful thing I've clapped eyes on for as long as I can remember.'

'You liked her, then.'

'Oh, Paul. She's perfect. She's so perfect.'

'They let you see her?'

'I didn't just turn up. I thought that might backfire. I sat near the flat for a while, and when Andrea came out with Ella, I watched where they went and just struck up a conversation. Then I told her who I was and handed over some presents, and she was a bit suspicious at first, but actually I think it went very well.'

'Rebecca wasn't there?'

'No. Andrea says it's her who doesn't want me.'

'So what's going to happen?'

'That's what I wanted to ask you,' said Helen.

'Well it's out of my hands, now, isn't it? If you're in touch with them directly.'

'I'm not talking about me. I'll find a way to see Ella. Andrea seems like a reasonable person. I'm sure we can work something out.'

311

'So what are you talking about?'

Helen stopped slicing and placed her knife flat on the chopping board. She turned to face Paul. 'You,' she said.

'What about me?'

'What you're going to do.'

'About what?'

'About being a father.'

'I'm not a father. We've been through this. That's not the arrangement.'

'Paul! I'm not an idiot. Please don't talk to me about arrangements when I'm trying to be serious.'

'The arrangement is the arrangement, and it *is* serious. That's what we agreed, and that's what's going to happen. If I was the kind of man who wanted to be in there every day changing nappies, they wouldn't have wanted me. They would have gone somewhere else.'

'But they didn't go somewhere else, they came to you, and they had your baby. Ella is your baby.'

'She's their baby.'

'You're her father, whether you like it or not.'

'I do like it, but we've agreed what my role is, and it's to keep my distance, so that's how it's going to be.'

'Who's agreed?'

'Me and Andrea and Rebecca.'

'What about Ella?'

'What about her?'

'Has she agreed to this?'

'Don't be stupid.'

'I'm not being stupid. I'm being deadly serious. Has Ella agreed to this?'

'She's a baby!'

'Exactly, so no one's asked her her opinion.'

'Now you're just being insane.'

'I'm not saying you should ask her. What I'm saying is, you should try and imagine what it would be. What it will be. When she's old enough to mind and to wonder where she came from, and who looked after her, and who cared for her, what's she going to think then? What's she going to want?'

'Well, we'll find out, won't we? When the time comes.'

'Then it will be too late.'

'No, it won't. If she wants to see me, she can see me.'

'It will be too late, Paul. Because by the time she's old enough to know that she wants a father, and to wonder if her father ever loved her, and if not why not, by that stage the question will already be answered, won't it? And if in fifteen years' time you want to say to her that you didn't think it was your job to show an interest in her, and you were too busy and you couldn't be bothered, then go ahead. Do what you're doing now. But if you want to say to her that you cared what happened to her, and you did your best to give her what you thought she might want from you, then you have to start doing that right now.'

'Mum, she's got two parents. If I didn't trust them and think they were loving and honest and stable and caring, then I wouldn't have done it. Yes, in some way she's my daughter, and I wouldn't have let a child of mine be brought up in a nasty environment, but I don't think I have.'

'She could have ten mothers for all I care, and all the attention in the world, but she's only ever going to have one father, and it's you.'

'Mum, this really isn't any of your business.'

'It is my business. It's absolutely my business, because you and her are all that is left of my family, and I'm damn well going to do my best to make sure that you don't neglect her.'

'She's not neglected, Mum. She's extremely well looked after.'

'Stop passing the buck, Paul. This is about you. It's about you and your daughter.'

'But . . . that wasn't the arrangement.'

'Right. That's it.'

'What?'

'I'm leaving.'

'What?'

'I'm leaving. I don't want to hear that word again. I've had enough of it. I'm going home.' Helen roughly untied her apron and threw it on the floor.

'Mum, don't be like that,' said Paul, but she was already walking up the stairs. He followed, heavy-footed and weary. 'Mum, don't make a scene.'

'I'm not making a scene. I'm just going home. I've had enough.'

'What do you want me to say?'

Without acknowledging that Paul was speaking to her, Helen strode into her bedroom and began to throw her clothes and shoes roughly into a suitcase.

'You want me to beg you to stay?' he said, from the doorway. 'Is that why you're behaving like this? You can't feel important until I've begged you not to leave?'

'You can beg all you like, I'm not staying.'

'I'm not going to beg!'

'Good, then that'll save us some time.'

'This is ridiculous. If you don't want me to talk

314

about the arrangement, I won't talk about the arrangement.'

'That's twice more. I told you, I don't want to hear that word.'

Helen shouldered past him, banging her suitcase firmly into his knee, and stamped downstairs to the front door.

'So go! Fine!' he called after her.

'I am going, and please don't shout.'

'YOU'RE THE ONE THAT'S SHOUTING!'

'I'm not shouting, Paul. I think you'll find that I have not raised my voice once in all the time I have stayed here, despite extreme provocation.'

'Even if you're not shouting, you're angry. You're the one that's getting angry, and it's ridiculous, because I haven't done anything,' said Paul, descending to join his mother in the hall, rubbing his knee as he went.

'Precisely. You've put your finger on it. I am angry. Yes. And I'm angry because you haven't done anything. There is a little girl that needs you, and you have done nothing.'

'Mum—'

'I'm not going to argue. I've said my piece, and nothing you can say will change my mind, so I'm going, and I don't want to hear any more of your excuses. I just want you to think about what I've said, and remember that Ella is going to be alive, God willing, for the rest of your life, and one day you are going to have to look her in the eye and account for what you've done. Or haven't done. Bye. Thanks for having me.'

She pecked him on the cheek and left the house, closing the door behind her. Paul walked to the living-room window and watched her figure recede

315

down the street. If they hadn't been together a minute earlier, he might not have recognised her. The mother he had grown up with didn't walk like this. His mother never walked this fast, with such bounce and purpose. This was not a woman he knew.

ONE YEAR LATER

WHATEVER MADE HIM HAPPY

Daniel and Erin's wedding was unusual not only because it took place in the London Eye, but also because the best man was their three-month-old son, Joseph. As the huge Ferris wheel climbed up from the Thames, ascending over the city, the registrar gave a short speech to which no one listened. Everyone either gazed at Daniel and Erin, who were gazing at one another, or at the vast roofscape slowly coming into view below, glistening in the crisp spring sunshine.

Daniel was wearing a suit that cost twenty times more than any other item of clothing he had ever bought. Erin had persuaded him to try it on 'for fun', then, when he had seen himself in the mirror, and had realised for the first time in his life that he was capable of dressing smartly without looking like a waiter, if only he spent enough money, he gritted his teeth and handed over the credit card. Erin's outfit was a green vintage Ossie Clark dress that had been the subject of a brutal and frantic bidding war on eBay, from which Erin had emerged steely and triumphant. It looked simple enough, but performed an astonishing, subtle feat of concealment and accentuation, hiding the after-effects of her pregnancy while making the most of her milk-swollen breasts, in the process restoring her to a strangely enhanced version of her physical prime. When she put it on and examined herself in the mirror, she began to believe, for the first time since the birth, that she would eventually be herself again. She would not feel like a cow for ever.

The glass pod in which the ceremony took place contained only relatives, with a small number of invited friends crammed into the pod behind, pawing at the glass and waving whenever they caught anyone's eye across the narrow void of London sky. This was not a solemn affair.

Gillian had worried that it would seem like too much of a joke, but now, as it was happening, she felt reconciled. Happy, even. No, she was ecstatic. She had been allowed only two guests of her own, and had chosen, of course, Carol and Helen. In a manoeuvre plotted by Gillian, but never discussed with Daniel, both women were accompanied by their sons rather than their husbands. Gillian felt it was appropriate, not because there was any real friendship still alive between the three boys, but because, somehow, this wedding felt like the culmination of a joint enterprise undertaken by all six of them.

Daniel had been stunned to see Matt and Paul walking into the pre-wedding reception with their mothers (though nothing Gillian did was ever entirely shocking), and he would have been angry if he hadn't found himself buoyed up by an impenetrable bubble of wedding euphoria, and also strangely pleased to see them both.

He hadn't seen Paul for more than ten years, and since hearing from Gillian about the lesbian-parented daughter scenario, he had wondered how the experiment was progressing. A smirk of mischievous curiosity was playing on his lips as he walked over to Paul and shook his hand.

Paul seemed strangely similar to how he had always been, and was as gay as ever, with the same detached reserve, but with a calmer, happier air to him than had ever been apparent in the past. After having made enough small talk to prevent the question sounding prurient, Daniel asked Paul how often he saw his child.

'Every week,' Paul replied.

'Really?'

'Yeah. I didn't think I would, but . . . you know . . .'

'What? Tell me,' said Daniel. From his mother, he had heard extensive details about Helen's intermittently successful struggle for contact with Ella, but had gleaned little trustworthy information about Paul.

'Just . . . once I started, I couldn't stop. It was tricky at first, but we've slowly figured something out that keeps everyone happy. I think we all found that . . . that the idea of a baby is very different from the reality. It sounds stupid, but—'

'It's not stupid,' said Daniel. 'You expect them to be a baby, not . . . a person. I mean, not straight away. Actually, maybe it is stupid, but I felt it, too.'

'And they learn all this stuff all the time,' said Paul, suddenly animated, 'soaking everything up, and they change every week, but the one thing they don't learn is a personality. That's the amazing thing. It seems like it's all there from the start, and

318

all you do as a parent is . . . is slowly find out what it is.'

'You think?'

'You'll see. Joseph will be someone completely different a year from now, but he'll also still be exactly the same.'

'That's a weird idea.'

'I never knew it would be so interesting,' said Paul, his mouth curling into a hint of a smile, touched by some private thought of his child—a memory, perhaps, or simply an anticipation of their next meeting.

As Daniel was dragged away to greet another guest, he turned back to Paul and told him, squeezing his arm for emphasis, that it was great to see him again, and to find him so happy. Paul blushed, and when Daniel insisted they should make sure they didn't lose touch again, he handed over a business card with his email address. Daniel slid it into his jacket and, smiling as he turned away, gave the pocket two gentle pats.

Gillian was in the midst of a garbled explanation of the son-for-husband swap made by her two friends, involving an illness and an invitation lost in the post, with Daniel all the while trying to interrupt and let her know that he didn't mind, when Matt grabbed him from behind and hoisted him into the air.

'Weheeaaaaaaaaaayyyyyyy!' said Matt. 'What a man!'

'Get off,' said Daniel, wriggling free.

'Nice suit,' said Matt, turning to Gillian. 'All it takes is a wedding, and he finally dresses like a grown-up.'

'Hello, Matt,' said Gillian, 'so nice of you to step

319

in at the last moment.'

Matt gave her a blank look.

'Instead of your father,' she went on, visibly urging Matt with a clenched jaw and bulging eyes to back up her lie.

'Always ready to please,' said Matt, leaning forwards to kiss her on both cheeks. 'You must be so proud,' he went on. 'And all these years, I thought he was firing blanks.'

'Firing blanks?'

'He's talking about Joseph,' said Daniel, who was beginning to wonder how much longer this conversation could progress with neither his mother nor his friend understanding a single word the other one said. 'Do you want to meet him?'

'Er . . . OK,' said Matt.

Gillian watched as Daniel led Matt towards Erin, took the baby from her arms, and placed him in Matt's stiff embrace.

While Matt greeted this new life with the words, 'He's not going to chunder on my clothes, is he?', Gillian turned and saw Carol standing alone at the edge of the room, watching her son cradle his friend's baby. Carol's features were clenched, frozen with what Gillian sensed was an intermingling of jealousy and regret.

One year on from their week with their sons, only Carol's life remained unchanged. While Gillian and Helen were both active grandmothers and, for the first time in years, active mothers, Matt still had the same job, lived in the same flat, and was as uncommunicative and evasive with his mother as ever. There was never a girlfriend who lasted long enough to merit a mention. When he failed with Julia, Matt had seemingly reverted without a thought to his old tastes.

Carol had unearthed in her son a desire to improve himself, but he apparently lacked the will to act on it. Her pressure, in the course of their week together, had forced him to admit to a dissatisfaction with his life, and to a yearning for something less shallow, but ultimately the life he lived appeared to offer a close enough approximation to whatever made him happy for Matt to lack the will to undertake any disruption.

Her intrusion had rippled the surface of her son's life, nothing more. He wanted to change, but he also wanted to stay the same, and, as for almost everyone, the latter was a more powerful urge.

Carol's week with her son had not been a waste of time. She had, at least, learned a little more about him. They had become reacquainted, briefly, which was worth doing, but she had no desire to go again. She now knew as much as she wanted to know.

*   *   *

Rings were exchanged at the apex of the Eye's rotation, the Thames now a glinting silver thread far below, squirming through a vast landscape of brick and concrete, of human struggle. As they climbed through the air, the levity of the occasion slowly tailed away, a wave of emotion spreading from Daniel and Erin through to all the guests. This was not, however hastily and casually the event had been planned, however outlandish the location, a joke. Few things in life were more profound or serious than this.

It was Daniel, as a thin platinum band was

placed on his finger, who cried first. Erin's voice wavered throughout her vows, but she remained in control as Daniel slid the ring into place. They kissed immediately, their first married kiss, deep and tender, the first, without doubt, of many thousands. Daniel felt a tear drip from Erin's cheek on to his lips. Then the muffled sound of a cheer from the neighbouring pod penetrated the glass, and they turned to see their friends waving manically, blowing kisses and saluting them with champagne glasses. Daniel and Erin blew back a joint kiss, brandishing their newly ringed fingers, causing another wave of cheers, accompanied by the popping of champagne corks.

'What I usually say at this point,' said the registrar, 'is, "You may now kiss the bride."'

Amid waves of laughter, Daniel and Erin kissed again, her fingers pushing tenderly up over his neck and into his hair. Without letting go of one another, they tumbled towards Gillian, who handed them their best man. As Joseph entered their embrace, Daniel momentarily felt the world beyond his wife and son recede away to nothing. This, right here, right now, in his arms, was as much as he would ever need. This was the pinnacle of happiness. He felt the sensation percolate through him, burying itself into his heart, a seam of purest joy locked for ever into the landscape of his body.

Barely a minute into the marriage, Joseph began to wail, a loud, hungry protest, angrily claiming back his mother. Erin sat and put him to her breast. He drank with his eyes wide open, barely blinking, gazing at her with something more than love or hunger or need or trust, with a look that seemed to speak of some other appetite, as if she held the answer to everything, as if, just by staring at her, the universe would be revealed to him.

The Eye continued to turn, carrying them all slowly back down to earth.

ACKNOWLEDGEMENTS

Thanks to Felicity Rubinstein, Alexandra Pringle, Mike Jones, Leah Schmidt, Susannah Godman, Jane Finigan, Emily Sweet, Richard Sved, Kate Webb, John and Sue Sutcliffe, and also to Saul Venit and Caroline Bourne. And thank you above all, more than I can express, Maggie O'Farrell.